LIFE FORGOTTEN

LAYNE DEEMER

For Jeanne & Mary
I am so lucky to call you both Mom

Playlist

"Hot in Herre" by Nelly
"Life in Mono" by Mono
"Hey, Ma" by Bon Iver
"Have You Ever Seen the Rain" by Creedence Clearwater Revival
"My Little Ruin" by Glen Hansard
"Hey Jude" by The Beatles
"Into the Mystic" by Van Morrison

Chapter One

"NELLIE, did you hear what I said?" How could I not? She's only repeated herself three times in one phone call. I take a deep breath, keeping my irritation at bay.

"Yep, Mama, I got it. I'm at the store now, and I already have your juice in the cart."

"Oh, good, okay. Love you. Bye." *Click.*

I drop my phone back into my purse and let out a groan. I need an outlet for all of this pent-up frustration. As a kid, whenever I was stressed out, I would sneak into my sister's room and swipe something tiny off of her dresser—the back of an earring or a small barrette. I knew it was wrong, but I loved the rush it brought me. The adrenaline was a much-needed escape from the tension I had been feeling. She never knew I took anything. No one did. It's a dark secret that I'm not proud of, but I'm also not strong enough to ignore the pull.

My eyes scan the beauty aisle for the perfect sized item and land on the mascara on the bottom row of the display. I squat down so that I can see it more closely. The words on the packaging promise voluminous lashes that are dangerously long. Bold claims in bold print, but I don't care about any of that. The mascara tube is slim, and the cardboard and plastic surrounding it is petite—easy to conceal. My fingertips glide along the top of the packaging making each one swing like a pendulum. The tubes of blackest black sway to the left and back again as I rifle through them, choosing the perfect one.

I find it, the third from the back. It has no blemishes or bent corners. *Unlike me.* I slide each tube off of the metal hanger until I'm holding the one I want. My breathing intensifies and I feel tingling in my fingertips. I replace the tubes I've deemed not good enough and stand, taking my new mascara with me. If someone was monitoring my heart right now, it would be a dead giveaway—the steady beating has increased as though I just finished a high-impact workout. As I push my cart along the rows, I pass my right hand—the one holding the mascara—over my purse that's been carefully positioned in the child seat of the cart. It's wide open and ready for what comes next. I open my fingers letting the package tumble out into the waiting mouth of my gold leather purse. It falls deep into the black abyss. I don't watch it happen. I don't look down to make sure it hit my intended mark. I know it has. I've been doing this long enough. If there's an eye in the sky, it'll never rest on me for more than a second. I'm entirely too ordinary for anyone to ever suspect me of stealing. And if, on the off chance, someone does catch me in the act, I have my response all worked out.

Clutching my right hand to my chest, I'll appear completely dumbfounded. "What do you mean? I put the mascara right here in my cart, see?" I'll lean over and survey the contents in my basket, shifting items around, frantically trying to locate said mascara. When I don't find it and it's suggested I look in my purse, I'll place my hand over my mouth in horror as I realize it's inside. "Oh my goodness! I must have dropped it there by accident! Thank you so much for telling me! I would never have been able to forgive myself if I made it home without paying for something!" How can you fault someone who's just as surprised as you are? You can't. It's a solid plan of attack, but, so far, I've never had to use it.

Like I said, I'm pretty unremarkable. My only redeeming quality is the mass of copper curls on my head, but, on most days, it's more frizz than ringlets. My blue eyes are not the crystal clear, ocean kind. Mine are murky, like swirling storm clouds covering up a picturesque sky. Not that it would matter if they were more exceptional, since today they're hidden behind thick-rimmed glasses. I chose them over contacts this morning because that's all I had the energy for.

I'm not a bad person. I'm not entirely sure that I'm a good person, either, but I don't steal because I'm evil. The things I take never amount to more than a few dollars. I'm not a thief. Well, I guess I kind of am, but not in the orange jumpsuit way —more in the *I'm just trying to feel something* way. It's a relief— a momentary release from a world in which I have no control. Even if the feeling only lasts a few minutes, it's still worth the risk.

When I reach the paper products aisle, I pause and survey the contents in the cart. I think I have everything, but I pull out my list just to be sure.

Cranberry juice—check
Poise pads—check
Tastykake Butterscotch Krimpets—check
Tissues—

That's why I'm in this aisle. My feet took me here before my brain could catch up. I hate when that happens. For most people, it's normal to go to a room in their house or an aisle in a store and forget why it was they went there in the first place. But I'm not most people, and I can't help the worry that bubbles up to the surface whenever it happens.

I look over the vast array of tissue boxes on the shelves

and compare the price per box. I find the best value and toss a few in the cart. I'm only saving seven cents, but when you're watching every penny, everything counts.

I amble toward the checkout and choose the U-Scan line. I slide each item across the scanner and pack it neatly into a plastic grocery bag. I hate using plastic. If I could, I'd use my cloth bags, but Mom wants, no, *needs* more bags, so I don't have a choice.

There's a young girl, maybe seventeen-ish, stationed near the registers. I'm pretty sure her purpose is to help shoppers when they have a problem, but from the looks of things, I'm not so sure she knows that. There's an older man off to my left who's been struggling with the UPC code on his box of bran flakes, but she hasn't noticed. She's too engrossed in a conversation with a boy who looks to be about the same age. They're both wearing red Smart Shopper T-shirts. He's on his break. I know this because I'm eavesdropping. I'm not even being discreet about it, but it doesn't matter. They aren't paying attention to anyone but each other. I watch them so intently, I'm at a complete standstill. I hear my register tell me to insert my credit card, but I can't look away. I heard him ask her if she wanted to go to Dairy Queen after her shift and I need to know how this plays out. I'm living vicariously through them and I have no shame.

Bran flake guy clears his throat loudly enough that we all turn to look at him. "I'm sorry to interrupt this, uh, love connection." He moves his hand back and forth between the two of them, and I cringe. Why do older people always say exactly what they're thinking? Their flushed cheeks confirm that he has their attention. "This cereal won't scan. Can one of you two youngsters help me out here?" Checkout girl nods and solemnly walks over to him the same way a death row inmate might walk to the electric chair. The boy watches her and looks like he might want to say something, but he decides against it and sulks away, deflated.

I let out a sigh. I'm reminded of when I was a kid and my older sister would snatch the remote control from my hands and change my *Looney Tunes* to *The Real World*. Bran flake guy changed the channel and I have to bite my tongue so I won't yell, "Hey! I was watching that!"

There's nothing else to see—no more distractions. I turn my attention back to my groceries and open my wallet. I look at my mom's Visa card just waiting to be used, but I can't do it. These are things she wants but doesn't need. I can't use her money for that. I slide my debit card out of its holding sleeve and send it through the machine. It's not that much money, but it's still more than she should spend. This is the least I can do for her after all she's done for me.

Chapter Two

SHADY VILLA RETIREMENT COMMUNITY sits parallel to a local park. Its sprawling campus boasts enough trees to qualify as a mini forest with plenty of benches to accommodate nearly every resident. It's the best of its kind within a fifty-mile radius. I wouldn't have it any other way.

Before my mom moved here, I scoured the area for places like this one. I called at least a dozen different senior living centers and visited half of them before settling on this one. No, settling isn't the right word. That makes it sound like I picked the least offensive place out of a shit hole line up. Honestly, the moment I set foot on these grounds, I knew. See, I wasn't just searching for a place for Mom to live; I was looking for a home. And I don't mean home in the dreaded *nursing home* sense. If my mom had to move, I wanted to be certain that she would feel comfortable and taken care of, but more importantly, I wanted her to feel loved. I never want her to feel discarded. I couldn't live with myself if she did.

The parking lot is packed with cars. It's 2:30 p.m. on a Saturday afternoon. The sun is high in the sky and there's a slight breeze stirring up the smell of cedar and pine. It's a picturesque day and nearly every bench on the grounds is occupied. As I approach the front door, I spy Mavis and Gerry McConnell, a sweet couple who live in the apartment across the hall from my mom. Mavis is leaning against Gerry; her blueish silver hair is pressed to his shoulder. I'm certain she'll regret that position once she wakes and finds her perfectly coiffed curls asymmetrically matted on one side. Gerry lost a leg in Vietnam, and as his body ages, the wear and tear on his remaining leg has made it difficult for him to move around. But what he lacks in mobility, he makes up for in personality. He's always quick with a joke, offers the best advice, and keeps a close eye on my mom for me when I'm not around. He looks up at me with bright eyes and brings a bony finger to his lips. He makes a slight *shh* sound and then winks at me. I wink in return and shoot him a playful grin. Reaching into my purse, I pull out a Kit Kat bar and hand it to him. His eyes light up with excitement and, at that moment, he looks about twenty years younger. His joy is palpable and I feel it zing throughout my body.

I give the heavy doors a shove and am immediately greeted with the sounds of slightly off-key singing. A man and woman wearing matching gold lamé vests over black button-down dress shirts are singing a duet of "I Got You, Babe" in the lobby. They're each holding microphones with tangled cords plugged into a tiny amplifier. The background music blares from an ancient boombox perched on a coffee table. The sound of the woman's voice cuts in and out, but she smiles and keeps on singing despite the technical difficulties. A few residents surround them on folding chairs. For some, this is the perfect naptime opportunity; for others, it's a great excuse to mingle and collect the latest gossip. My eyes sift through the crowd and spot Simon immediately. His box-dyed jet black hair is impossible to miss. He's leaning in toward June while simultaneously holding Dottie's hand with his arm stretched behind his back. Eighty-six years old and still a player. There's an eighty-twenty ratio of women to men at Shady Villa, but the majority of that twenty percent gets around. Men are in high demand here and the ladies don't mind sharing. No one wants to talk about elderly people "getting down to business," but sometimes I swear a better name for this place would be Viagra Villa.

I don't look for my mom down here. I know I won't find her anywhere near this crowd. There's live entertainment here every Saturday afternoon, but she's very selective, preferring most days to stay in her room watching old reruns of *The Match Game* and *Hollywood Squares*. I move through the maze of walkers and wheelchairs toward the elevator. I'm stopped in my tracks when I notice yellow tape across the doors. Out of order again. I groan for the poor residents who will be forced to take the stairs, but mostly I groan for myself because I'm in for quite an earful when I get to my mom's room.

The stairwell is empty as I make my way up to the third floor. It's a short walk, but for older people struggling to move around, it's an arduous task. I feel the weight of their frustration as I try to imagine what it must be like to be forced to do something that used to be so easy, but now, thanks to the cruelty of time, has become very hard. They must feel like their bodies are traitors. I turned twenty-seven this year, but in my head, I still feel like a teenager. It's not a huge leap so it doesn't feel so unrealistic, but is it the same for an older person? Does someone in their eighties still feel mentally like they're in their thirties? How humbling it must be to feel young in your mind when your body starts to fail you. That's not the case for my mom.

Room 346 sits on the left and down the hall a bit from the stairwell. I walk briskly toward my mom's apartment. Richard Dawson must be one of the actors on *The Match Game* today because I can hear his inappropriate sexualized comments all the way out here in the hallway. I have to knock with force and for at least twenty seconds straight to ensure

Mom can hear me. I told her I was coming, but that was almost an hour ago, so she may not remember. I hear the lock on the other side of the door disengage and then click to the lock position once more. I smile and wait until I hear it unlock one more time, and then the door slowly glides open. My mother stands before me in a long blue floral nightgown with billowy sleeves that hug her wrists with elastic. I spy a small stain on the collar. I could examine it more closely, but I don't need to. I know it's mint chocolate chip ice cream. It's the right shade and size.

It's been nearly a year since she moved in here, but I still find myself looking at her with wonder every time I visit. My mind struggles to connect the woman standing before me with the one who raised me. They look nothing alike and they behave even less alike. At sixty-three years old, she shouldn't need to live in a place like this. She should be taking trips and visiting with friends. She should be back in our old house whipping up a batch of her famous rocky road brownies and dancing to Creedence Clearwater Revival on the radio. But that's not the card she was dealt. Alzheimer's disease had other plans for her. It had other plans for me, too.

She squints up at me through thick glasses. I have her to thank for my near-sightedness. Her eyebrows turn down and her face twists into a grimace. "Oh, I didn't know you were coming today." I feel disappointment wrap around me like a weighted blanket, but I don't say anything. I could remind her that I called her earlier, but it won't change anything. I just smile and hold up the bag from the grocery store and watch as the perturbed expression on her face morphs into delight.

She's all smiles now as she moves aside and yanks the door wide open. Her glee isn't for me; it's for the cranberry juice and Tastykakes in the bag I brought for her, but my foolish heart is so deprived it latches on to any form of happiness it finds.

A pungent smell is the first thing that hits me as I enter the darkened room. I scrunch up my nose and survey the space to find the source. My eyes zero in on a Styrofoam bowl wrapped in tinfoil sitting precariously on an end table. Without looking, I know it's responsible for the overwhelming aroma permeating the air. Mom often brings extra desserts up to her room with her at night, and I suspect this might be one she's forgotten about for a few days. It happens far too often than I care to acknowledge.

If this were my mom five years ago, I could waltz right over and scoop up the offensive smelling bowl and toss it right into the trash. But if I were to do that now, it would set off a domino effect. She would ask what I was doing, but my answer wouldn't matter. I would be touching her things and altering the state of her space. She has everything where she wants it and I am not allowed to change a thing. Her voice will rise like waves in the ocean, gentle at first, but growing rapidly until her fury crashes down on me with extreme force. Her temperament is like a delicate flower. The wrong sort of breeze will cause the petals to curl and drop. Her calm demeanor will scatter in the wind and I'll be left with a woman so distraught, she cannot be soothed. This is how she is most days—a stem without a flower.

Every time I come here, I give up all control. It's like we're dancing and I'm just a placeholder. I stand in the small hallway and let her take the lead. She reaches out for the bag, and I give it to her. The smile on her face is wide and makes her cheeks appear full. While she's distracted, I let my eyes roam over her face. My gaze lingers on her cracked lips. If I had to guess, I'm pretty certain she hasn't had anything to drink today. It's a constant battle that the aides here and I always have with her. Even Gerry's tried to get involved. There are two containers of cranberry juice in the grocery bag she's holding. She asks for them every week, but that doesn't mean she'll drink them. She just likes to pour the juice into small glass cups and then line them up on her coffee table.

I glance over there now and count six glasses, all of which are about half full with red liquid. I let out a small sigh because I know how this conversation will go even before I ask the question. Still, I have to try.

"Mama, have you had anything to drink today?"

She doesn't look up at me. She keeps her eyes glued to the bag while her hand roams around and probes each item inside. "I swallowed some of the water when I was brushing my teeth this morning. That's plenty. Plus, I had my ice cream and that's made with milk."

My head shakes involuntarily. Frustrated isn't even the right word for this situation. Exasperated. That's a better way to describe how this feels. I continue speaking gently to her even though I know it's no use.

"Listen, it's important that you actually drink fluids. Water from brushing your teeth and liquid from melted ice cream isn't enough. We've been over this. Remember what Dr. Ezra said—"

"I told you I don't like him!" She levels me with a glare that leaves me speechless. Her sharp tone is something I'll never be able to get used to. When I was little, she had to scold me if I did something wrong, but there was still love in her voice. I never doubted that for a second. But now, when she reprimands me, I can only hear the scorn. There's no warmth.

She looks past me toward the elevator. "Was the elevator fixed when you came up here? It's been broken since this morning!"

I inhale deeply. I knew this was coming, but it still isn't any less bothersome. "No, it's still out of order, but they're working on getting it back up and running." I add that last part to appease her. I didn't see anyone working on it.

"For what we pay to live here, we deserve an elevator that

works. I had to take the stairs for breakfast this morning and again for lunch. It's too hard on my knees!"

But good for your waistline, I think to myself. Mom has put on a considerable amount of weight since moving here, and her sedentary lifestyle isn't helping.

I've only been here for five minutes, and I've barely made it into the room, but I know I've reached my limit. My heart *and my nose* can only take so much. I decide to take the coward's way out and tell one of the aides about the foul-smelling bowl. It's one less war for me to wage.

I force myself to smile so she can hear it when I speak. "Okay, Mama, well, I guess I better get going. Do you need anything else?"

She looks up at me, and I can tell she's really seeing me. It's as if she didn't even know I was here before this moment. The right corner of her mouth hitches up and her eyes crinkle slightly in the corners. "Thank you for all of this, Bells. I'm gonna go watch my programs."

She sets the bag on her bed and pulls me into a lopsided hug. When I'm this close to her, I can tell her nightgown hasn't been washed recently, but I pinch my lips shut. I'll save that argument for another time.

She pushes out of the hug and holds me at arm's length. "Now, be a good girl and bring me some donuts next time you come."

I nod solemnly. "Sure thing, Mama."

Chapter Three

"SWERVE! WHAT ARE YOU UP TO?"

The sweet little cat sits perched on the concrete stairs in front of my apartment building. Her orange fur is a little matted from living outdoors and the slight curve of her spine makes her lean a bit to the left. She's been coming around my building for the past year and often brings a few friends with her whenever she visits. Today she's alone and lets out a small mew when she sees me approach.

I reach out and scratch the soft patch of fur under her chin. She purrs in response and leans into my touch. "Hi-ya, sweet girl. How've you been?"

My eyes scan the top of the landing and notice the empty bowl. The sunlight gleams off of the stainless coating. "Hungry?"

Swerve eyes me with a look that could only be translated to "Duh!"

I let out a small chuckle and scoop up the bowl. "Hang on one second! I'll fill this up for you."

I key in my code and slide the door open. I'm careful not to let Swerve sneak her way inside. She's tried a few times and even succeeded once. I shake my head as I recall the nearly two-hour search and rescue mission when she found herself trapped in a tiny heat register in the upstairs hallway. Truthfully, I would love to let her come inside. If I could, I'd bring her into my apartment and let her live with me. But, Brad, my land/slumlord, says otherwise. He has a strict NO PETS policy, which I suspect has more to do with his cold, black heart than for any other reason.

I hustle up the stairs to the second floor and grab my keys from inside my purse. They're tangled up with something. I give the ring a sharp pull and free my keys. Something else comes tumbling out with them and lands on the floor at my feet. The tube of mascara still confined to its packaging stares up at me. I bend down to retrieve it and once I have it in my hands, I feel my legs give out. I flop down onto my bottom and lean back against my door, holding the cardboard package up in front of me.

This happens every time. The guilt. I took something without paying for it. I took something when I very easily could've shelled out the $4.95 that it costs. My mind is alive with thoughts like *I'll never do this again.* Or *I can take it back and tell them I took it by mistake.* But it's all a lie. I *will* do it again and I'll *never* give any of it back. I close my eyes and feel the shame that always comes. I wish things were different. I wish life were different. I breathe deeply and blink away the remorse. I can't wallow or I'll lose myself completely.

I toss the mascara back into my purse and stand abruptly. The keys in my hand collide with the stainless bowl, and a loud gong sound reverberates throughout the hallway. Shit! I don't want to wake up Jodi. She lives in the apartment across the hall from me and works third shift. Jodi Lynch is raising her fourteen-year-old daughter on her own, and between juggling work and teenage angst, that poor woman is always exhausted. She wouldn't appreciate being woken up by her

"Goddamn neighbor." I've heard her refer to me by that term of endearment multiple times. The walls in this building are thin and Jodi doesn't like my "shitty" taste in music, but she forgets that if she can hear me, then I can hear her, too. Or maybe she hasn't forgotten. Maybe that's the whole point.

I grip the bowl with my other hand to stop the sound while I simultaneously unlock my door. Rushing inside, I plop my purse on the small table by the door and hang my keys on the hook above it.

My apartment is small, but it's more than enough for me. The main living area is set up in an open floor plan that makes the tiny space feel much larger than it is. My decor is a modge podge of hand-me-downs and thrift store finds. The living room doubles as a dining room, but I don't have much company so a large eating area isn't necessary. I much prefer eating at my kitchen island. If I angle the barstool just right, I have the perfect vantage point for watching episodes of *Queer Eye* on Netflix.

There's a gray corduroy loveseat in my living room, and next to that is a small wooden wine barrel that I use as an end table. Instead of a dining room table, I have an antique rolltop desk with two cherry wood filing cabinets on either side. Two seem excessive, but I like my mom's paperwork separate from mine. It's far less confusing that way.

My walls are painted a stark white and lined with photos from a much happier time. Faces of people that I love stare back at me from their permanent stillness. My grandfather, whom we called Poppy, holds up a winning lottery ticket, his gummy smile rife with joy. My older sister, Meg, blows out the candles on her twentieth birthday cake. Her eyes are squeezed shut and her mouth is pursed. Mom laughs with uninhibited glee. Her head is tilted back and her eyes sparkle with youth and vigor.

I took those photos when we had an overabundance of joy

in our lives. There were still wishes to be made. Time was on our side. We had nothing to worry about. I keep these images on my walls as a reminder that nothing in life is permanent. Everything can and will change whether we like it or not. And when we find ourselves at the mercy of time, all we have left are our memories—and sometimes, we don't even have those.

Padding over to the kitchen, I set Swerve's bowl on the counter. I keep a cabinet well stocked with canned cat food in several different flavors. After all, if I enjoy variety with my food, why shouldn't every living thing have that same luxury? Today Swerve is in luck because I have her favorite— savory salmon. I tug on the tab of the can and glide it open. The contents slide into the bowl with a wet plop.

I find Swerve exactly where I left her, roosting on the cement pad by the door. Her front left paw is raised to her mouth as she meticulously cleans each pad with her tiny pink tongue. She may be a stray, but she's not a savage. This cat has manners. She knows the importance of washing your hands before eating. The heavy glass door opens with a squeak, startling Swerve out of her bathing ritual. She turns her head and observes me over her shoulder.

"Here you are, sweet girl." I set the bowl in front of her and pat the top of her head. And then I quickly head back inside. In the months that I've known her, she's never eaten in my presence. I think it must have something to do with trust. She has enough to eat what I bring her, but not enough to let her guard down and eat in front of me. I can respect that.

I stroll over to the stairs to head back to my apartment, but when I reach the bottom step, I turn my head ever so slightly and peer out the glass door. Swerve is bent over the bowl eating with unabashed fervor. I smile and allow the feeling of contentment to wash over me. It feels good to take care of her and that's a welcomed reprieve from the helplessness I felt visiting my mom. Even if I can't give Swerve a roof over her head, I can rest easy tonight knowing that her belly is full, and for now, that's enough for me.

A loud crash in the upstairs hallway pulls me out of my reverie. Taking the steps two at a time, I rush to the second floor. I'm out of breath and clearly out of shape when I reach the top. A lone can of chicken noodle soup rolls toward me, stopping when it hits my foot. I bend down to pick it up and glance down the hallway. Claudette Sharp is on her hands and knees grasping at other wayward cans like the one in my hand. She sighs audibly and mutters a few profanities under her breath.

"Claudette? Are you okay?"

Her shoulders jump at the sound of my voice and she cranes her neck to look my way. "Oh! Nellie, hunny! Yes, yes, I'm fine, sugar. This old paper bag finally gave out, is all."

I give her a sympathetic smile as I head in her direction, scooping up cans along the way. Claudette is seventy-three years young, but she doesn't look a day over sixty. She keeps her mind sharp and her body sharper with a social calendar more active than a seventeen-year-old. Every Saturday morn-ing, she collects canned goods and drops them off at the soup kitchen on the corner. She keeps that same bag outside the door of her apartment with a handwritten sign taped to the front asking for donations. It's always close to overflowing by the end of each week. If I'm honest, I'm responsible for at least half of the food she collects. I sneak extra cans into the bag when no one is around. It's a noble cause, but selfishly, it's just another way to dull the heartache I feel most days.

"Here you are." I hand over the last can I picked up. "Looks like you could use a sturdier bag. Hold on. Let me run inside and grab one for you real quick."

Her face erupts in a smile that makes her cheeks look like oversized plump cherries. "Nellie, you are a lifesaver."

I dash inside my apartment and fling open my pantry door. I keep a few reusable cloth grocery bags on the bottom shelf. I reach down and select one with a solid bottom and durable straps.

"Here. This one should hold up well." I hand the bag over to her and begin transferring the cans from the pile into the new carrier.

"Thank you, hunny. I'll give it right back to you after I deliver these." She motions to the cans in front of her.

"Oh, no worries. I have more of these bags than I need. Please keep this one and use it for your donations."

She pauses and takes my hand in hers. Her eyes find mine and I watch her pupils dance back and forth like she's trying to see inside a foggy window. "Thank you, sweetie." I give her a nod. I'm not looking for praise. It's just nice to feel useful. She gives my hand a pat and then pushes herself back up to standing. "Okay, then, off I go."

"Need any help carrying that bag? It looks awfully heavy." I give her a wry smile.

"Nellie, girl, do you know how much weight I'm up to now?"

I shake my head as my smile grows wide. I set her up and she can't resist.

"Well, then, let me tell you. As of last Tuesday, Alfonse has me lifting three hundred pounds." She beams with pride and bats her eyelashes playfully.

We both pause and then we can't hold it in any longer. My body shakes with silent amusement while Claudette howls with laughter. She has a personal trainer and visits the gym every morning. She is the strongest woman in this entire building and we both know it, but it's fun to tease her and she's always a good sport about it.

"Catch you later, hunny." She pats my arm as she sidles past.

"Bye, Claudette." I watch her walk down the hall. Her hips sway back and forth as though they're balancing an invisible hula hoop. *She's ten years older than my mom.* The thought comes out of nowhere and settles over me like a storm cloud. The unfairness of my mom's diagnosis is never far from my mind, and from time to time, it manages to break through in tiny bursts just like this one. I close my eyes and give in to the despair just for a moment, and then I blink and let it go.

Chapter Four

I HOLD my phone out in front of me and groan. I can't put it off any longer. Before I can change my mind, I scroll through my contacts and tap on my sister's name.

Megan Campbell is five years older than I am, but you would never know it. She lives her life with a freedom that I've never known. She was always the carefree one, but over the past few years she's grown more reckless. I used to try to reason with her, but after being shut down a half a dozen times, I stopped trying. What I can't seem to stop doing is worrying about her.

"Hey-lo?" Meg's smooth voice croons over the phone.

"Hey, Megs. It's Nellie."

"Oh, Belly! How's it going, little sister?"

When we were just kids, our poppy gave me the nickname Belly because when I was a toddler, I had one and it was impressive. My mom was so proud of my rotund middle attributing roughly ninety percent of it to the power of breast milk. The name stuck and I never minded when my poppy or mom used it, but something about the way Meg says it makes it sound degrading. She may be my sister, but she's definitely not above insulting me. In fact, lately it seems like it's a full-time job for her.

"I just came from visiting Mom and wanted to give you an update."

She hums into the phone. "Why bother? It's never positive news. What's the point of dwelling on something we can't change? Honestly, Belly, you could use some more *aloha* in your life." She laughs, but it's more like a cackle.

Meg moved from California to Hawaii three weeks after Mom was diagnosed. She packed a bag, and I drove her to the airport in a daze. Before she got out of the car, she put her hand on my shoulder and told me she knew Mom was in good hands. And then she was gone, leaving me to make all of the life altering decisions by myself. I'm reminded of Claudette and how she's been after me to join her at the gym. I already do enough heavy lifting.

"I know that, Meg, but she's still here and sometimes I catch a glimpse of the old Mom. As a matter of fact, just the other day she brought up that time the three of us took that day trip to the beach. You remember—I was maybe five or six so you would've been around ten. We were so excited that we went running right into the ocean with all of our clothes on. Mom was yelling at us to wait, but as usual, we weren't listening."

She lets out a small chuckle that sounds breathy over the phone. "That *was* a great day, wasn't it?"

"It really was. When Mom brought it up, she looked like she was reliving it right in front of me. You should've seen her face, Megs. I swear, in that moment she looked at least ten years younger."

Meg clears her throat, and when she speaks, her voice is laced with emotion. "It's too bad that all we have are memories. The mom we used to know is gone. I don't know how you can stand being around her the way she is now."

Well, for starters, I don't have a choice. You moved away, remember? The words are on the tip of my tongue, but they never see the light of day. The truth is, I don't blame my sister for leaving. I would've left, too, if I could have. But these are our roles in life. She's unpredictable and I'm dependable. There's no other way this situation could've played out and we both know it.

I open my mouth to update her on Mom's lack of drinking when I hear a man's voice in the background. "Come back to bed, baby." His voice is deep and gravelly. I haven't heard this one before. He must be her latest flavor.

"I'll be right there, baby. Promise." Her voice is muffled like she has her hand over the phone. It masks the sound, but doesn't block it. A fact I'm sure she's aware of.

"Uh, I gotta go now, Belly. Call ya later?"

I shake my head. Some things never change. "Aren't you going to tell me his name?"

She giggles and speaks into the phone in a hushed tone. "His name is Austin, and Belly, get this—he's actually from Austin! Isn't that just too funny?" She doesn't wait for me to respond. "Anyway, he moved here to practice circus yoga on the beach. That's how we met. I saw a sign advertising the class so I decided to give it a try and now here we are!"

"Hold on—did you say *circus* yoga? What even *is* that?"

"Oh, Belly! I don't have time for details. He's waiting for me! Aren't you always researching things online? Just go Google it or something. I will say this—he's *very* flexible, if ya know what I mean!" She falls into fits of laughter and all I can do is roll my eyes. She's hopeless.

"Okay, Megs, I'll let you go. Call me later, when the Ringmaster takes a nap, okay?"

"You got it," she lies. She never calls me. "Bye, Belly."

As soon as she hangs up, I head right over to my desk and flip open my laptop. I type *circus yoga* into the search bar and am astounded by all of the information that comes up. I honestly thought she was making it up, but as I sit here scrolling through countless images, I see that she was not lying. Circus yoga does, in fact, exist. The photos of kids bent into crazy shapes together make it look like a fun gymnastics class. But the pictures of adults with their bodies twisted together in various pliable positions make it seem more like something that should be happening in a bedroom instead of on a public beach. *Oh, Meg. What are you doing?*

My sister has been switching up boyfriends the same way you might change up your skin care routine. Everything seems to be working out well until something shiny and new comes along and throws off her whole plan. Before the yoga instructor, there was Xavier, the professional surfer and before him, there was Tom, the scuba instructor. Each one more fabulous than the one before, and the only thing they have in common is that she's never stayed with any of them long enough to form a real connection. I could hope, for her sake, that Austin will be different, but I know better.

My phone lights up and the sound of a drumbeat fills the air. My mom chose that ringtone for herself. This may sound dramatic, but it's one of the last real choices I can remember her making when she was still in total control of her own thoughts. Even though a deep drum doesn't seem to fit who she is now, I know I'll never change it.

"Hi, Mama. Everything okay?" It's a question that I already know the answer to. She wouldn't be calling me without a reason.

"When are you coming back over to visit me?" Her voice sounds impatient. It's as if we haven't seen each other in weeks.

I take a deep calming breath. "I was just there a few hours ago. Remember? I brought you more juice and your cakes."

There's a pause on the line. "Oh, yeah, that's right." She doesn't sound convinced. "Well, listen, when you come over next time, I'm going to need more socks. I only have a few pairs."

I could remind her that she has a full drawer in her dresser reserved for socks, but it would only upset her. Instead, I placate her with half-truths. "Okay, I'll bring you some next time I come." I won't bring her more, but I will show her where she has a full supply.

"Oh, good." She sounds content with my response and that's all that matters. "Okay, love you, bye!"

"Love you, too, Mama." I end the call and think about Meg. She doesn't get phone calls like that. Mom doesn't remember her number. She barely remembers her at all. Is it worth it? The tradeoff? She gets to live in relative peace while I'm here picking up the slack. But I get the bits of Mom that are still her. I think I'd rather live in reality than hide from it.

Chapter Five

WHEN I WAS in my freshman year of college, my philosophy
professor asked us to write a short paragraph detailing where
we saw ourselves in ten years. When we were done, he told
us to crumple up the paper while he walked around the room
with a small trash can, telling us to toss them in. He said our
aspirations didn't matter because free will doesn't exist. We
can't choose our fate; all we can do is stay morally sound
whatever the outcome may be. At the time, I shrugged off his
words as determinism. He was a philosopher. Those beliefs
were part of his code, but they didn't have to be part of mine.
But here I am, nearly ten years later, wondering if maybe
there was some truth to what he told us. I can't quite
remember what exactly I wrote on that paper, but I can definitely remember what I *didn't* write.

For starters, I never planned on being a college dropout. I
never thought I'd be working as a call center representative in
the billing department of Hope Community Hospital. And I
never could've predicted my mom's diagnosis and my sister's
subsequent abandonment. My life, as I know it now, is a
product of the situation I found myself in five years ago. I had
one semester left for my degree in Photojournalism. Mom

was always absentminded, but her forgetfulness was starting to disrupt her life and ours. She was still working full time at the flower shop when Liz, Mom's best friend and the owner of the shop, pulled me aside to express her concern. I'll never forget that conversation. It set off a chain reaction that moved so fast, I could hardly catch my breath. And, at times, I still can't. I close my eyes and let my thoughts drift back to that day.

Reaching for the doors to Flowers by Liz, I noticed a small canary-yellow bird eating bits of bread from a fast food wrapper that had been tossed into the trash can outside. I smiled at him thinking how he must feel so lucky to have discovered such a treat. Holding my mom's lunch bag in my left hand, I pushed open the door with my right. She had packed herself lunch that day but left it on the kitchen counter again. I laughed when I saw it sitting there. I didn't realize the significance of it or I never would've reacted so nonchalantly. Liz was behind the counter when I came in. Her eyes seemed to dim a little when she saw me, but I thought I must have imagined it.

"Hey, Liz! Is Mom around? She forgot her lunch again!" I held up the bag and chuckled.

Liz didn't return my amusement. Her face remained stoic and her jaw clenched. "Hi, Nellie. Your mom is in the greenhouse, but before you go back there—I've been meaning to talk to you for a little while now. It's about your mom."

"Uh, oh, what's she done this time? Did she talk another lovesick Romeo into telling his girl how he feels with words instead of flowers? She means well, Liz, but she can be so bad for business sometimes!" I laughed. Mom was always worried about people spending money on frivolous things. The fact that she worked in a flower shop, where most purchases were more of a want than a need, wasn't lost on me, and I teased her about it constantly.

Liz smiled at me, but it was the kind of sad grin you might give someone when you're about to deliver bad news. And that's exactly what she did next. "Honey, listen, I don't know how to say this so

I'm just going to say it. I think there may be something seriously wrong with your mom."

She may as well have punched me directly in the gut because her words knocked the wind right out of me. "What are you talking about?"

"I love Charlotte. You know that. And I know this isn't easy to hear, Nellie, but she's been overly forgetful lately. You must have noticed. Just the other day, she was in the middle of helping a customer look for pink daisies when suddenly she was in the front window fixing the display. The customer was confused, of course, and asked Charlotte if the pink daisies were part of the display. She turned to face him and looked stunned to see him standing there. I saw the look on her face, Nellie. It was as if she had never laid eyes on him before, and yet she had been helping him not more than three minutes earlier."

I waved my hand, dismissing her concern. "Oh, Liz, you know how Mom hasn't been sleeping well. It makes her brain foggy just like it would any of us. I'm sure she was just having an off day."

Liz wasn't convinced. "I wish that were all it was, but this is just one incident in a long list of many. And it's getting worse. Maybe I'm wrong here, but—"

"You are wrong." I didn't want to hear any more of her nonsensical theories. She was one hell of a florist, but the last time I checked, she didn't have a medical degree.

"I hope I am wrong, trust me. Just please do me a favor and make an appointment for her to see the doctor. If it's what you say it is, and she just isn't sleeping well, then maybe the doctor can help. Either way, what have you got to lose?"

The answer was everything. We had everything to lose.

I made an appointment for my mom to see her family doctor, and he referred us to a specialist. At the start of the visit, the doctor asked her to remember three words—banana, sunrise, and share, and at the end, he asked her to repeat those words. She only remembered banana. One-third of her memory worked at full capacity. The other two-thirds brought forth words that I will never forget. Early onset Alzheimer's disease.

I remember my initial reaction because it was so irrational, and yet, I couldn't help myself. I was mad at Liz. I may have even blamed her. No, if I'm being honest here, I *did* blame her. Not for the disease, but for the diagnosis. Before Liz spoke up, I was living a happy, carefree life. I was ignorant. That day marked the beginning of the end for so many aspects of life that I had come to know. That was the day that I lost everything and I've never been able to get it back.

Chapter Six

COLUMBIA HEIGHTS, California, population 8,263, sits on rolling hills near the southern end of the state. Hope Community Hospital takes up four blocks in the center of the small town. The billing department is part of the business office, which is located in a two-story stone building that sits catty-corner from the emergency room. This locale offers a medley of ear-splitting sirens off and on all day.

My apartment building is a quick two-block walk to the hospital, which I'm grateful for since most days I'm running late. I don't mean for it to happen. I set my alarm every night, but try as I might, I just can't seem to wake up without hitting the snooze button at least 102 times. Okay, maybe I'm exaggerating. It's probably more like ninety-seven times, but whatever the number, it's one too many because I'm always left scrambling.

This morning is no different. I only have myself to blame. I stayed up way too late reading about a new clinical trial for Alzheimer's. There's a new drug that's currently in the testing phase, but it sounds promising. Since Mom's diagnosis, I've subscribed to every mailing list I can find to stay up to date on the latest research.

When I look at the clock, I immediately shove the covers off and spring from my bed. It's 7:35 a.m. and my workday starts in twenty-five minutes. Last night's pajamas are propelled from my body as I frantically flip through the clothing in my closet. Dresses and skirts blaze past me until I eventually settle on a lightweight black and gray sweater, pairing it with a mustard-colored corduroy skirt. Charcoal tights and black boots complete the outfit. I imagine I probably look like the Tasmanian devil as I spin through my apartment brushing my teeth and finger detangling my hair. I grab a breakfast bar from my pantry and I'm out the door at 7:50 a.m. I shake my head as I race down the stairs and shove the front door open. Will I ever get my act together?

I'm hustling along the concrete path in a walk that's almost a jog. A couple of ill-timed "don't walk" signs throw off my commute, but I still manage to make it to the front door of the business office with a minute to spare.

My heart rate is slightly elevated and there's a sheen of sweat at my hairline. I tap my watch and notice I earned some exercise time from this morning's activities—the one silver lining to waking up late. I make a mental note to try harder tomorrow, but it's in the same ballpark as my New Year's resolution to eat healthier. Behind every good intention is an easier option. My life is so full of difficult decisions that sometimes I just can't handle one more complication, even if it is to my own detriment. *Especially* if it is.

Lila sits behind the vast receptionist's desk with the phone pressed to her left ear. Her long red manicured nails weave through the strands of her silky, wheat-colored hair. She nods absentmindedly as she pops a small bubble of gum with her teeth. Her eyes are glued to her computer screen. She doesn't notice me as I walk up and lean over the counter to peek at what has her so captivated.

Aha! Looks like Liam Hemsworth was spotted at a cafe not far from here. I make a show of my mock surprise as my lips form an obnoxious O. I lean back and my feet make contact with the carpet below. Tapping my index finger on the screen, I make a sizzle sound with my tongue as though Liam's hotness has managed to radiate through the computer. I have her attention now, and she's covering her mouth with her hands to keep from laughing. I wink at her as I sashay away from her desk and push my way through the doors that lead to the billing department.

As soon as I'm inside the office, I'm greeted with a wave of familiar voices, all speaking variations of the same script. We are the mecca for every billing related phone call that comes in to the hospital. The number that's printed on every bill prompting people to call with questions patches them here. Our phones take turns ringing in a carefully synchronized order. Everyone gets a turn; several turns, actually.

My station is the third one on the left, just as soon as you enter the door. Tan partitions separate us, and behind each one is a countertop with a computer and a headset. Our tools are minimal, but our workload is not. Most, if not all, of the calls that come in here begin with an irate person. Generally speaking, they're calling because they've received an astronomically high bill and they are usually wondering one of two things, and sometimes both.

1. I have insurance; why haven't they paid the bill?
 And
2. Am I *actually* responsible for this entire amount?

On the best days, I find a typo in their insurance group number. And once it's fixed, their entire bill is taken care of, and I come out looking and feeling like a hero. But on the worst days, their insurance company found a loophole, and, sadly, they *are* responsible for the entire bill. Those days far outnumber the good ones.

It's not an easy job, and it isn't for the weak at heart.

Compassion is a necessity, however—at least I've found that to be the case. Because these are people, and their feelings matter. I take the least amount of calls among all of my coworkers here, but it isn't because I'm lazy. I speak to less people because I spend more time with the ones I do speak to. I let them vent. I listen to their woes. I empathize because their problems are very relatable. I know what it's like to be faced with an impossibly large number on a bill. Shady Villa sends me one every month. It can feel crippling like you're buried under a mound of dirt with no shovel in sight.

I open the bottom drawer of my filing cabinet and slide my purse inside while reaching up and powering on my computer. The screen blinks to life as I plop down on my chair and glide toward the keyboard. With my password entered, I'm logged into the system and ready to take calls.

I'm in the middle of fastening my headset when a slight knock startles me. I turn and find Shane lightly rapping his knuckles against the metal molding on my cubicle. I smile warmly at him. He works at the station across from mine. He's in his mid-forties and has worked here for nearly twenty years. His dark brown hair is dusted with silver, and he keeps it cut close to his scalp to hide the baldness that's beginning to set in.

"Good morning, Shane! How was your weekend?"

He smiles brightly as he recalls how he spent the last two days. "It was great, actually. And do you know why?"

I smile and shake my head.

"Because I didn't do anything. Absolutely nothing at all. I'm telling you, Nellie, it was incredible. There were no soccer games, no trombone lessons, no mall drop-offs. Nothing! I know it was a fluke and I probably shouldn't get used to it, but I'm just glad I got to experience it once in my lifetime."

I chuckle. "Well, in that case, I'm glad for you, too!"

His smile turns sheepish.

I cock my head and give him my best "mom" look. "Okay, out with it. What's on your mind?"

"It's just, well, it's your turn to make the coffee run this morning, but you were just getting situated, and I hate to bother you." He waves his hand at me as though he's absolving me from my duties. "You know what, don't worry about it. I can go get it."

I pull my headset off and slide my chair back so I can stand. "No way! You went three times last week. We're supposed to take turns. It's the only way the system works." I level him with a playful glare. "Don't mess with the system, Shane."

He laughs and bends at the waist to slap his knee. Shane always laughs with his entire body, and when he really gets going, it's impossible not to laugh right along with him.

I hold out my hand palm side up. "Alrighty, hand over the order and I'll go get the petty cash."

I know he was already planning to go pick up the coffee himself, which is why I know he's already collected everyone's order. He gives me a toothy grin and places the paper in my hand.

* * *

EVEN THOUGH THIS town is relatively small, there's still a Starbucks on practically every corner, so my walk isn't far at all. Truth be told, I don't mind making the coffee run. I'm almost as bad as Shane with how often I volunteer to do it. I enjoy getting out of the office for a little while, but mostly, I just like Kathy, the barista at this location. She's always so quick-witted and full of clever anecdotes. Plus, she makes the best mochas around, so that doesn't hurt, either.

It's a Monday morning, so the inside of the coffee shop is bustling with activity, but oddly enough, there's no line at the register. I stroll up and see Kathy with her back to me and her body halfway inside a cabinet where they store extra bags of coffee.

I clear my throat loudly and announce my presence. "Are you playing hide and seek again, Kathy? Come on. We've been over this. You know there's no time to play games when caffeine is involved," I tease.

She slides out of the cabinet and stands, turning to face me, only it isn't Kathy. It's not a woman at all. Standing before me is a man who looks to be in his late twenties with a shock of dark brown wavy hair and those ocean blue eyes that I wasn't blessed with. The green Starbucks apron makes it hard to tell what his true build is like, but there's a definite shadow of a bicep under the sleeves of his black button-down. And I'm pretty sure I'm staring because now he's cleared his throat. I blink slowly and take a quick breath before peeling my gaze away from his arms, letting it travel back up to his face. He's regarding me with amusement. His arms cross in front of his apron, and I have to fight the urge to glance back down at them.

"So, you might've noticed, I'm not Kathy."

The corner of my lip hitches up. He may not be Kathy, but he has similar wit. "Yep. I noticed."

He's grinning at me, and my stomach dances with butter-flies in response. "But, just so we're clear, I'm not above playing hide and seek." He winks, and I'm suddenly grateful that I didn't have time for makeup this morning because my face surely has enough color all on its own.

"But I'm also not about to get between a person and their morning coffee. What can I get you?" His facial expression is one of warmth and kindness.

His smile reaches down into the darkness and awakens something in me that has been dormant for years. I feel my mouth turn up to match his as though I have no control over my own facial expression. And in this case, I definitely don't. "Oh, well, it was my turn to make the coffee run for my coworkers this morning. I have a list!" I hold up the paper I've unknowingly been crumpling in my hand. "Should I just hand it over to you, or would you like me to read it off?"

His eyes scan the mangled list and slide back up to meet mine. "Maybe it's better if you read the order to me. Plus, it'll give me a chance to listen to you talk some more." He smirks. I'm incredibly flustered, and I'm pretty sure he's enjoying every minute of it.

I tear my gaze from his and force my eyes onto the list as I smooth it out on the counter. My eyelids rise in shock from his comment, but I keep my head down so he can't see how he's affecting me. Of course, once I speak, I'm sure he'll hear it in my voice.

"Um, sure, I can just tell you the order. No problem." I try to sound confident, and it almost works if not for the slight waver in my tone. Damn nerves.

I manage to recite the long list of beverages, which is no easy feat considering this is Starbucks where no drink is ever simple. There are far too many descriptors like tall, nonfat, two pumps of peppermint, salted cold foam. When I reach the end of the order, he looks up at me, his eyes fixed on mine and a small smile playing on his lips. "What name should I put on the order?"

"Oh, it's, um, Nellie."

"Nellie."

I've always liked my name, but I like it even more when he says it.

"Yep. Like the rapper, only with an *-ie* instead of a *-y*." I add that last part and immediately wish I could take it back. I don't listen to Nelly. I hate rap music. But what if he thinks I'm a huge fan and realizes we have nothing in common? He looks like he might listen to Bon Iver, and I *love* Bon Iver. Music can make or break a relationship, and now I've ensured that we're dead in the water. What am I saying? Relationship? I don't even know his name. *Get a grip, Nellie.*

I'm afraid to look up at him, scared I might see disgust in his eyes because he thinks I groove to "Hot in Herre." When I finally find the courage to glance in his direction, he doesn't look disgusted. He looks thoroughly entertained. Maybe that isn't much better, but for now, I'll take it.

I move to the end of the counter and stand under the *pick up order here* sign. My fingernails are all bitten off—a repulsive habit that I always swear I'll quit but never do—but despite their blunt length, I still manage to tap out a nervous rhythm on the marbled laminate. Every so often, I let my eyes roam over him. He moves with purpose and confidence, frothing milk into art. I try to make myself stay quiet and just observe him, but my curiosity gets the better of me.

"So, what happened to Kathy? Is she okay?"

He glances up at me as he wipes up some foam from his workspace. "Yeah, she's fine. She just took some time off to go visit her brother in Toledo. She's been gone a week, actually, but I guess you must have missed her announcement." His eyes dance with humor, and I let out a chuckle. Anyone who's ever met Kathy knows that the woman loves to talk, and if she has news of any sort, everyone within a five-mile radius hears about it.

"Yeah, looks like I somehow managed to miss out on that." I pause for a beat to try to make my next question sound casual. "Will you be filling in for her then?"

He smiles widely, and I have a feeling I wasn't as smooth as I tried to be. He nods as he speaks. "Yes, I'll be here most mornings during the week while she's gone. I'm one of the managers here, but I usually work nights and weekends, so filling in for her was too good to resist. I'm Jude, by the way."

I feel a tingle when he tells me his name. He was real before, but now that I know his name, it puts him on another level. Now he's moved from being someone I'm talking to in passing to someone I can get to know.

Gripping the cardboard carrier with both hands, I smile

up at him. "Well, it's been nice meeting you, Jude." I turn toward the door and hear the thumping of his shoes as he comes up quickly behind me.

"Here, let me get that for you." He gives the door handle a tug and holds it open. I pass through it easily while balancing the multitude of coffees in the holder.

"Thank you. I was wondering how I was going to pull that off." I chuckle.

"Sure thing, Nellie with an -*ie*. Hope to see you again soon." His smile is wide and it reaches his eyes, making them gleam. There's something more behind them, but I've stared enough already.

I press my lips together in a small smile and look down at my boots as they take me away from him. When I'm a few feet away, I glance back and find him standing just inside the glass doors watching me walk away. My eyes find his, and he doesn't try to hide the fact that he's staring. He raises his hand and waves it slightly. With my hands full of coffee orders, I tip my head back at him, and then I face forward and let my feet propel me back to work. Back to reality.

Chapter Seven

I ONLY LET myself think about Jude for a moment on the walk back to work, but it's enough to ignite something within me. *Harmless flirtation, that's all it was,* but even as I say this to myself, I'm not sure I believe it. Or more importantly, I'm not sure I care. My interactions with men have been pretty asexual over the last few years. Charlie, my on-again-off-again college boyfriend, was a friend with benefits for a little while, but I could only stomach that relationship for a short time. I'm not cut out for a no-strings-attached arrangement. Sooner or later, there are always strings. I ended it about three years ago and have been close to celibate ever since.

I've been far too preoccupied taking care of my mom to focus on much of anything else. I'm not complaining. It's the way it has to be. But I won't lie—I've missed the charge I get from a wink or a second glance. That's not to say it hasn't happened, but this time, the feeling was mutual, and that was very new. I'm not sure what to do with these feelings, and I definitely don't have time for them, so I push them aside as I shove open the door at work.

* * *

WE AREN'T SUPPOSED to take personal calls when we're on the clock, but everyone here knows my situation, so they look the other way when I put my phone on hold and answer my cell. About three hours into my workday, my phone vibrates on my desk and a picture of my mom and me from a trip to Sequoia National Forest nine years ago illuminates the screen. I'm between work calls at the moment so I tap my hold button and scoop up my phone. I stare at our faces smiling back at me and close my eyes for a moment.

The woman on the other end of this call is not the same one who gasped in awe at the giant sequoias and then squealed in fright as a scorpion crawled over her boot. Even though I know all of this, I still need the reminder, and it breaks my heart every time. I don't want to be right. I want to answer this phone and hear delight in her voice as she tells me every minute detail of her day. I want to hear her laugh as she recalls something funny Liz said or tells me how many clueless boys she helped choose corsage flowers for their homecoming dates. I just want to answer the phone and hear my mom, my best friend.

I let out a deep breath and answer. "Hello, Mama?"

"Belly, I hate it here. I hate it so much!"

I sigh. Calls like this come in waves. Even though I've heard this many times, there's no way to gauge when she's feeling this way, so I'm always thrown by the desperation in her voice.

I try to speak slowly as though the calm tone of my voice will help to soothe her. It never works. "What happened?"

"Ohhhh," she moans. "They didn't bring me my chocolate pudding like they always do! They know I eat it right after I finish my tuna salad, but today they tried to give me vanilla! Vanilla, Belly! You know I hate vanilla!" She whines into the phone, sounding more like a toddler than a grown woman.

"Remember when this happened before? They were just out of chocolate pudding, but they ordered more and in two days it was back in the kitchen." I leave out the part about how those were the longest two days of my life. I swear it was the reason I switched to the unlimited call plan on my cell phone.

"No, they didn't give it to me out of spite! I didn't see Stacy in the kitchen, and I think they fired her. She would've given me my chocolate pudding! Now I'll never get it again because she's gone and it's their fault! I hate this place!" She expels the word "hate" from her mouth like it's a spoiled piece of meat. I can hear her gasping like she's trying to catch her breath.

"Mama, please, try to calm down."

"Why did you do this to me, Belly? Why did you put me here? I was a good mom, wasn't I? I don't deserve this."

Her words cut me wide open. Fat tears stream down my face and I frantically swipe at them. *This isn't your mom. She doesn't know what she's saying. This isn't your fault. You're doing the right thing.* In situations like this, you need a mantra. Something to keep you grounded. I often find myself repeating those few phrases over and over again. The problem is, despite knowing I'm right, I still don't believe what I'm saying. It all feels wrong. To my mom, it must seem like I've systematically taken control over everything in her life. Her house is gone; her car is gone; her autonomy is gone. I'm her child and I've robbed her of her free will. I know Alzheimer's is the thief, but buried way deep in my head is the worry that I'm not an innocent bystander, either.

"You're right. You don't deserve any of this. I wish I had a magic cure, you know? If I could fix it all, I would do it in a heartbeat. Hell, I still haven't given up hope that it can't be fixed. But for now, Shady Villa is the safest home for you. I promise you that."

"Belly, I need to go now. Paul Lynde is the center square, and I don't want to miss it."

And just like that, she's shifted gears. She's transitioned

from outrage to blame to watching *Hollywood Squares* in the span of a few minutes. The problem is, she might be no worse for the wear, but I most definitely am. I can't shrug conversations like this one off so easily. I can't forget the words she said or the finger she pointed. It feels as though, deep down, there must be a part of her that holds me responsible for her situation. She jumps to that conclusion way too easily. I take a deep breath and let it all go as I speak into the phone.

"Okay, Mama. Call me if you need anything."

"All right, I will. Love you." *Click*.

I'm left with nothing but my thoughts. These are the times when I miss her the most. My mom was my person. I always called her whenever I was upset about anything. She always knew when I needed her advice or when I just needed an ear. Now, she's the source of my upset and I have nowhere to turn.

Chapter Eight

AS I ROUND the corner and head down my street, I notice a figure slumped over on the front steps of my apartment. I pick up my pace, and as the person comes into view, I can make out Claudette's favorite lavender plaid scarf hanging loosely from her neck.

"Claudette? What's wrong?" My voice comes out in gasps.

She peels her head up and turns to look at me. Her eyes look a bit glazed over, but her mouth splits open into a wide grin. "Nellie! I'm all right, hunny. I just didn't drink enough water today and I got a little lightheaded." She cups her hand in front of her mouth as though she's going to whisper a secret. "Between you and me, I'm more embarrassed than anything else. I know better!"

I reach into my work satchel and find my water bottle. "Here," I say, handing it over. "Drink some of mine."

I plop down on the step next to her and watch as she takes long gulps from my bottle. When she empties it, she screws the cap back on and tilts her head to look in my direction. Her eyes no longer seem dazed, and her skin has more color to it. I let out a little sigh of relief.

She hands the bottle back to me with a coy look on her

face. "Looks like I was even thirstier than I thought. Thank you, hunny."

"Sure thing. I'm just happy that you're okay."

She laughs, and it's a throaty, guttural sound. "Oh, hunny, gonna take a lot more than a little dehydration to take me out!"

I chuckle. "I'm sure you're right about that." I stand and offer her my hand, but she waves me off. Placing her hands on her knees, she pushes up to standing with very little effort. She's so resilient.

We say our goodbyes in the hallway upstairs, and I stop in front of Jodi's apartment. She may have to endure my music through these walls, but I've had to endure her stifled sobs when she thinks no one can hear her. When my dad left, Meg and I were young. Our mom shielded us from the hardships of single-mom life much in the same way Jodi protects Annabelle. But as the years went by, my sister and I realized how much our mom had done for us and she had Poppy's help for most of that time. As far as I can tell, Jodi doesn't have anyone. I'm overwhelmed with the desire to help her, but she isn't always receptive. She doesn't want to be a charity case. Sometimes I slide a grocery store gift card under their door when I know that no one's home. Other times, like tonight, I pack up leftovers and pretend I've made too much, hoping she'll take the food with little complaint. It's worth a shot.

Once I'm inside my apartment, I crack open the fridge and locate the extra-large Tupperware container that I filled to the brim with potato soup. There's a bag of toppings resting on the lid so I grab those as well.

On my way out the door, I notice my keys on the floor. Sliding my index finger through the ring, I pick them up and raise my hand to return them back to the hook, but it's not there, or at least not all of it is. The hooked part appears to have snapped off, leaving just the base screwed to the wall.

Well, that's just great. I groan. Looks like a trip to the hardware store is in my immediate future.

It's just after 4:30 p.m., so I'm sure Jodi's awake. I rap my knuckles against the door, and within a few moments, I hear the deadbolt unlock from the other side. The door cracks open, and chestnut eyes peer out at me. Jodi spied me through her peephole, no doubt, or else she never would've opened the door. Even still, she hesitates to open her door fully until her eyes land on mine.

"Yeah?" Despite the exhaustion in her voice, there's no mistaking the disdain in her tone. Her eyes are ringed with dark circles and her jet-black hair is pulled back into a severe ponytail.

I smile at her and try to keep the pity from infecting my tone. "Hey, Jodi. I'm sorry to bother you. How's it going?"

She sighs deeply. "Oh, I'm just peachy. Can't you tell?" She waves her hand in front of her face.

I feel my resolve falter a bit, but I do my best to ignore it. "Um, well, I made a little too much soup last night and I'd hate for it to go to waste." I lift up the container in front of me as though it were a shield to protect me from the daggers her eyes are shooting my way.

"Well, isn't that just the sweetest little coincidence." She eyes me with distrust.

"Yeah, so here." I thrust the container at her. "Why don't you take it? You and Annabelle would be doing me a favor."

She glares at the soup but makes no move to take it.

"Mom?" Annabelle calls out from inside the apartment.

Jodi pulls her head back and pushes the door so that it's mostly closed. "What is it?"

"I'm hungry, and there's nothing in the fridge. Can we order a pizza or something?"

Jodi's face reappears in the doorway looking more weary than combative. She glances back down at the Tupperware in my hands and then lifts her eyes to the ceiling, sighing loudly.

She reaches for the container, glances up at me one last time, and then she shuts the door.

"You can just return the container when you're done or keep it," I say to no one.

* * *

MY LITTLE VOLKSWAGEN GOLF waits for me in the parking lot across the street. Brad, the slumlord, owns a few apartment buildings on this block as well as the parking lot. Each tenant is allowed one numbered space, and there are a few extras meant for visitors. My sky blue hatchback is in spot twenty-seven. The driver's side door opens with a low screech. This old car has just over one hundred forty-seven thousand miles on it, but the engine still turns over every time I turn the key, so I have no plans to replace it. If it weren't for visiting mom on a regular basis, I'd have no real need for a car. I can walk to work, and Smart Shopper is just around the corner. Plus, the public transportation system isn't half bad. But my current situation requires a car so that's why I have Emma.

Yeah, I'm one of those people who names her car, but in my defense, she's made life a little easier for me. It only seemed fitting to give her a name. Bon Iver released "For Emma, Forever Ago" in 2008, the same year my car was made, and so Emma was the obvious choice.

The Home Depot is a ten-minute car ride from my apartment. As I enter the store, I hear the drumbeat of my phone. I move off to the side of the entrance and out of the flow of foot traffic. "Hey, Mama. What's up?"

"Nellie?"

"Yep, it's me."

"Oh, this is Mom calling."

I let out a slow exhale. "Yes, I know. Is everything okay?"

"Uh-huh. Everything's good. Listen, what day is it today?"

I bought her a calendar earlier this year once these calls became a daily occurrence, but every so often, she forgets to look there first and calls me instead. "Today is Tuesday." I chuckle. "Hey, Mom, remember what Poppy used to say whenever he burped? 'Excuse me, today is Tuesday.'" I say the last word the same way he did, with an *e* sound making it rhyme with "me."

She doesn't say a word, but her silence is answer enough.

"Okay, Bells, it's time for my dinner now."

"All right, I'll talk to you soon," I say, trying to keep the dejected tone from my voice.

"Love you, bye."

I stare at the phone in my hand, wishing that conversation had ended differently or better yet, that it never happened in the first place.

I pass by a small display of pocket-sized flashlights. They're unencumbered by plastic packaging and sorted into bins by color. I pick one up and marvel at how easily it fits within the palm of my hand. If I close my fist, you would never even know I was holding it. There's no one around me, but just in case I'm being watched, I lean down and sift through the bins along the bottom shelf, all the while keeping my hand closed tightly around the flashlight. When it feels like the right amount of time has passed, I stand and begin walking away. With each step, I feel the effects of the phone call slide away, replaced with a temporary adrenaline rush. I stealthily reach into my purse and let the flashlight fall inside. Then I scoop up my ChapStick from an internal pocket and uncap it. While I glide it onto my lips, I move my eyes around the store to make sure no one saw what I just did. Once I'm satisfied that I'm in the clear, I pop the cap back on and slide my ChapStick back into my purse, being careful not to stop moving.

I quickly navigate to the aisle where hooks are sold. Brad isn't super efficient when it comes to small repairs, so over the past few years, I've come to know my way around this store. I'm not the handiest of people, but my poppy made sure I knew how to use a few basic power tools, and where I'm lacking, YouTube has proven to be a pretty useful resource.

I'm not looking for anything fancy, and honestly, this hook isn't a real necessity. I could just keep my keys on the table next to my purse, but the broken hook would drive me nuts. I installed it three years ago and I've become very accustomed to using it. I can't stand when things are out of place. And this is just one of those small problems that I can solve. Those are few and far between these days, and so, when I encounter one, I act on it immediately. I like the feeling of knowing I fixed something.

I'm holding up two hooks, trying to decide between an oil-rubbed bronze or a satin nickel, when I hear the faint sound of humming behind me. It's barely noticeable at first but starts becoming increasingly louder as though the "throat musician" is moving closer to me. I know this song. I lift my eyes to the ceiling and try to remember the words. And then it hits me. It's "Hot in Herre" by Nelly. This can't be a coincidence.

I turn my head and find Jude standing behind me wearing a shit-eating grin. I can't help but laugh at the absurdity of the situation. I give him a smirk. "I bet you think you're so clever, don't you?"

He chuckles. "Trust me, Nellie with an -ie, I *am* clever. There's no question there."

"Uh-huh." I nod. "I'm becoming aware of that pretty quickly."

He leans in to inspect what I'm holding. "So, need some hooks, huh? What are you planning on hanging from those?" His eyebrows rise to his hairline with interest. I try to suppress a giggle, but it still manages to squeak out. I clear my throat and try to recover my composure.

"Yeah, my key hook that I keep by my door broke, so I need to replace it." I look down at the two choices in my hands and sigh. "I've been trying to decide which finish to go with. It should be an easy decision, but sometimes those are the hardest to make."

He eyes the hooks for a split second before speaking. "Oil-rubbed bronze."

"Really?"

"Really," he says with confidence.

"You seem pretty sure of your choice."

He's wearing a smug look. "I am sure because as far as I'm concerned, it's the *only* choice."

I cock my head and study him, but his expression gives nothing away. "Okay, now I'm intrigued. How can you be so sure?"

His eyes sparkle. "Because, Nellie, bronze is the perfect shade for you. It adds to the depth of your eyes and brings out the natural highlights in your hair."

This is only the second time we've seen each other, and our flirtation and back and forth banter has felt natural, but his casual admission stuns me. I can't seem to form any coherent thoughts, which is probably for the best because at that very moment, a leggy brunette with waist-length hair sidles up alongside Jude. She playfully pushes on his shoulder and says, "I leave you alone for five minutes and you've already found someone else to annoy." She rolls her eyes in mock irritation.

I feel my stomach plummet the way it might if I had just been given devastating news. And in a roundabout way, I have. This gorgeous girl leaning on Jude is clearly his girlfriend, and my ability to read signals needs obvious work because I've been all wrong.

The need to remove myself from this situation is overwhelming. I frantically try to come up with a reason to leave immediately, but Jude speaks up before I have the chance.

"Don't worry, Sam, I've saved all of my best jabs for you." He winks at her. The same way he winked at me in the coffee shop. I feel nauseous.

The girlfriend shakes her head and looks my way. Her eyes scan the length of me as though she's sizing up the competition. I want to raise my hands and back away with my tail between my legs. I despise confrontation of any sort and will always run in the opposite direction when faced with it.

"Jude-y, where are your manners? Aren't you going to introduce me to your friend?" Did I imagine it or did she practically spit the word "friend" from her mouth?

Jude groans. "I was trying to save her from actually having to speak to you, but now since you've left me no choice—Nellie, this is my sister, Sam. Sam, this is Nellie, like the rapper only with an -ie not a -y." He looks so proud of himself. I should smack him for adding that last part, but I barely heard anything he said after "sister."

I feel giddy and my body vibrates with adrenaline. I just experienced an entire medley of emotions in the span of about five minutes. That has got to be a new record for me. I hold out my hand, and Sam takes it in hers. "It's nice to meet you, Sam. And you have my sympathies."

She looks confused for a moment before my joke lands. "Oh, girl, growing up with this guy"—she arcs her thumb in his direction— "my skin is at least seven layers thick."

We share a laugh at Jude's expense. He wears an insulted look on his face, but there's a glint in his eyes. He feels no shame.

I hang the satin nickel hook back and hold up the oil-rubbed bronze. "Well, I should get going."

The corners of Jude's mouth turn down slightly. If I were

the type of person who analyzed subtle details like that, I might think he looks disappointed.

He juts his chin out toward the hook in my hand. "So you're going with the bronze, I see." He looks pleased with himself.

I purse my lips to try to contain the urge to smile at him like an idiot. "It seemed like the obvious choice." We share a knowing look and it's like we have a secret. "What about you? You never told me what you were looking for."

He studies my face, and I watch his Adam's apple bob with a swallow. "I'm pretty sure I found exactly what I was looking for."

* * *

I'M LISTENING to an audiobook on the car ride home, but I couldn't tell you a thing about it. I've been replaying the conversation I had with Jude over and over in my mind, specifically the last thing he said. What did he mean he found exactly what he was looking for? He couldn't have meant me, could he? I never had a chance to ask him because right after he spoke, we were rudely interrupted by an employee asking if we needed help. As it turned out, Jude was there to pick up a few boards to repair Sam's deck and they had been searching for someone to cut them. The next thing I knew, they were being whisked off to the lumber aisle, and I was left standing there clenching my teeth to keep my jaw from dropping open.

I'm normally not a very astute person. In fact, I often misread situations, but it's hard to misinterpret this one. I may have been out of the dating scene for a while, but I think I know when someone is interested in me. And Jude is most definitely interested.

I think about what that might mean for me. Can my life

handle a new development? Is there room in my heart for a relationship?

I give my head a shake. I'm getting way ahead of myself here. I hardly know him and here I am analyzing what it might be like to be in a relationship with him. *Oh, Nellie, you are so out of practice.*

* * *

THE LIGHT above the mailboxes is barely suspended by the wires above. It's holding on for dear life, and with the wires beginning to fray, it's only a matter of time before it comes crashing down. I've already told Brad about it, but like everything else wrong with this place, he has yet to address it.

I flick through the contacts on my phone until I find his name. I would rather have root canal than call Brad, but this problem poses more of a danger so I suppress my disgust as I listen to the ring on the other end.

"Talk to me."

It's just three words but uttered by that man, they are the three most irritating words on the planet. I'm instantly on edge and I let my mood filter through my voice. "Brad, it's Nellie."

"Nellie, huh? Remind me again who that is?"

This is just one of his many stall tactics. "I live in one of the apartments on Elmwood."

"Oh, yeah, I remember you. You're the one with the noisy shower, right?" He coughs out a chuckle.

I roll my eyes up to the ceiling and silently beg for strength. "That's right, and it's still screeching, by the way. But that's not why I'm calling."

"Of course, it ain't. So, what is it this time? Is the beeping on your microwave too loud." His raspy laugh fills the line and singes my last nerve.

"As a matter of fact, there's a light fixture just inside the front door that's barely hanging on. I'd hate for it to fall on the wrong person. You could wind up with a huge lawsuit on your hands."

"Whoa, whoa, now!" My lips curl into a grin. That got his attention. "I'll come over this week and get it fixed."

"Thank you."

"But you know what you need, doll? You need to get yourself a boyfriend. Then you won't have to call me every time you need a light bulb changed. Ha!"

Before I can even form a coherent response, he dismisses me. "Hey, listen, I gotta go. Yours ain't the only building I own, you know. I'm a busy man in high demand. I'll get to your light bulb when I get to it." *Click.*

Defeat settles on my shoulders as I peer up at the mangled light fixture. I shouldn't be at all surprised by the way that conversation went. If I've come to know anything about Brad, it's that he's predictably bad at his job. Still, I naively thought it might be different this time. I do this same thing with my mom—put unrealistic expectations on a person. I'm setting myself up for heartache every time, but I can't seem to stop myself from hoping. And I can't stop the despair that always follows the letdown.

Chapter Nine

MY HANDS SLIDE on the chilled metal handle of the glass door and I give it a tug. As I step inside Starbucks, the wafting aroma of freshly ground coffee beans overwhelms me. It's a scent I wish I could bottle up and keep in my pocket to experience any time I wanted.

I spy Jude before he sees me. He's at the register keying in an order from a tall man wearing a gray suit. There's a line this morning, but I'm grateful for it. Now I have some time to collect my thoughts and calm my nerves. I give my head a shake. This boy is supposed to be my recipe for calm, not the final ingredient in a chaos soufflé.

There are three people ahead of me. A girl with a short blond bob who looks to be in her early twenties is next in line. Her eyes haven't left Jude's face. I can feel the lust radiating off of her in waves. My shoulders pull back, an involuntary response of defense. *Actually, this is good,* I think to myself. If Jude responds to her the same way he does with me, then at least I can prevent any further embarrassment on my part.

I keep my back to them as I pretend to investigate a display of mugs on a shelf. I probe the raised lettering while tilting my head so that their conversation is in earshot.

"What can I get for you?" Jude asks this same question of every person in line. It's the first thing he says to everyone, *except me*. Our interaction was instantly flirtatious, and I smile triumphantly knowing that "blond bob girl" didn't get the same treatment.

"Oh, well, that depends..." She lets her voice trail off seductively, and I steal a glance over my shoulder to find her exactly how I pictured her to be—leaning down with her elbows on the counter and her chest on full display. I peek at Jude and am shocked to see his eyes remain fixed on the screen of the register. She's setting a trap, but so far, he's not taking the bait.

He looks bored, and when he speaks, the disinterest in his voice is impossible to ignore. "Depends on what?"

She chuckles like she's the cat that caught the canary when really she's the splinter in someone's finger. "On you, of course."

He sighs audibly. "I'm sorry, but as you can see, there are a lot of people waiting. If you could just tell me what you'd like, I'll get it ready for you and then we won't be holding anyone up."

Point for Jude! The ball is in her court now. I angle my head so I can hear what she'll do with it.

"I was just hoping you might have a suggestion for me. You seem trustworthy. What's your favorite thing to drink here?"

I've gotta hand it to her, the girl has tenacity. Even if it does make her seem desperate, she's not giving up easily, that's for sure.

Now it's Jude's turn to respond. "I'll tell you what, why don't I just make you a Mocha Frappuccino. Every kid who comes in here orders one, so I don't think you could go wrong with that."

Game, set, match. Ladies and gentleman, we have a winner. If she thought she might be able to win him over before, she definitely knows she can't now that he just lumped her into a group with children.

I catch a glimpse of her crestfallen face before she solemnly shuffles over to the pickup area. I almost feel sorry for her. Almost. But mostly, I feel invigorated knowing that flirtation isn't just a part of Jude's job description. Everything he said to me, the way he responded, it was all meant for me. The realization makes me feel warm all over.

I'm so engrossed in my feelings of triumph, I don't even notice the man in front of me give his order. But suddenly, it's my turn, and Jude's tumultuous eyes are fixed on mine.

"Well, well, well, if it isn't Nellie with an -*ie*." He playfully crosses his arms and leans back, his eyes assessing me like he's trying to memorize my face. "What brings you here on this fine Wednesday morning?"

You. It's on the tip of my tongue, and maybe I should just say it, lay my cards out on the table face up for him to see. But I decide to play it coy for the time being. "My turn for the office order again." I lift my right shoulder in a half shrug trying to seem nonchalant, but judging from the smug look on his face, I think I'm failing miserably. Maybe my enormous smile gave me away. I can't help it. I have zero poker face.

"You know, you don't strike me as the office type."

I bristle a little. "I don't? Why not? What's wrong with working in an office?" My job is a bit of a sore subject for me. It's not that I hate what I do. It isn't my favorite line of work, but it's tolerable and I love my coworkers. It's just not where I pictured myself working. I was backed into a corner and left with no other choice. I could be miserable and feel sorry for myself or I could just accept things for what they are and make the best of my situation. Wallowing seems pointless. I don't spend a lot of time thinking about how I've fared in everything that's happened. Nothing good will come of that. Jude's comment makes it sound as though he sees through all of that, and it sets me off balance.

He furrows his brow and steadies his gaze like he's trying to discern why I've suddenly turned defensive. When he finally speaks, he does so slowly and with care as if he's afraid he'll scare me off. "There's nothing wrong with working in an office, Nellie. I mean, I'm a twenty-nine-year-old barista at Starbucks. We all have our own stories and this is just a chapter in mine. All I meant was, when I look at you, I picture you outside. You just don't strike me as someone that walls could easily contain."

I have no clue how he could know all of that from the few encounters we've had. I'm quiet for a moment as I try to collect my thoughts. This conversation suddenly took a very deep turn, and if I'm not careful, we'll head down a road that I'm not ready for. I can't seem to find the words to respond, but luckily, I don't have to.

I'm pretty sure Jude can see me struggling so he decides to throw me a bone. "So, this office where you work, is it nearby?" He watches me with interest.

I look down at the counter and smile, glancing up at him through thick eyelashes. I watch his throat bob and feel victorious. I know what I'm doing, and I know how it's affecting him. I couldn't stop even if I tried. And I'm having far too much fun. "Yeah, I suppose you could say it's nearby."

He gives me a sly smile. He's definitely on to me. He prods me for more. "Close enough to walk?"

I reach over and run the tips of my fingers along the edges of the gift cards on display. "Uh-huh." I nod. I can feel his searing glare burning a hole in my face, but I keep my eyes on the cards.

"Interesting."

My gaze snaps to his and I can see that I've given him what he wanted. My full attention. "What do you mean, interesting?"

He shrugs and tries to appear casual. "It's just obvious that I was right, that's all."

My face scrunches with confusion. I feel like I'm walking into a trap, but curiosity gets the better of me. "Right about what, exactly?"

"That you don't like to be boxed in. The first chance you get, you're pushing open those doors and breathing in the fresh air." He crosses his arms and looks so sure of himself.

I laugh at his self-righteousness. I can't help myself. "Oh, wow, remind me never to play a board game with you."

He juts his chin back pretending to be offended. "Why? Because I'd win every time?"

I shake my head. "You're impossible."

A loud throat clearing snaps both of us out of our cozy little bubble. We turn our heads and see blond bob girl eyeing her nonexistent watch and looking very put out. Jude shoots me a sheepish half-smile and holds up his finger.

He preps her Frappuccino and the other man's latte at lightning speed and places them onto the pickup counter. Then he sidles back over to me, placing his hands on the counter and leaning forward. "So, where were we?"

I hold out the list of drink orders from my coworkers. "You were just about to make these for me." I wink at him and he grins in return.

Once Jude has the various coffee beverages secured in a carrier, he slides it over the counter, but just as I reach down to take it, he tugs it back.

I raise my eyes to his, an expectant look on my face. His expression matches mine. We're both looking for something from each other.

"Where was it that you said you worked again?"

I curl my lips into my mouth and press them together, trying to contain my smile. He's so into me, and he's not even trying to hide it. I have no idea what he could possibly see in me, but I'm just going to enjoy the ride while it lasts. "I didn't." I pause just long enough to make him wonder if I'm going to answer, and then I give him what he wants. "I'm a call center rep in the billing department at Hope Community."

He nods, a contemplative look on his face. When he hands me the carrier, his fingers graze mine. I feel the floor shift below my feet. Our eyes lock, confirming he felt it, too.

I turn to leave and call over my shoulder, "I'll see you around, Jude."

"Without a doubt, Nellie."

My cheeks flush as I move toward the exit. Blond bob girl beats me there and holds the door open for me. I thank her, and when we're outside, she turns to face me.

"Your boyfriend is super cute. You're a lucky girl."

I shake my head. "Oh, he's not—"

She holds up her hand. "Please. Have you seen the way he looks at you? If he's not your boyfriend yet, he will be soon. Trust me." And with that, she spins on her heel and walks away.

Do I want a boyfriend? I peek through the glass doors and watch Jude pour coffee beans into the top of the industrial espresso machine. I can't help but smile. *If the boy is Jude, then yeah, I think a boyfriend is exactly what I want.*

Chapter Ten

INSIDE MY APARTMENT, I can't stop thinking about Jude. My thoughts are all over the place. I need to talk this through with someone.

I'm reminded of the monster crush I had on Mike Reilly in ninth grade. He was giving me whiplash with all of his mixed signals and it wasn't until I sat down with my mom and hashed everything out, that I realized it was a one-sided "romance." Mom was always straightforward with me, but with a delicate tone to ease the harshness of her words. "Nellie, I know you like this boy, but he hasn't been fair with your heart. He likes you one minute and he's ignoring you the next. I don't think he's earned the right to take up so much of your time. You deserve more." A faint smile touches my lips. She always did have a way of making me feel better.

I reach into my purse and grab my phone. Without thinking, I just dial. The phone rings four times before her answering machine picks up. My voice greets me on the other end.

"Hello, you've reached Charlotte's phone. She's unable to answer your call right now, but please leave a message. Chances are she's listening." *BEEP*

"Hi, Mama, are you there? It's me, Nellie." I wait a few seconds and then hear the familiar sounds of the receiver being picked up followed by my mom's voice.

"Belly? Is that you?"

"Yep, it's me. How are you?"

"Oh, sorry, I was in the bathroom."

This is her standard reason for never answering her phone when it rings. It's a lie, but I never call her out on it. She always lets her machine pick up, and then she sits by idly screening the call and deciding whether or not to pick up. Sometimes she answers and sometimes she doesn't. I've been on the receiving end of both responses so I consider it a good sign that she chose to answer today.

"That's okay. Hey, listen, I wanted to talk to you about something. I met this guy, and I think he may actually like me. And…well, I like him, too. I want to get to know him better. Is it weird if I ask him if he wants to have dinner with me?" I pause and wait for her answer, but it never comes. Not in the way I was hoping for, anyway.

She sighs into the phone. "Belly, I'm almost out of cranberry juice. Can you bring me some next time you come?"

I close my eyes and sit in absolute stillness for a breath. I used to tell my mom everything. Nothing was sacred. No stone was left unturned. Irrational hope led me to pick up the phone. Memories of past conversations pushed me to dial her number. But it's not the same, and it'll never be the same again. I'm not doing myself any favors by pretending.

"Sure. I'll bring you some next time." I dig my fingernails into my palms to keep the emotion out of my voice. I used to think if I let her see how affected I was, it would tap into some hidden part of her—that the small bits of her that were still my mom would awaken. But the mom who raised me never emerges and I'm always left feeling worse. Now I just swallow it all down, all the pain and disappointment.

"Thank you, Belly. Okay-I've-gotta-go-now-love-you-bye!" The long stream of words is her typical way to end phone conversations, and it's also an effective way to cut off any further comments from the person on the receiving end. She's still clever despite her condition.

As usual, she hangs up before I have a chance to say good-bye. I'm used to it, but it doesn't make it hurt any less.

* * *

THE SHOWER IS the only place I ever allow myself to *feel* things. I spend most of my day either repressing my sadness and frustration or trying to mask it by doing something nice for someone. I can't let those emotions overwhelm me because I'll shut down, and I don't have time to shut down. When I'm in the shower, I let the steady stream cascade over me while I grieve the mother I'm losing piece by piece. This disease is death in slow motion. It acts like a parasite feeding off of its host, draining their memory and personality.

The water rains down from the showerhead and mixes with my tears, taking them down into the drain where I'll let them stay. This was my fault tonight. I set myself up for disappointment by calling her. I found myself needing to work through my thoughts out loud and calling my mom was my natural response. Some habits are just really hard to break.

I lean my head against the wall. The cool shower tile feels soothing on my temple. I close my eyes and give in to the first thought that pops into my head. *Jude*. My eyes spring open in surprise. My mom is always the central focus of all of my thoughts. This is the first time in a few years that I've thought about anyone besides her.

I'm in the shower, my sacred space, so I'll indulge for a moment. What is it about Jude that has me so transfixed? It's a question that needs no answer because I already know. Jude is attractive. Let's just get that out of the way. His hair is thick and dark with unruly waves that make it lie in a sort of haphazard perfection. His eyes are the sort that you read about. My mom and I took a trip up the Pacific Coast once. The sky was dark and menacing, and the ocean reacted with choppy swirling movements. Deep blues mixed with cobalt and cerulean. Each color stayed true but also took on an entirely different hue. Jude's eyes are exactly like that. They aren't just beautiful; they're otherworldly. And if I'm not careful, I could fall right into them and get lost for hours.

I could stand under this water mentally listing all the ways in which Jude is the most beautiful man I've ever seen, but that would take forever and I'd only be scratching the surface. I don't know him. Not really, anyway, but the parts I do know make me desperate to know more. He has confidence, but he's not cocky. He is witty and charming, and he speaks with an honesty that completely disarms me.

When I think about how he makes me feel, there's only one word that fits. Comfortable. Despite my attraction to him, I feel relaxed when I'm in his company. He makes my reality blur at the edges and my worries all but vanish. When I'm with Jude, it's the only time since my mom's diagnosis when I've felt truly at ease.

I let out a deep groan. I know I'm in trouble now. Peace has evaded me for years, but now that I've had a small taste of it, I'm desperate for more.

Chapter Eleven

SWERVE IS WAITING for me outside of my apartment. She's not alone today. A timid, rail-thin, black cat with pale green eyes hides behind her, using Swerve's body as a shield. I'm slow in my approach, careful not to scare the little black cat off. When I reach the steps, I lower myself onto the top one and lean back against the wrought iron bars of the railing. Swerve wastes no time sauntering over to me and pressing her bony orange head against my hand. I run my fingers along her face tracing the bottom edge of her jaw. She purrs with approval and eyes the little black cat huddled in the corner. "Who's your friend, sweet girl? Are you two hungry?" Swerve's friends aren't always as cordial as she is. I learned that lesson the hard way when I once tried to pat the back of a gray cat she brought with her and earned myself a neat little row of bloodied scratches on the top of my hand. Now I just follow their lead. If they want to be touched, they'll let me know; otherwise, I just offer food and water.

While I'm spooning out the canned food into a bowl, my phone chimes inside my purse with an incoming text. I rest the spoon on the lip of the metal bowl and pull my phone from its pocket. It's Meg, which is unusual, considering I'm almost always the one to text or call first. I swipe at the screen and open my message app.

> **Meg:** Belly, Mom left a message on my phone today.
> Can you please call me as soon as you get this text?

Uh-oh. I have a feeling this won't end well. I tug the corner of my lip into my mouth and mindlessly bite at it. A couple of weeks ago, while I was visiting Mom, I mentioned Meg. Mom said she hadn't spoken to her in a while so, without thinking, I jotted down Meg's phone number onto a scrap piece of paper and put it on Mom's side table next to the phone. I just assumed she'd never call, and after several days passed, I figured it must have gotten tossed into the trash. Apparently, I was wrong.

It's not that Meg doesn't care about her. I know she does. It's more that she'd rather not have to deal with any of this. Mom's messages are never ordinary. She doesn't call to see how you are or to tell you about something fun that she did that day. She only calls if she needs something, either a physical something or worse—the kind of something that neither of us can give her. Relief.

I set my phone onto the counter and take the food and water out to the waiting cats. I give Swerve a few quick pats, and then I head back inside to deal with my sister.

Given our tumultuous relationship now, it would probably surprise most people to know that when Meg and I were little, we were inseparable. But isn't that always the story? Two siblings are the best of friends until trauma yanks them apart. The cataclysmic event in our lives was our mom's diagnosis, but if I'm honest with myself, Meg started distancing herself even before we had any answers. For lack of a better word, or maybe it's the only word that works, our mom started *changing*. It was barely noticeable at first, but one of the first things to go was her humor. Our mom had the best sense of humor. She would laugh at anything and everything, and more often than not, she was the butt of her own jokes. Her laugh went first, followed by her smile. I thought she might be depressed, and I even suggested to Meg that we should get Mom into therapy. Meg shook it off and told me I was looking for problems where there weren't any, but I saw the doubt in her eyes even as she said the words. She knew something was happening, but Meg's best defense has always been avoidance. She moved nearly three thousand miles away to pretend that everything was still normal. If our mom is calling her, then the protective little haven she built around herself isn't so safe anymore.

I close my eyes and breathe in, holding my breath for the count of five, and then I exhale. I tap Meg's name on my phone and the screen lights up in response. She answers on the first ring.

"Belly! I'm assuming you got my text?"

"Hello to you, too, Meg. And yes, I did. I called as soon as I could."

She sighs with annoyance. "So, then you know Mom called me?"

She insists on this dance even though we both know that it isn't necessary. Of course, I know that Mom called her. Didn't I just say that I got her text? But I know this is how Meg needs this conversation to go. She has to feel like she's in charge, and so I let her guide the conversation. "Yep, I read that in your text, Megs."

"Annnd, any ideas on where she got that idea?" She draws out the "and" like it's necessary. It isn't. I'm the only one who could've given Mom Meg's number. I'm where the idea came from. Meg knows it, and I know it.

I chew on my lip and take a few seconds to decide the best method to handle this. I think about my mom and what life must be like for her now. She was a single mother with a job and two children. She never had much, but what little she did have, she gave to us. Now she's living in a state of confusion at a home she doesn't recognize with people she doesn't know. And I feel angry. I'm furious on her behalf. So I channel those emotions and I empty them onto my sister. "Let's just call a spade a spade here, Megs. You know where Mom got your number. *Our* mother got *her* daughter's phone number from her *other* daughter. She misses you, Meg. She was asking about you and talking about how long it's been since the two of you last spoke. What else would you have had me do in that situation? I didn't know she'd actually call you, but honestly, I didn't think it would matter much if she had. Giving Mom your number seemed like the right thing to do at the time. It was the only thing I could do."

I hear her quick intake of breath over the line that connects us despite being miles apart. "Oh, Belly, I know this is hard for you. Trust me, I know. But you're living so close to Mom and I'm so far away. How can I help her from here? I just feel helpless, you know?"

Yeah, I know, Meg. And who's responsible for that distance, again? I don't say any of that even though I probably should. "I know all about feeling helpless, Meg. You feel like you can't help her from where you are, but honestly, I can't help her much from here, either. Distance doesn't matter in this situation."

"She said they ran out of chocolate pudding again. I can't believe she still eats that every day!"

I shake my head. She wouldn't know what Mom eats because she never calls her. And whenever I call, Meg barely lets me tell her anything about Mom.

"Habits bring her comfort, Meg. It may not be the healthiest choice for her, but if it brings her a modicum of peace, I don't see the harm in it. The biggest issue, the one I've been struggling with for the past couple of months, is her refusal to stay hydrated. She drinks just enough, but not enough." I know Meg doesn't want to hear about any of this, but she opened a door when she chose to text me, and I won't be the one to close it.

"Hmm, have you tried just telling her how it is?"

"I'm not sure I follow, Meg."

She chuckles. "Of course, you don't, Belly. You're *way* too nice too much of the time."

My hand tightens around the phone. I've changed my mind. Maybe I don't want this door to be opened anymore. "What else would you suggest I do, Megan?"

"Tell her exactly why she's living there. And don't sugar-coat it." She speaks so matter-of-factly, as though her proposal is innovative.

I once tried telling my mom she has Alzheimer's. I was at my wit's end. Everything I had in my arsenal wasn't working. I was out of tricks up my sleeve. There were no more rabbits in my hat. I thought that maybe if I leveled with her and told her exactly why she needed to stay there, she'd understand. The problem is reasoning doesn't work with someone who has lost their ability to reason. Telling her she had a disease made things so much worse. She became belligerent, calling me cruel. It was the first time she used that word to describe me, and I wish I could say it was also the last, but sadly, it's a word I've heard more times than I can count. Lucky for me, if you can call it luck, short-term memory loss is a symptom of Alzheimer's. She's forgotten all about what I told her that day, but I never have. And I won't be making the same mistake twice. I'm not going to tell my sister any of this. There's no point. She wasn't there to see our mom's extreme reaction, and nothing I say will convince her that her idea won't work.

"Great idea, Meg. Maybe I'll give that a whirl and see what happens." There's no life in my voice, no inflection. I'm sure Meg notices, but if she acknowledges it, then she'll have to acknowledge everything else—our mother's disease, our strained relationship, how she deserted me and left me to go through all of this alone. "I'm sorry if Mom's call caught you off guard."

"It's no problem, Belly. I know you were just doing what you thought was best. I'll call her soon to check in." It's an empty promise, and we both know it. I make a promise, too, but it's not one I say out loud. The next time I visit my mom, I'll find that scrap of paper with Meg's number on it and I'll throw it away.

Chapter Twelve

CLAUDETTE and I leave our apartments at the exact same time. I lock my door and notice that she's still fumbling with her keys. My eyes land on her right hand and watch as it seems to tremble. The movement is subtle, but it's still hard to miss. She reaches over and clasps her left hand onto the wrist of her right and manages to control the quaking long enough to insert her key into the lock. I avert my gaze when she turns to face me.

"Good morning, Nellie, hunny!" Her voice is bright and cheerful, but it doesn't match the look on her face. Her brow is creased with worry, and her eyes look sullen. Her skin is ashy and lacks its usual glow. Something is wrong. I can feel it in my gut the same way I felt it when I made that doctor appointment for my mom.

It's obvious by the forced smile on her face that Claudette isn't looking to go into any details this morning. I'll mind my own business for now, but I won't be able to remain silent for long. If there's a problem, I can't help her solve it if she won't talk to me.

"Morning, Claudette. Where are you off to today?"

She fidgets with the straps of her tote bag that keep sliding down her arm. "I was just heading out to make my morning visits. Did I tell you we added another parishioner this week?"

Claudette makes weekly rounds visiting the homes of some of the elderly people from her church. She spends quality time with each person—praying, talking, listening. The woman is truly a gift to everyone she meets.

"No, I didn't hear that! How many people are you up to now?"

She looks up at the ceiling, making a tally in her head. "Six now that we included Pat." Her eyes regain some of their sparkle when she speaks about the work she does for her church. Maybe I was wrong. Even though she seems a lot younger most days, Claudette *is* seventy-three. It's also pretty early, and I imagine it probably takes some time for her muscles and joints to wake up in the morning.

We leave the building together, and when we reach the sidewalk, Claudette turns to the left while I head to the right toward the hospital. "Have a good day, Claudette!" I call after her as she strolls away.

"You too, dear!" She waves over her shoulder.

* * *

I TRIED to convince Shane to let me make the coffee run this morning, but his reasoning was ironclad. He had a prescription waiting for him at the hospital pharmacy and the building was on the way to Starbucks. I couldn't argue with that logic, but I could pout, which is exactly what I'm doing now. It's juvenile, but so is this tremendous crush I have on Jude.

Waiting for Shane to get back with my coffee feels like watching paint dry. Just when you think it's been long enough, you swipe your finger along the wall and it comes up coated in color. I give up staring at the door and lose myself in my work.

My first phone call of the day was an easy one. A middle-aged woman received a bill with a zero in the total amount due box. She was sure it was a mistake because she fully expected to have to pay for the blood work she had done. But when I investigated things, it turned out her original bill was correct. She owed nothing, and in my line of work, that is the best news you can give to someone. Actually, that's probably some of the best news for anyone to receive no matter what the situation is.

When I hang up, I turn to find my latte waiting for me on the side of my desk. Shane must've stopped by while I was taking the call and didn't want to disturb me. I reach for the cup and turn it around, examining it from every angle, but I find nothing. I'll admit, I was hoping for a secret message from Jude. Shane is quite the talker, so I assumed he'd spout off where he worked when he placed the office order. The previous two times I've visited Jude, I ordered the same thing—a grande mocha latte with two pumps of vanilla and a sprinkle of cinnamon. It's not a very common request, and that's on purpose. I'm not normally a fan of standing out, but with Jude, I don't mind so much.

Glancing at my office phone, I notice the light for Shane's line isn't lit. I lean back in my seat and spy him typing away on his computer. He's wearing his headset, but he isn't talking to anyone, which makes it the perfect time for me to *thank* him for my coffee. Thank him and nudge him for any morsel of information I can get.

I amble over to his station and bounce my knuckles on the metal edge of his cubicle. He spins his chair around to face me and slides his headset down to rest around his neck. "Hey there, Nellie. Did I get your coffee order right?"

I smile warmly at him. "You sure did. It's perfect. Thanks, Shane."

He grins. "Sure thing. You drink an interesting concoction —even the barista thought so, and I bet he's gotten some crazy requests working there!"

Oh, he thought it was interesting, did he? I feel heat rise to my cheeks at the thought of Jude talking about me even if it was just about my unique latte order. "That's funny that the barista commented on my drink." I try to make myself sound casual with a bit of disinterest thrown in. I'm not so sure I was successful, but Shane doesn't seem to notice.

"He did more than just comment on it." He laughs, and I feel my stomach churn with anticipation. "When I told him what you wanted, he got this funny look on his face. He said whoever thought of combining vanilla and cinnamon with mocha must be a fascinating person and he'd love to sit down and pick their brain for more ideas."

Yeah, Jude's on to me all right. I can't hold in the chuckle that escapes my mouth. "I can't imagine my drink is that innovative, but maybe I should pick up the coffee tomorrow so that I can wow him with more crazy concoctions." I wag my eyebrows up and down, and Shane lets out a belly laugh, slapping his knee.

When he regains his composure, there's a gleam in his eyes that wasn't there before. "Sounds like a plan, Nellie."

* * *

I'VE HAD a few disheartening phone calls today from people I couldn't help. That's the worst part of my job because when I hear the disappointment in their voices, it's hard not to feel responsible. I'm not the doctor who performed the tests or the insurance company who refused to pay. And even though I may work at the hospital, I'm also not the one who sent out the bill. I'm just the unlucky asshole who listens to the complaints, the doormat for them to wipe all of their frustrations on. All of my coworkers struggle with this same thing, but for most of them, it's just a job. When they hang up the phone, they disconnect from their emotions. It's self-preservation. I wish it were as easy for me. I'm a fixer. It's who I've always been. Problems are meant to be solved, and resolving them is what I live for. But even as I sit here in between calls, I can't ignore that I feel a bit lighter today. I'm still riding the high from the comments Jude made about me to Shane this morning.

I close my eyes and try to picture his face as he heard my order. Just as I had hoped, he knew that drink was for me. Did he also know that Shane would tell me everything he said? Maybe that was his goal. I don't know Jude very well, but from what I've gathered, he seems pretty sure of himself. I don't think anything he does or says is by accident.

The light on my office phone blinks red and alerts me with a ring. I let out a sigh. I'll have to come back to my thoughts after I finish working.

I press the button on my headset and answer with my best helpful voice. "Hello, and thank you for calling Hope Community Hospital. This is Nellie. How can I assist you today?"

It's quiet on the other end, and just when I'm about to repeat my greeting, a rough sounding cough breaks through the silence. A gruff voice follows. "Uh, yeah, hi. I have this bill here that you guys sent me and I don't think it's right."

No one ever does. I hear this all the time. "Okay, let me help you get to the bottom of this, Mister…?"

"Hargrove, er, uh, yeah, Mr. Hargrove." It almost sounds like he made a mistake when he gave me his last name, but I know people are often flustered when they call us. It wouldn't be the first time someone stammered when saying their name.

"Okay, Mr. Hargrove. First thing I'll need is your account number. It should be printed in the upper right corner of your invoice."

He mumbles a response that sounds like, "I forgot about that." I'm sure I misheard him, so I ask him to repeat what he said.

"Sorry, I was talking to myself. So, uh, yeah, the account number. See, the thing is, I'm not sure where I put that bill." I can hear the telltale signs of paper shuffling in the background. "It's around here somewhere. You see, what happened, is I, uh, broke my ankle."

"Oh, no, that's terrible. I'm sorry to hear that. I hope you're all healed up now." My response comes easily. Part of my job is to sound like I care, but I never have to pretend.

"Well, that's very kind of you to say, Miss, uh, what did you say your name was again?"

"It's Nellie."

"Oh, right, right, Nellie. Nice name. I think I may have heard it somewhere before." *Probably when I said it the first time,* I think to myself as I shake my head and chuckle silently. "Anyway, you asked about my ankle. It's getting better, but it should'a never broke in the first place."

"In my experience, broken bones never usually happen on purpose. I guess that's why they call it an accident, right?"

"You're right about that, Nellie. This was definitely an accident. A ridiculous accident, if I'm honest. See, the heater was broken in my apartment, but instead of not working at all, it worked too well. Damn thing heated up my place so much I was starting to get delirious. It was so hot I didn't know what the hell to do. So I took off my clothes and got my foot stuck in the leg of my jeans. I fell over sideways and busted up my ankle. I'm just glad I was alone because I don't think I ever would'a lived that one down if my roommate was home, you know what I mean?" His deep laugh reverberates through the phone. There's something familiar about him, but I can't quite place it.

"So, let me see if I follow you here. Your apartment got so hot that you needed to take off your clothes?" As soon as the words leave my mouth, everything snaps into place. "Oh. My. God. Jude? Is that you?"

He starts humming Nelly's song, and we both laugh. "I can't believe you. How'd you pull this off?"

He chuckles. "Well, if I were you, I'd be a little leery of a coworker who's so easily swayed by free coffee." *Shane.* I glide my chair back and peek into his cubicle. He's talking through his headset, but when he senses my eyes on his profile, he turns his head. He smiles wide and gives me a half shrug before angling his body back to face his computer. I want to shove him and hug him at the same time. Okay, I mostly want to hug him.

"I can't say I blame him. I'd do just about anything for free coffee."

I hear a catch in his throat. "Anything, huh?" He sounds amused.

I smack my face with my palm. Clearly, I need to weigh everything I say around Jude before it leaves my mouth. "O-k-a-y, moving on, Mr. Hargrove. If that's even your real last name."

His laugh is breathy as he answers, "Actually, it is. I didn't mean to use my own name, but when you asked me, it just slipped out."

I snicker. "Was there a particular reason for your call, or are you just bored on your lunch break?"

"Nellie, Nellie, Nellie. I know you don't know me very well, but know this, there's always a reason. And you will never just be an escape from boredom."

I swallow hard. Any coherent thoughts that were forming inside my brain have all dissipated. He's so good at leaving me floored.

"The reason I called"—his voice takes on an almost melodic tone as he continues— "was to ask if you'd like to have dinner with me tomorrow night."

Wow. I don't know why I'm so surprised. We've been

overly flirty with each other every time we've spoken, but I guess I just assumed it wouldn't lead anywhere because nothing ever does.

"Dinner? With you?" The words stumble out of my mouth.

When he replies, his voice is filled with humor. "Well, yeah, that *was* the idea. So what do you say?"

"Umm…" My mind immediately fixates on my mom. I've put everything in my life on hold because I don't know how to balance my concern for her with my own happiness. I close my eyes and try not to overthink the question, after all, it's just dinner. I have to eat anyway, right? I may as well be in good company. "Sure. I'll have dinner with you. I'd love to."

I hear the smile in his voice as he speaks. "How does Bella Vita sound? Around seven o'clock?"

"That's right near my apartment. It sounds perfect."

"Great! Then, it's a date."

Chapter Thirteen

WELL, it's official. I hate all of the clothes in my closet. I've spent the last hour parading around my room like a runway model trying on every article of clothing I own in every combination I can think of, and nothing comes close to the impossibly high standards I've set for myself.

I trudge over to my closet and stare at my reflection in the full-length mirror on the door. I'm still wearing the green plaid pleated skirt I tried on with a cream-colored camisole and a Kelly green cardigan. I scrub my hands down the length of my face. I look like I'm bending the rules of a parochial school uniform. I roll my eyes at the ceiling. Come to think of it, Jude may actually appreciate this outfit. I laugh at the thought.

This is the first date I've been on in nearly three years. And it's with Jude. I don't know what I was thinking when I agreed to this. I'm grossly out of practice and insanely attracted to him. How can this end in any way other than a disaster?

I back away from the mirror until my calves hit the edge of my bed. Giving in to gravity, I flop back onto the mattress. My body bounces from the force as I keep my eyes fixed on the ceiling above me. *What am I doing?* I should just cancel. We exchanged cell numbers yesterday; I could just shoot off a text and tell him I'm not feeling well. It isn't the truth, but it's also not exactly a lie, either.

I think about that for a moment. What would happen if I called it off? Nothing would change. My life would continue on just as it had before we met. I would walk to work every day, secretly try to help Jodi and Annabelle, bother my sister with phone calls, fill Claudette's collection bag with canned goods, visit my mom every Saturday, answer her phone calls, quell her worries—the list goes on. It all may sound horribly dull to most people, but it's what I know, and it's what I'm used to. But if I bailed on this date, there's one thing I would lose. Jude. Sure, maybe he'd give me another chance. We could always reschedule. But I know how statistics work and they wouldn't be in our favor. The likelihood that I would cancel again would be far greater, and somehow I don't think Jude is a multiple chances kind of guy.

I let out a low groan. The few times I've been in Jude's company, I've felt immense relief. All of the never-ending to-do's fade off into the background. They may never go away, but I'm able to ignore them for a little while. It's why I said yes to this date in the first place. And it's why I'm going to snap out of this funk, pick myself up, and get dressed.

Jude saw me wearing business casual skirts and sweaters when I came into Starbucks and ultra-casual jeans and a sweatshirt when I ran into him at Home Depot. That's the girl he asked out to dinner, so that's the girl he's going to get.

I decide on a camel brown tunic sweater with black leggings and chestnut suede booties. I refresh my curls with some mousse and manage to tame the frizz into submission. I enjoy wearing makeup, but I usually reserve it for special occasions. I think dinner with Jude qualifies so I apply a small amount of eyeshadow and top it off with winged liner and mascara. I dust my cheeks with a bit of blush and finish off the look with a light nude gloss. I step back from the mirror and assess the final look. Not half bad! I can't believe I almost canceled. I feel tingly with anticipation.

* * *

BELLA VITA IS a short walk from my apartment. I didn't want to be late, so I left a little earlier than I needed to. I arrive at the front of the restaurant at 6:50 p.m. I don't see Jude yet so I stand to the left of the doors and try not to appear nervous. Even though things have been pretty easy between us, I can't seem to get my body to relax. My palms are sweaty, and despite the warmth in the air, I can't control the shiver in my back and shoulders. I shift my weight from side to side to help calm my jittery legs, but it's no use.

"There you are. Ready to go inside?" Jude walks up behind me. His voice does little to control my nerves. I turn to face him, and his eyes widen. "On second thought, maybe we should just order takeout. I'm not so sure I want to eat where everyone can see us."

His words knock the wind out of me and I rear back from the impact. "Why don't you want to eat inside?" Oh no, did my mascara run? I lift my finger up to pat the space below my eyes, but he catches my hand before I can reach it.

He links his fingers with mine and his eyes drift slowly up from our clasped hands to settle on my face. He blinks a few times as if he's trying to see through fog. "So beautiful." His voice is barely a whisper. I'm not sure he intended for me to hear him.

I still my expression, trying not to let him see how his admission is affecting me. He takes a deep breath and reaches his free hand up to rub the back of his neck. He almost looks embarrassed. It's strange to see him appear anything other than confident.

He lets out a chuckle. "I'm sorry, Nellie. It's just, you look incredible. Everyone in that restaurant will agree and I'm not sure how I feel about that."

I suck my lower lip into my mouth to keep from grinning like a nitwit. "Well, I appreciate the compliment, but I'm starving. Do you think you can put your worries aside for the time being for the sake of my stomach?" I wink at him. I have no idea where this confidence is coming from. I sound so self-assured when in reality, I'm the polar opposite.

"I guess I can't argue with that, can I?" My boldness seems to spark something in him. He keeps our hands locked and angles his head, nodding it toward the door. I smile with approval, and we remain joined as we enter the restaurant.

It's a busy Friday night at Bella Vita, but Jude is prepared. He made a reservation and gives his name at the hostess station. The hostess drags her eyes up and down the length of him. Jude was worried that everyone would be looking at me, but I hadn't even considered that the same might be true for him. Standing a few feet away, I let myself admire him. He's wearing fitted deep green pants and a charcoal gray V-neck sweater with a black T-shirt peeking out from underneath. His shoes are hybrid hi/low top Nikes in forest green with black trim. His style is simple, like it could've been thrown together casually and with little thought, yet it suits him perfectly.

He picks that exact moment to look at me. I don't hide the appreciation in my eyes, and from the smoldering expression on his face, I can tell the feeling is mutual. I glance at the hostess and find her openly gawking at him. I've never been much of a jealous person and I don't intend to start now. She can look all she wants. It's clear to me that I'm the one who has his attention.

Once we're seated, the brief fortitude I felt starts to waver. Since Jude and I don't know much about each other, I can easily guess the kinds of questions that will arise. Did I go to college? Do I have any family close by? Do I have any plans for my future? Unfortunately, for me, those are all topics that I tend to avoid. Maybe if I can keep the conversation focused on Jude, I won't have to spend much time discussing myself.

"You okay over there?" Jude eyes me with concern. He's so perceptive. I need to be careful or this whole thing could blow up before it even begins.

I try to reassure him with a smile. "Yep, I'm just thirsty, and if I'm honest, I'm worried they might run out of breadsticks. This place is pretty packed!"

He looks relieved and laughs at my confession.

Before I can even formulate my first question, Jude fires one off at me. "So, how long have you worked at the hospital?" Okay, that's fairly harmless, at least.

"Hmm, let's see…" I tilt my chin and try to do the math in my head. My mom was diagnosed a little under five years ago. I was almost finished with my degree, and I remember thinking that I might still be able to graduate. Things started rapidly progressing and within a few short months, it was clear that she could no longer be left alone. Everything from that point forward became a blur of snap decisions, and once the dust settled, Mom had moved into Shady Villa and I had left college, sold her house, moved into an apartment, and started working at the hospital. "It's been just over four years and nine months." The words fall from my lips. I hadn't even realized how closely I was counting the days.

Jude looks intrigued. "That sounds like a countdown, like you have some grand master plan. Care to elaborate?" He leans in, resting his chin on the palm of his hand.

Shit. How did we get here so fast? I was hoping to keep myself from becoming the topic of conversation, but here we are, five minutes into the date, and already, Jude is tossing out the heavy hitters.

I laugh off his question as though it were meant as a joke. "No, it's nothing like that. I just started working there the day after my sister moved to Hawaii. It was a pretty emotional day, and so it's hard to forget." I hadn't planned my answer before I spoke. It's the truth—at least, part of it. I just hope it doesn't lead to more tough questions.

"Is your sister older or younger?"

"She's five years older."

"Going by what you said, I'm guessing you two are close."

This is dangerous territory. I need to shift the focus. "Sure. I mean, we're sisters so it isn't always sunshine and rainbows, but we get along okay. What about you? I've met your sister, Sam. Do you have any other brothers or sisters?" Good. I've put the spotlight back on him. Now I just need to keep it there.

He looks away, fixing his eyes on the menu in front of him. His shoulders pull up and the thumb and index finger on his right hand tap out a haphazard beat on the edge of the table. Everything about his demeanor has shifted. Where he once was carefree, he's now drawn and closed up. It looks like Jude has his own set of taboo subjects.

I'm not sure what to do. If I could, I'd take back the question, but it's already out there, floating in the air between us. I know what it's like to feel trapped by something that's out of your control. I slide my hand across the table and place it on top of his, stilling the movement of his fingers. He glances up; his eyes search mine. "I have an idea. Let's set some ground rules."

His eyebrows draw down in confusion. "Ground rules?"

"Mm-hmm." I nod. "From now on, if I ask you a question that you don't want to answer, all you have to do is say, 'Pass.' And that same rule applies to me, too. Deal?" I lift my hand from his and reach it out toward him.

He looks down at my hand and then slides his into mine, clasping our palms together in a firm handshake. "It's a deal." He pauses briefly like he's considering saying more.

"Nellie?"

I keep my gaze fixed on his. "Jude." My name is a question and his is the answer.

"What if I don't want a pass?"

"What do you mean?" My arms break out in goose bumps. I'm not sure where this is headed, but it feels like we're straddling a fine line.

"What I mean is, I like you, Nellie. Enough that I don't want to hide from you. And I don't want you to hide, either." He levels me with a look so intense, it feels like he must be able to see inside my brain. I cringe when I think of what he might find in there.

We're locked in a stare down when our waitress approaches our table to ask if we're ready to order. My mouth rounds in an *o* and I lift my hand up to conceal it. "Oops, I haven't even opened my menu yet."

Jude glances up at our waitress and eyes her name tag. "Jessica? Can we have just a few more minutes, please?"

Jessica looks flustered from Jude's attention, and I can't say I blame her. I've been the main focus of his scrutiny lately, and I still haven't gotten used to it yet. "Uh, yeah, sure. I'll, um, just come back in a couple of minutes then," she stammers and then flits away to the next table.

I peel open the menu; the faux leather cover is heavy and hits the top of the table with a thud. "Hmm, let's see...what am I in the mood for? I usually order the lasagna, but I feel like trying something different. Any recommendations?" I try to brighten the atmosphere. Things were getting much too heavy only a moment ago.

Jude scans the inside of his menu. "I've eaten here a few times with Sam, and I always order the cannelloni. I've never had better." He doesn't look up when he speaks. I glance at him out of the corner of my eye and see him working his jaw back and forth as though he were clenching it.

I hate the feeling that I've disappointed him somehow. I don't want to hide who I am from him, but I also like that I can be around him and not see sympathy reflected back at me every time he looks my way. I know it can't last, but I guess I was hoping I'd have more time before I had to introduce him to my disaster of a life. I stay silent as I let my eyes roam over the entrée options. It's all just words on a page. I can't focus on any of them long enough to read what they say.

"I had a brother—*have* a brother. His name is Dylan. We're twins. Dylan was born first. He's older by six minutes and twenty-three seconds and never let me forget it." Jude chuckles softly. His eyes remain fixed on the menu. I don't say a word, but I angle my body toward his so he knows I'm listening. "He died three years ago." He looks up; his eyes find mine. "Drunk driving accident."

I suck in air on a gasp and take his hands in mine. "Jude, I'm so sorry. God, I had no idea." He gives me a sad smile and shrugs his left shoulder.

"I know you didn't, Nellie. And normally, you still wouldn't because I don't talk about him very often. But that's what I meant when I said I didn't want to hide who I was from you. Dylan is my brother, and he's a part of my life even though he's no longer here. It's important for me that you know about him." His gaze is soft and searching.

I let my thumb slide back and forth across his knuckle. "I'm glad you told me about him. Wow, twins? You and Sam seem so close; I'm guessing you were just as close with Dylan."

He nods solemnly.

"What happened to the drunk driver? Were there any charges filed?"

Jude's face falls and the corners of his mouth turn down. "Dylan *was* the drunk driver."

I pull my chin back in surprise. That piece of information makes this whole story infinitely more tragic. "Oh, Jude. I can't even begin to imagine how hard that must've been for you. Was anyone else injured?"

"Thankfully, no. Dylan crashed his car into a retaining wall. There were no passengers and no other cars involved."

I think about the way he phrased his words and it strikes me as odd how we often say things like "thankfully" in situations like this. When in reality, there's nothing to be thankful for. Sure, it's better that no one else was hurt, but Dylan was, and it's not the sort of injury that someone can recover from.

Jude lets out a long breath. "I haven't talked about that day in so long. I can't change what happened. I couldn't talk Dylan out of getting in that car because I wasn't with him. I was at home trying to fight off a cold. He tried to convince me that I should go out barhopping with him and a few of our friends, but I chose to say no. I don't blame myself." When he looks at me, I see the sincerity in his eyes. "I used to, though. I was sure if I had gone with him, I could have talked him out of driving. I know now that I'm not to blame for someone else's actions." He smiles warmly. "Years of excellent therapy taught me that."

I return his smile. It feels strange to feel even a minuscule amount of happiness after hearing such a tragic story, but for some reason, I feel a little lighter having heard it—if not for any other reason than knowing everyone has painful seasons in their lives. It helps me feel not so alone.

I clap. "Okay, let's play a game." I steeple my hands together and try to look thoughtful.

Jude chuckles. "And what kind of game would you like to play, Nellie?"

I do my best to ignore the insinuation in his tone, but I still feel the heat rising to my cheeks. "Um, well, why don't we take turns asking each other fast facts?"

"Fast facts?"

"Uh-huh, I'll go first so you can see what I mean." I pause until I see his head tilt with intrigue. "All right, Jude, tell me your top five favorite musicians or bands in no particular order. Just list them right off the top of your head."

He scratches at his temple with his index finger. "Wow, and here I thought you were trying to lighten the mood. You're obviously not messing around." He winks at me and we share a laugh. "Okay, if you're asking about musicians, then I'd have to go with Joshua Radin, Novo Amor, Glen Hansard, the Shins, and Bon Iver." He ticks off his list with his fingers, and I'm left stunned. His list could easily be mine. "Your turn, although you only have to list four because we both know who's in your top spot." He mouths the lyrics to "Hot in Herre" with a smirk on his face.

I swat at his arm. "This may come as a shock to you, but I hate that song."

He rears back and places his hand over his heart in mock horror. "No, Nellie! Say it isn't so!"

I let out a giggle. "I'm afraid so, Jude. Although, I'll admit, lately, it's starting to grow on me."

Chapter Fourteen

THE REST of our dinner conversation is easy. We keep things light, and I'm grateful. As much as I appreciate Jude opening up to me, I'm enjoying the flirtatious banter between us. When I'm fixated on the back and forth with him, I'm not focused on anything else. I can let everything fall away. It's liberating, even if I know it has an expiration date.

"So let me get this straight." Jude leans over, resting his elbows on the table. "You love the movie version of *Great Expectations*, but you're not a fan of the book? Oh, Nellie, that has got to be against some kind of literary law." He makes a tsk-tsk sound and shakes his head.

"Come on, that movie has Ethan Hawke circa 1998, way before his face turned mousey. You can't blame me there." His mouth opens, preparing to argue with my point, and I raise my hands up. "Besides, it's more than just that. The soundtrack is everything, and the entire movie has this incredible feel to it. The cinematography is extraordinary. There's a green hue that's present in nearly every shot, and it just creates this mood. It's earthy and natural and tranquil. And if I'm honest, I never finished the book, so I guess I can't really say I like the movie better. I just like the movie period." I bite my lower lip, feeling slightly embarrassed for never having completed the Charles Dickens classic.

His expression turns serious, and he speaks in hushed tones. "Want to know a secret, Nellie?" He turns his head from side to side as though he's making sure no one can hear him. "I've never read the book, either. But you're right about the movie. It's fantastic."

I shake my head and laugh. It's so refreshing to be in the company of someone who makes you feel so relaxed. So free.

As if the universe needs to ensure balance in my world, my phone picks that very moment to ring with my mom's drumbeat tone. I close my eyes briefly and take a quick breath. I don't want Jude to see how that sound affects me, but I also can't ignore the immediate reaction I have every time I hear it.

He bops his head to the rhythm of the percussion. He doesn't know the significance of this ringtone or the stress that will surely come when I answer the call. "That's a fun ringtone. Is that a special tone for someone?"

Yeah, it's a fun ringtone, all right. "It's my mom. Will you excuse me for just a sec? I need to take this." I stand and crane my neck in search of somewhere private to take the call.

I can already feel the apprehension building inside of me, but Jude doesn't seem to notice. "Sure thing. Take your time, but also, please hurry back." His smile is like a warm blanket shielding me from the cold reality waiting for me on the phone line.

There's a little alcove near the restrooms with a small wooden bench tucked into the corner. It's probably meant for nursing mothers, but it also works well for private phone calls, too.

I'm anticipating the worst, but maybe I'm jumping to conclusions. My mom rarely calls me unless there's an issue, but it could be something simple, like she just wants me to bring her donuts tomorrow. I already bought some at the store this afternoon, so I'm prepared if that's why she's calling. I take one final calming breath, and then I answer.

"Hi, Mama. How's it going?"

"Ohhhh," she whimpers into the phone. "Belly? Belly? Are you there?" She sounds frantic. There's a fake potted fern on the floor next to me. I rub one of the leaves between my fingers and concentrate on the smooth, waxy texture.

"Yep, I'm here. You sound upset."

"Well, I *am* upset! Someone took all of my clothes!" She's practically screaming into the phone. I pull it away from my ear to adjust the volume.

Ordinarily, if someone told me all of their clothes were stolen, I would react in shock and dismay, but there's nothing ordinary about this situation. In fact, I've heard these exact words from her many times.

"Do you mean they took your clothes to the laundry room?" I try to keep my voice even, despite knowing it won't do much good. If she's upset, she'll stay that way until she's ready to move on to another emotion.

"I don't know where they took them! All I know is, I came back to my room from dinner and all of the clothes I had on my table were gone!" Since moving into Shady Villa, my mom consistently won't allow her clothes to be washed. It's a battle with no end in sight. No amount of convincing has been able to sway her, which means I get phone calls like this one every few weeks. The staff is trying their best, but they can't allow her to wear dirty clothing, so they wait until she's not in her room, and then they scoop everything up and get it washed. They'll return it in a couple of hours, but until that happens, she'll be inconsolable.

It's times like these when I find myself wishing Meg was around to help. Having a sibling should mean I have someone to tag in when I'm feeling overwhelmed, someone to help shoulder the burden when it gets to be too much for me to handle. But that isn't the arrangement. Even if she lived twenty minutes away, I'd still be picking up every piece, cleaning up every mess, putting out every fire. "Mama, listen to me, they're just washing your clothes for you so that they're clean. They'll bring them back soon. I promise."

"I should've known you'd side with them! You must really hate me to make me stay in a place like this." If only she knew how wrong she was. My love for her is alive in everything I say and everything I do.

"Mama, you know that's not true at all. I love—"

"If you won't find my clothes, then I will! Goodbye!" I only hear the slight click of the call disconnecting, but I know she slammed the headset into the base. I can still feel the impact, even if I can't hear it.

I sit alone on the bench outside of the restroom with my hand over my face. My cell phone falls from my ear and lands on my lap. *I just want this to end.* It's a thought I have often but never verbalize because there's only one way for this situation to end. I can't say the words out loud. It hurts enough just to think them.

I slide my hand from my eyes and blink a few times. Looking up, I notice Jude standing in front of me. I wonder how long he's been standing there. From the sympathetic look on his face, I'd say it was long enough to get the gist of my conversation with my mom.

He gives me a sad smile and places his hand on my shoulder. "So, I guess that's a no on dessert then, huh?"

I breathe out a small laugh, grateful for his attempt at trying to cheer me up. "Yeah, I think I'm going to have to pass on that tonight." I pat my stomach, pretending to be full when we both know that isn't why I'm skipping dessert. I make a show of checking the time on my phone. "I should probably get going."

Jude's face falls a bit, but he nods as though he was expecting me to say that.

The truth is, I don't want this night to end, but the call

from my mom soured my mood. I'm afraid I probably wouldn't be much company.

Jude extends his hand out, and I take a hold of it, allowing him to pull me up to standing. When we're outside in front of the restaurant, I realize we're still holding hands.

"I had a great time. Thank you for dinner."

He looks down at our clasped hands and places his free hand to rest on top of them. "Hold on a second, Nellie. I'm not letting you go that easily." He winks at me.

"What do you mean?"

His grin is wide as he brings my hand up to his mouth and places a quick kiss on the back of it. I'm certain my face turns three shades of crimson. It's a simple romantic gesture, but it reaches me in places I didn't know I could feel things. "You live close by, right?"

I nod. "I do. I walked here. I'm only a few blocks away."

He looks pleased with my answer. "Then it's settled. I'm walking you home."

"You don't have to do that." I don't know why, but I'm feeling slightly nervous about him knowing where I live. I'm not afraid that he'll turn into a stalker or anything like that, it just feels like a big step.

He tilts his head regarding me with earnest eyes. "Lead the way."

* * *

OUR WALK to my apartment starts off in silence. It's not the comfortable kind. This is the kind of quiet that makes you consider breaking it by baring your soul. I know I should address the phone call that Jude overheard, but I'm taking the coward's way out for the moment.

Jude glances over at me every so often and I can feel his eyes assess me. He's wishing I would divulge something, and why wouldn't he? He opened up at dinner, telling me all about his brother who died. The least I could do is match his story with one of my own.

On a deep exhale, I open my mouth before I can think twice. "So, my mom has Alzheimer's disease, and that phone call that you heard part of back there?" I turn my head and nod in the direction of the restaurant. "Well, that was just her calling to tell me she thinks the staff at the retirement home robbed her of all of her clothing while she was down in the dining hall." I lift my head up to search his eyes and realize we've stopped walking. Jude is still holding my hand, but now he's angled his body toward mine, and his other hand is clasped on my elbow. He doesn't offer any comforting words or fill the void with nervous laughter, and I'm so grateful for it, I almost hug him. "No one stole anything from her. They just needed to wash her clothes, and since she won't let them do it voluntarily, they have to sneak in when she isn't there." I let out an exasperated sigh.

"Does that happen often, Nellie?" His voice is soft when he speaks.

"At least once a month, sometimes more." It strikes me then, how defeated I sound. I've been feeling that way for a while now, but I'm usually better at concealing it. I think I'm starting to understand what Jude meant when he said he didn't want us to hide from each other.

"That must be so hard." He surveys my face as though all of my scars are in full view.

I feel my eyes well up and I try to blink away the tears before they can fall. A lone one escapes and cascades down my cheek. Jude reaches up and cups my chin, tilting my face so that our eyes meet. He swipes his thumb across my skin, catching the tear before it rolls down my neck.

"Yeah, it's hard." I choke on the words. I don't like to admit when it's difficult because this is my mom. She took care of me when I needed her, and now it's my turn to take care of her. I'm sure it was hard for her at times, especially being a single mom with a full-time job, but she never complained. At least not in front of Meg and me. If I give a voice to my frustration, it makes me feel like a failure. My mom didn't ask for this life. The least I can do is be there for her. It isn't fair for me to complain. But with Jude, it's different. I feel like I can admit things to him, dark things that I usually try to keep buried, and he won't judge me for it. My secrets feel safe with him.

We stand together under the glow of a streetlight, holding hands and keeping secrets, forging a silent pact. I feel a little less lonely, a little more connected. From the look in his eyes, I think Jude feels it, too.

The rest of our walk is quiet, but the amicable, introspective kind. We've unearthed something unexpected and now we're left trying to work out what this budding relationship means for each of us.

When we reach my front stoop, Swerve leans out from behind the cement steps and struts over to me, weaving her lithe body through my legs. I reach down and brush my hand along her back and she arches into my touch.

"Who's this?" Jude leans down, offering Swerve his hand. She nudges it playfully with her tiny nose and he responds with a few strokes under her chin.

"This is Swerve. And Swerve, this is Jude." I cup my hand up to my mouth as though I'm whispering a secret to the little cat. "He's one of the good ones."

Jude beams at my words. "Swerve, huh? Did you name her?"

I nod with pride.

"That's an interesting name. Any particular reason why you went with that instead of something like Fluffy or Greg?"

I shake my head and laugh. I don't think I'll ever get tired of his wit. I squat down until my bottom rests on one of the steps leading up to the door of my apartment building. As if on cue, Swerve pounces up the steps and perches right next to me. "See how her back is angled? She looks almost like she's *swerving* to the left." I raise my hand and make an *s* shape in the air above her.

"Okay, that makes sense." He leans down and takes one of Swerve's white paws into his hand, giving it a little shake. "It's nice to meet you, Miss Swerve." She lets out a small mew.

Aside from me, I don't think I've ever seen Swerve allow anyone to touch her. Claudette has left a few catnip toys for her, but as far as I know, she's never tried to pet her. Since she's a stray cat, I'm certain Swerve has seen more ugliness than most of us could stand. Her wariness of people is certainly justified. I've been feeding her for a little while now, building up her trust over time. They say animals are very perceptive and can smell evil from far away. Jude has been in Swerve's company for all of ten minutes and they've already progressed to physical contact. I find myself watching him interact with this little cat and feeling a sense of wonder. I don't know where he came from, but now that he's in my life, I really hope he'll stay.

He catches me studying him, but rather than feeling embarrassed and turning away, I keep my gaze fixed on him with a confidence I didn't know I had. His stare matches mine in intensity. Something has shifted tonight, something neither of us saw coming.

I lift myself up to standing, and Jude follows. The toes of our shoes touch. My arms rest down at my side, and he reaches out, taking both of my hands in his, holding them between us as though we're sharing a silent prayer. "Tonight was..." His voice trails off, and I find myself inching my head closer to his hoping he'll continue his thought. He doesn't make me wait long. "Well, it was perfect, Nellie. I'd love to do this again soon with you." His eyes lock with mine, imploring me with a silent plea.

My head starts nodding before I can speak. My heart answers ahead of my thoughts. "I would love that."

He gives my hands a squeeze before releasing them. I turn away and head up to the front door. I can feel his eyes on me as I enter my code on the number pad. The door unlocks with a click and I pull it open. As I glide through the opening, I pause and look back over my shoulder to find Jude standing statue-still on the sidewalk below, a look of awe painted on his face. His eyes seem to shimmer under the muted glow of the lamp above my door. I want to memorize the way he's looking at me, like I'm some kind of ethereal being that has him captivated. I lift up my hand in a small wave, and he smiles in return. "Good night, Nellie."

"Good night, Jude."

Chapter Fifteen

THE SKY IS overcast and there's a faint mist of rain in the air. In this light, the campus of Shady Villa takes on an almost ominous appearance. The needles of the tall pine trees glisten, and the walkway leading up to the main doors is littered with moist grass clippings, leftover from the lawn service that comes by every Friday. The air is damp and thick, making the curls on my head open up like a crown, tiny tendrils reaching out in search of moisture.

I place a tentative hand on the front door, feeling the clear glass-like finish smooth on my skin. Everything at Shady Villa was built to withstand destruction. There's a wide variety of residents here; some who need memory care, like my mom, a few who have more physical restrictions, and there are others who don't want to live alone and prefer the constant company of a retirement home. No matter what their reason, every one of them has one thing in common—they stopped giving a shit about the small things in life. If their walker clips the corner of a wall and chips up the molding—oh well! If they slam into one of the many decorative pieces of furniture in the hallway and leave a dent in the wood—too bad! The extra coats of lacquer on doors, trim, and cabinets are insurance against excess damage.

Gerry sits inside the lobby with his hands wringing together in his lap. He's lost in thought and I touch his shoulder gently when I approach so as not to startle him. He flinches ever so slightly and lifts his head to look up at my face. His grin is wide, but his eyes are etched with worry. I sink into the cushion beside him and retrieve a Milky Way from the pocket of my jacket. When I hand it over to him, the lines and wrinkles around his eyes and forehead seem to smooth for a moment. He silently accepts the candy and tips his head in thanks.

"So, what's the story, morning glory?" I use his favorite phrase, eliciting a small chuckle out of him. His movements are slow as he peels back the wrapper on the chocolate and pops the whole miniature candy into his mouth. I wait for him to finish. Gerry never savors his chocolate. He has it down to a science of three chews and a swallow.

"How's life treatin' ya, Nellie girl?" Gerry reminds me of my poppy. It's one of the reasons why I was instantly drawn to him. They look nothing alike. Where poppy was round in his middle, Gerry is slender. Poppy lost all of his hair early on, but never went without a carefully trimmed mustache. Gerry is always clean-shaven, but still has enough hair on his head to require a comb every morning. His similarity to my grandfather lies more in the way he speaks. Just like my poppy, he would much prefer to talk about someone else's problems than his own, and he's super quick to dole out advice. I lost Poppy nine years ago, but when I'm with Gerry, it feels like a part of him is still with me.

"Oh, same ole, same ole, Gerry. My mom calls and I come running." I let out a laugh, but he doesn't join me. His eyes may be milky with age, but it's only a facade. He rarely misses anything.

"Oh kiddo, don't let her get you down. She'd be proud of

you if she could be, you know that, right?" He gives my knee a pat.

"I sure hope so." I cast my eyes down and suck in a shaky breath. "So…" I turn to face him, surveying his eyes with my own. "Care to tell me why you're sitting here alone? Where's Mavis?"

Now it's Gerry's turn to look forlorn. He gives his head a sad shake. "Today's not a good day, Nellie. She woke up that way, but you know this weather never helps any." He juts his thumb toward the door.

I know all about how much outside conditions can affect someone like Mavis or my mom's ability to cope. Just like my mom, Mavis has Alzheimer's, but for her it usually means comical confusion instead of hurtful indifference. Not comical in a sense that it's truly funny; more in the way that she mistakes a container of butter for ice cream or tomatoes for apples. She's easily confused by everyday things, but generally, she's in pretty good spirits about it. She even laughs at her mistakes, although she has no idea why she's making them.

I didn't know much about Alzheimer's disease before my mom was diagnosed. Before that fateful day, I associated the condition with memory loss, but I never stopped to think about what all that would entail, and I never considered what it might be like for the family members and loved ones of the afflicted. Now that it's part of my everyday life, I've become somewhat of an expert on the subject. But one glaring thing I've learned is, Alzheimer's doesn't look the same on everyone. My mom spends much of her time feeling angry and like the world is out to get her, whereas Mavis is mostly happy. She doesn't always remember Gerry, but even on those days when she can't seem to recall his name, she still manages to associate him with love. I could say that Gerry is one of the lucky ones, but the reality is, he's forced to live in an environment where his wife of over fifty years doesn't recognize him and often tries to eat her soup with a carrot instead of a spoon. I'm not sure I'd call that lucky.

One unfortunate side effect of Mavis' disease is depression. She takes daily medication for it, but on her worst days, it still manages to peek through. Today is one of those days, and all Gerry can do is wait it out.

Depression isn't something my mom has struggled with, but Alzheimer's commonly brings a myriad of symptoms along for the ride, and we haven't been left unscathed. Crippling anxiety, on the other hand, is a condition that has been known to render my mom completely out of commission. When it strikes, she'll remain frozen in one spot, wiping her hands with wet rags as they become sticky with nervous sweat. When she's like that, you can't convince her to move, much less eat or drink. Luckily, steady doses of medication have kept those attacks at bay, but I still live in fear of the day she'll be struck with another one.

I rise to my feet and look down at Gerry. He's a fairly tall man, but from this angle, he looks so frail. He may not have Alzheimer's, but he's not immune to feeling his own set of symptoms. None of us are. "I better head up to my mom before she starts to wonder what's taking me so long." The smile on my face is a mixture of false hope and resignation. It's one I know he'll understand.

He nods. "Yeah, you best get on up there. Don't want to get you into any trouble!" He wags his finger and lets out a small laugh. "Now, Nellie, remember what I told you. You've done right by your mama. I know she would be grateful for you if she understood."

I feel the warmth of his words settle over my heart like a tiny barricade ready to ward off any ill intentions that might be coming my way. "Thank you, Gerry. Please give Mavis a hug for me."

His smile is wide, but it doesn't quite reach his eyes.

"Maybe she'll be down here before you leave and you can give her that hug yourself."

We both know the chance of that happening is about as likely as matching every number on the Powerball.

As I walk away, I hear Gerry call out to me, his gruff voice reminiscent of the commanding tone he probably used as an army lieutenant in the war. I spin around to face him and fight the urge to throw my hand up to my brow in a salute. "I talked to your mama this morning, and she sounded almost happy. They have her chocolate pudding in the kitchen again." He gives me a reassuring thumbs-up and I feel the tiny seeds of relief begin to take root. It may not seem like much, but when small victories are all you have, you take them wherever you can get them.

* * *

THE DOOR to room 346 is slightly ajar. It's unusual to find my mom's door any way other than dead bolted from the inside. Finding it unlocked would be strange; finding it open is unheard of.

"Mama?" I call out as I push the door fully open. The TV is tuned to the Game Show Network, but the volume has been muted.

"Just a minute!" Mom's voice is coming from the bathroom, and I sigh with relief. I notice a light shining out from under the door, followed by the sound of the toilet flushing. The door is shoved open immediately after and my mom emerges, looking surprised to see me. I'm so glad to see her and my first instinct is to gather her in my arms for a hug, but I've learned to adjust my instincts. It's always best to gauge her mood before reacting.

"Um, Mama? You washed your hands, right?" I know she didn't. Our roles have reversed over these past few years with me playing the parent most of the time.

A look of annoyance flashes on her face, but she turns around and trudges over to the sink. This is another one of those small victories. I smile. In spite of whatever else may happen during this visit, at least I won this battle.

When she's finished, she rushes back over to her sofa and unmutes the TV. I notice that her hands are still dripping wet, but I bite my tongue. At least they're clean.

The volume on the television is nearly at full volume, but I'm used to shouting over it. If I ask her to turn it down, or better yet, turn it off while I'm visiting, she will, but she won't be happy about it. I'd rather continue this upswing we seem to have going, so yelling over Chuck Woolery it is.

"Why was your door open, Mama?"

She looks over at me, but it's as if she's looking through me. This happens often and it used to upset me, but now I know she's just having trouble focusing on my words. It helps if I repeat myself, so I ask her the question again.

This time, there's clarity behind her eyes. "Oh, well, when I was in the bathroom, one of those ladies came in and brought me new towels. She said she put them on my dresser." She motions to the chest of drawers near her bed where I see a small pile of clean towels perched on the top. It's hard to know if the aide neglected to close the door or if my mom opened it for another reason and has since forgotten why. Most of the residents leave their doors unlocked and often propped open. It makes them feel as though they're living amongst family. My mom has yet to adopt that way of thinking, but maybe she had a change of heart. I'll check with one of the aides later and find out, but for now, my attention is on the stack of towels. If I don't put them away, she'll leave them right where they are and then get upset later when she thinks that no one brought some for her.

I scoop them up and take them into her bathroom. There's a cabinet above the toilet where clean towels, extra rolls of toilet paper, and boxes of tissues are kept. When I open the door, I find all of these things as well as a pair of socks, a wristwatch, and an unopened snack-sized bag of potato chips.

I could do one of two things here—I could remove all of these items and carry them out to my mom, or I could close the doors to the cabinet and walk away. I had already made the first choice a few months ago and it resulted in my mom yelling at me not to touch her things, which quickly escalated to her asking me to leave her apartment. She called me to apologize a few hours later, but I suspected it was because Gerry told her to. He heard her yelling from the hallway and saw me leave her room in tears. Her apology sounded rehearsed, like a script she was reading rather than a well-intentioned speech from the heart.

In this instance, those three misplaced items aren't harming a thing by remaining in the cabinet, so I let out a sigh and close the door.

She's still perched on her sofa, her eyes glued to the screen. She doesn't notice me enter the room; she doesn't see me walk over to her; she doesn't feel me take a seat next to her. Alzheimer's makes mothers ignore their children; wives disregard their husbands, friends neglect friendships. I have to remind myself that she's sick the same way a person who has cancer is sick. Her behavior is a symptom; it isn't personal. But sometimes it isn't so easy to separate the person from the disease, especially when the illness makes them cold and emotionless.

"Mama? I brought you some donuts. They're the powdered kind that you like so much."

She turns to me; her blank expression morphs into one of confusion. "I don't like powdered donuts. I never liked those." She sounds incredulous, like she can't believe I didn't know that bit of information.

"These are really good. Just give them a try, okay?" I leave out the part about how they're her favorite, how they were the only kind of donuts she ever wanted. Declarations like that will only confuse and upset her because, at this moment, she doesn't remember. To her, it will feel like I'm trying to trick her and she'll react the only way she knows how, with outrage.

She nods and turns away from me to face the TV. I stay there with her for the better part of a half an hour. We don't speak, but it isn't unpleasant. Sometimes when we sit quietly watching television together, I can almost pretend everything is how it used to be. I allow myself to live in those memories until they begin to blur around the edges. No matter how hard I try to fight it, reality has a way of creeping back in.

Once that starts to happen, I stand up and prepare to leave. She seems startled to find me there but tries to cover up her surprise with nervous laughter. These are the times that I feel the worst for her. It's as if somewhere deep inside of her she knows that something isn't quite right, but she can't seem to put her finger on it. She rises to her feet and gives me a hug. Her clothing smells of dryer sheets. Yet another small victory. This visit is shaping up to be one of best I've had in a long time, and I leave her room with a spring in my step, feeling a little less defeated.

When I'm inside my car, I sit in stillness for a moment and think about how much things have changed over the past few years. Before, a good day would have culminated with a marathon phone conversation between my mom and me, and now it consists of a visit where there's no complaining and even less talking. Today was an improvement, but it's also a sad reminder that life is fleeting.

I unzip my purse and slide my phone out. Today was a decent day with Mom, and Meg deserves to know about it. I tend to save the problems for her, but that's usually because all we have are problems. It's nice to have positive news for a change.

I bring up Meg's name and shoot off a text to her.

Me: Hey Megs! Today's visit with mom wasn't bad for a change. She was, actually, in pretty good spirits!

I watch as a text bubble appears almost instantly. I feel hopeful as I wait for her reply, but after a few seconds, the dots disappear, and a response never comes. Shaking my head, I toss my phone back into my purse and start up my car. I can't force Meg to be someone that she isn't. I guess it's time I stop trying.

Chapter Sixteen

SMART SHOPPER IS MOBBED. I've only been here a little over ten minutes, and I've already witnessed two shopping cart collisions. The second one sent an entire display of gift cards tumbling to the ground.

I was getting low on cans of cat food for Swerve, so I decided to stop in and pick some up. But now, as I watch the chaos unfold around me, I'm beginning to wish I had placed an order online instead.

With a few cans in my basket, I weave among the throng of shoppers until I find myself in the stationery section. Compared to the rest of the store, this aisle is a ghost town. A middle-aged man in gray sweatpants, cherry red Crocs, and a 49ers jersey is several feet away. He's crouched down, closely examining the wattage on packs of lightbulbs. He's staring at the packaging so intently, I don't even think he knows I'm here.

A neat row of gel pens and mechanical pencils dangle on hooks before me. I let my fingertips trace along the tops of each package and feel a familiar pang. I select a friction pen with erasable black ink. It's blister wrapped in plastic, and the cardboard surrounding it is minimal, making it the perfect size. Without turning my head, I shift my eyes to the right. The man is gone, no longer perusing the lightbulbs. I'm completely alone in the aisle.

My purse hangs off of my arm with a waiting open mouth. Like all the other times before, it would be so easy to just—oops!—let it fall down into the compartment. The feeling is there, but the pull is less severe. I can't explain it, but something is different.

There's a bend in the cardboard on the corner of the package and I probe it with the tip of my index finger. I'm still reeling from my unanswered text to Meg, and swiping this pen would ease the hurt. Or would it? Whenever I've stolen something in the past, I've only thought about the rush I'd feel when I got away with it. For the first time, I force myself to think about the guilt that always comes later. The remorse I feel far outweighs the momentary high. It's never worth it.

I smooth out the kink in the cardboard, and then I slide the package back onto the display. I move away from the temptation with a proud smile. I may not have experienced the jolt from taking something that didn't belong to me, but that thirty-second high doesn't even come close to the euphoria I feel as I walk away.

* * *

I KEY in my code on the pad outside my apartment door. My movements are almost robotic as I sift over the endless stream of thoughts that have been bombarding me since I left Shady Villa. Once I'm inside, I hear a text chime from inside my bag. I rush to pull out my phone, certain that Meg hasn't let me down after all. She probably just got caught up in something and it delayed her text.

Spinning the phone around, I scan the message and see that it's not from Meg. It's from Jude. Somehow seeing his name feels like a Band-Aid on a wound. I was hoping it was my sister, but I'm not unhappy that it's Jude instead.

Jude: Hey there, Nellie! How's your morning so far?

I smile at his thoughtfulness. I can't remember the last time someone called or texted just to check on me. I'm always the one doing the checking in. It's kind of nice being on the receiving end for a change. I take a seat on the last step of the stairwell and lean my back against the banister.

Me: Hey yourself! It's been pretty okay. How about yours?
Jude: Pretty okay, huh? I hope that's your way of saying it's been good *wink emoji* My morning has been mostly uneventful so far, but I'd like to change that.

Hmm. That's a lead in if ever I saw one. He's lucky I'm the curious type who can't let a conversation end on a cliffhanger.

Me: Oh yeah? And how do you plan on doing that?
Jude: Funny you should ask! I'm going to take you out again. Today. At 5 p.m.
Me: You seem so sure of yourself. How do you know I don't already have plans?
Jude: Wishful thinking? *grin emoji*

I chuckle at his admission. Last night was strange and unexpected and pretty incredible. I wouldn't mind a repeat again today.

Me: Well, as it turns out, you're in luck. What are you planning?
Jude: I'll tell you

His last text hangs like an ellipsis. There has to be more. Maybe he's typing a response, but I don't see any text bubbles. Just when I'm about to reply, another text pops up.

Jude: at 5 p.m., that is. *laugh emoji*

I share a laugh with his emoji and shoot off a quick reply.

Me: You have me intrigued. I'll see you then.

I have the goofiest grin on my face, and I don't even try to hide it. There's no point. Jude's texts make me feel alive and hopeful. I practically float up the stairs. I'm so deep in thought that I almost miss the bag of canned goods outside Claudette's door.

Huh? That's strange. I saw it there when I left to visit my mom this morning, but I just assumed Claudette was running a little behind schedule. I glance at my watch to find that it's a few minutes after noon. She definitely should've taken this to the soup kitchen by now. I don't want to pry, but I need to make sure she's okay.

I bring the back of my hand up to her door and knock my knuckles against it. I don't hear any movement, but I remind myself that she's older, and if she's ill, it may have slowed her down. I wait several seconds and then I knock again, this time I add in a, "Claudette?" for good measure. I listen closely and catch the faint sounds of footsteps shuffling along the wooden floor. The internal lock opens with a click and the door peels open. Claudette stands on the other side looking pale and slightly stooped over.

"Oh, there you are! Have you caught the flu that's been going around? I've been hearing all about it at work. The ER has been swamped with cases."

She lifts her head to peer up at me and her eyes look as if

they're having trouble focusing. Maybe I should take her to the hospital.

On instinct, I lift my hand to press it onto her forehead, but she stops me, clasping my hand in hers and bringing them to rest at her chest. I feel a quake in her hand as it loosely grips mine. My eyes scan her body for any signs of what's going on because I know that something isn't right. There's a somber expression on her face, and her mouth is the closest to a frown that I've ever seen on her.

"Claudette? Please tell me what's wrong. Do you need me to take you to the doctor?" I struggle to keep my voice even as concern invades every pore of my body.

She releases my hand and lets her arm fall down at her side. Her fingers nervously tug at the stretchy material of her leggings. "Oh hunny, I've been to so many doctors these past few days, if I never see another one, it'll be too soon."

"What do you mean you've seen so many doctors? What's going on?"

She lifts the corners of her mouth into a sad smile. "Well, they tell me I have Parkinson's disease, dear. Apparently, I've had it for quite some time, but other than feeling clumsy on occasion, I hadn't noticed."

"Parkinson's? Are they sure?"

"I'm afraid so, Nellie. I just saw another specialist yester-day, sent me home with a lovely assortment of pills in all colors and sizes!" She lets out a chuckle and I want to join her, but I can't. I feel like the floor beneath my feet has been yanked away. Claudette is the strongest, most vibrant person I know. I can't understand how this could happen.

She takes my chin in her hand. Despite the small tremor, her hold is firm as she tilts my head up. "Now listen here, sweetie, don't you go cryin' over me. I'm gonna be just fine. This is not a death sentence, and even if that's exactly what it ends up to be, I'm not going down without a fight. So dry those eyes and let me see that beautiful smile of yours. I could use a little more sunshine today."

I reach deep inside myself and give her what she asks for. It's one of the hardest things I've ever had to do. My smile feels forced, but I tell myself it's medicine for Claudette, and that helps make it feel more genuine. I have no idea how she can stay so positive after receiving such devastating news. I have so many questions swarming inside my head. What's her prognosis? Can she still exercise? Will she be able to remain living here on her own? Who will take care of her? But I keep them all to myself. Chances are those same thoughts are coursing through her mind, as well. She doesn't need me doubling down on her worry.

I glance down at the bag of canned goods. "I want to help. Can I take these cans down to the soup kitchen for you?"

She follows my gaze and seems to focus on a jar of salsa peeking out from the top of the bag. There's a wistful smile on her face. "That's sweet of you to offer, hunny. I still plan on walking down there, but Manuel, one of the volunteers, is coming by to meet me. He's going to carry the bag and we'll walk down together."

If I received news like she has, I can't imagine ever wanting to leave my apartment, much less go volunteer at a soup kitchen. But then I let that thought shuffle around in my head and realize I wouldn't give up either, not when so many people are counting on me. I guess Claudette and I have a lot in common that way. I smile warmly at her and take both of her hands in mine. "Will you promise me one thing?"

"What's that, dear?"

"Let me know if you ever need anything? I'm right next door to you and can be here in seconds. If you're struggling and you need help in any way or you just need a friend, please call me. Okay?" My eyes flick back and forth between hers, looking for confirmation that she's hearing me.

She pats my cheek. "Sure thing, hunny. But remember what I said, I'm a fighter. Don't worry about me."

I give her my best reassuring smile, but it's bullshit. If she notices, she doesn't say a word. Over the years, she's come to know that fretting is as natural as breathing for me. If I'm not fussing over my mom or distressed about Meg, I'm worrying about Jodi and Annabelle. Even Swerve hasn't been safe from my concern. Helping people is what I do. I can't change that about myself any more than Claudette can stop approaching every challenge with determination. These attributes are mostly strengths, but sometimes they can be weaknesses, too.

* * *

I MILL ABOUT inside my apartment, unable to sit for longer than five minutes. I try watching *Queer Eye*, but I'm so disconcerted even a "Yaass" from Jonathan isn't enough to bring me around. Maybe a shower will help. I can wash off the filth of this day. It started out fine and was even great for a bit, but then it took a huge nosedive and I don't know how to make it better.

I hear the sound of my own breathing as I undress and lumber into the bathroom. My bare feet meet the chilled tile, but the sensation barely registers. I catch my reflection in the mirror. My eyes are ringed in dark circles, and my lips are pale and dry. My eyelashes are stuck together in spots, cemented by unshed tears. Drawing in a deep breath, I lean into the tub and turn on the water. Before I can move out of the way, the spray pelts me on the back of the head, assaulting me with ice-cold water. I step back and give my head a slight shake. The cool temperature of the water jolts me out of my stupor for a moment. Water cascades from the shower nozzle, slowly warming as it hits the tub and spirals down the drain. I watch it swirl and think about how it often feels like my life shares the same fate as that water.

My phone perks up from my bedroom and sounds with a chirp. Another text. I could ignore it, but maybe it's Meg. On a sigh, I shut off the water and shuffle back into my bedroom.

Jude: I almost forgot—make sure you wear comfort-able shoes *monkey covering mouth emoji*

Jude. That's right, I'm supposed to go out with him again. No less than thirty minutes ago, I was elated over those plans, but now I don't see how I can muster up the energy.

Me: Sorry. Something's come up. Rain check?
Jude: I'll be right over.

Wait—what? Why is he coming over? I look down at myself and realize I'm still completely naked. No, no. He can't come over now.

Me: No, that's not necessary. Everything is fine. I'll text you later.

I wait for a reply that never comes.

Me: Jude?

Still nothing.

Me: Jude?? You haven't left yet, have you?

When he doesn't reply a third time, I make a mad dash around my room, tossing on clothing and hoping that it matches. I have no idea why he would insist on coming over right now, but if I had to guess, it's probably my own fault for being too vague when I canceled our plans. I give my fore-head a smack with the palm of my hand. Why couldn't I have told him I wasn't feeling well? It wouldn't have even been a lie.

I'm dressed in record time. I try to add some concealer under my eyes to mask the dark circles, but it ends up looking like a cakey mask, and I'm reminded of how Jude doesn't want us to hide from each other. I grab a makeup wipe from the cabinet under the sink and wipe off the evidence. If he's going to show up without being invited, he may as well see me as I am.

I'm in the kitchen downing a glass of water when I hear my phone chime.

Jude: I'm outside. Please let me in.

I never let anyone in. Maybe it's time to change that.

Chapter Seventeen

I SEE Jude before he sees me. He's standing on the cement pad. I spy on him through the glass pane as he looks down at his phone. He's wearing dark blue jeans and a brown heathered T-shirt with an unzipped army-green bomber jacket over top. He pulls off casual sophistication in a way that seems effortless. What would he say about my style? I look down at my mismatched clothing—a red plaid flannel shirt over purple leggings. I think it has a hobo-chic quality to it. I shake my head, wishing I had more time to survey my wardrobe and choose a better outfit. I don't know what I was thinking when I decided to let him see me this way, untouched and full of flaws.

He lifts his eyes from his phone and turns to look down the street. I watch as his neck cranes to peer up at my building. He's staring so intently, like he's searching for something. Suddenly, he's looking straight ahead, and he finds me behind the glass. His eyes widen slightly like he discovered what he's been seeking. He raises his hand in a frozen wave, and I swallow all of my reservations. I grasp the handle on the door and I let him in.

* * *

MY APARTMENT IS tidy because I can't handle unnecessary messes. I don't have much control over emotional chaos, but physical disorder is something I can manage. When I'm awake at all hours of the night, furiously channeling my frustrations into a mad fury of scrubbing and washing, this trait of mine can feel like a curse. For once, I'm grateful for the idiosyncrasy.

Jude takes a step into my apartment like a child might enter his first toy store. There's nothing tentative about it. I can tell by the look on his face that he's been anticipating this moment. His eyes are everywhere as he shifts his gaze to my loveseat and wine barrel table, over to the rolltop desk where he stalls on the two filing cabinets, followed by my wall of pictures. It's there that his focus remains. He moves closer, as though he has no choice. I imagine that Jude has a giant magnet hidden under his shirt and the framed images have the other half, pulling him toward them until he's standing right in front.

Other than a brief "hello" when he first walked into the building, we haven't said anything else to each other. We walked up the stairs in silence, as if we knew how this scene was supposed to play out. I'd open the door, Jude would come in, and then he'd eventually end up soaking in the photos I took so many years ago. I'll admit, I had talent, and there was a time when I thought I might actually be able to make a living out of my photography. Watching Jude stare so intently at these images, I feel a flicker of satisfaction in the way any artist might feel when their hard work is being appreciated. He hasn't mentioned what he thinks of my work, but he doesn't need to. I can see it written all over him. It's in the way he has his hands resting in his pockets, like he has to keep them confined so they won't reach out and touch the images. He doesn't rush his appraisal. He savors the time he spends assessing each picture, allowing his eyes to rest on every detail. After what feels like hours, but is probably less than ten minutes, he turns to face me. "These"—he frees his hand from his pocket and points at the wall—"are incredible. Did you take them?" He asks the question in a way that tells me he already knows the answer.

I nod. "Yeah, I took them a long time ago."

He turns back to the pictures. "This is your family." It's not a question. I'm not in any of the pictures, but there's a familiarity that couldn't exist if I didn't love the subjects.

"It is." I offer no other explanation, but he doesn't ask for one. He just stands there, silently observing the faces of the ones I love the most in this world. It feels intimate, like I'm baring a piece of my soul. The feeling overwhelms me, and the need to shift his focus compels me to speak. "Can I get you anything? Water? Orange juice? I think I may have a few cans of soda in my pantry, although they're not cold." I cringe at my pitiful offering. Playing the hydration game with my mom has me choosing water over most beverages. It feels insincere to preach to her if I don't follow through on my own advice. I have orange juice because I can't handle taking pills with thin liquid, and the soda is for Annabelle. I like to take over a can as a treat with dinner when I make it for her and Jodi.

Jude looks over at me, a thoughtful expression on his face. I think he may be on to my distraction tactic, but he's humoring me by not pointing it out. "Sure, I'll take some water. Thanks, Nellie." He strides to the kitchen and pulls out a stool at the bar. I feel his eyes on me as I move around the kitchen. I place a glass of water on the countertop and slide it over in front of him. He glances down at it and then back up at me. I can see so many questions behind his eyes. My hands find the edge of the bar, and I grip the counter, preparing for impact.

"So tell me, Nellie, what's your favorite color?"

I can't keep the surprise from my face as I reel back with shock. I definitely did not see that one coming. I was gearing up for the hard-hitting questions, and instead, he's talking about color. Sensing my confusion, he adds some clarification. "We covered a lot of ground last night, but there are still so many things I want to know about you."

"And my favorite color is one of those things?"

He nods. "Yep, it's one of those things."

I tilt my head to look up at the ceiling as though I might find the answer there. Huh, my favorite color…I'm not sure I've given it much thought. As a child, we live and breathe our favorites. Things like color and food and music are as important to our identity as our gender and ethnicity. As we age, we let the minor details fall to the wayside and shift our focus to the larger issues like social status and economic standing. We get lost in things that are outside of our control. Finding happiness in color and food is so basic, but also so vital. I close my eyes and try to picture my favorite color. It flashes in front of me as though it were always there. "Blue."

"Blue?"

I bounce my head up and down emphatically. "Uh-huh. Robin's egg blue, to be exact."

His grin is wide, like he was expecting my answer. "I like that color for you."

"You do?"

"I do." He's not giving anything away voluntarily, so I decide the only way to get the answers I want is to ask the questions.

"And why is that?"

He rests his elbow on the counter and his chin in his palm. He looks inquisitive and introspective. "Because blue is the color of serenity. It symbolizes trust and loyalty—qualities I've already seen in you." I open my mouth to ask for more of an explanation, but he raises his hand. "Before you ask, I took a color theory class in college." He shrugs. "I needed an elective and it fit into my schedule."

"Interesting. What was your major?"

He smirks. "Business management," he says with a shake of his head. "I know, I know, how original of me, right?"

I chuckle. "Hey, there's nothing wrong with playing it safe. And look at you now, you're putting your degree to good use by managing a coffee shop." I narrow my eyes at him. "However, choosing to take a color theory class as an elective tells me way more about you than your degree does."

He crosses his arms and looks at me with a challenging gleam in his eyes. "Does it now?"

I wasn't sure I wanted him here. I'm still not convinced it's the best idea, but now that he's sitting across from me, I want to pull back his layers like I'm peeling an orange. There's so much depth to him, and I've only scratched the surface.

"Okay, Jude. Quid pro quo. Now it's your turn to tell me your favorite color, although you'll need to include the analysis part, too, because color theory isn't in my repertoire." I flit my hand back and forth as though he's too fancy for me.

He laughs. "Well, that's an easy one. It's definitely red."

"Red, huh? I may not have the knowledge to back it up, but I'm gonna go out on a limb here and say that's an intense one."

He chuckles. "You'd be right with that assessment. Red is associated with extreme emotions and a driven personality. It's symbolic of an adventurous and active lifestyle."

Hmm. I've only known Jude as a barista. There's not much activity in that occupation. There's obviously a master plan at work that he has yet to reveal.

"So, you're adventurous? What type of activities are you drawn to?"

His eyebrows lift, and I feel a warmth in my cheeks. Thankfully, he doesn't seize the opportunity to make me blush even more. "Oh, I'm quite adventurous with the flavored syrups at work. Making lattes isn't as easy as it looks, you know." He looks at me pointedly, and I shift uncomfortably. I was sure he had a hidden agenda, but maybe I was wrong.

Without warning, he bursts into a fit of laughter. He's practically doubling over, and all I can do is stand by helplessly wondering what could possibly be so funny. He pushes through his amusement and speaks in gasps. "I'm sorry, but if you could see the look on your face right now, you'd be laughing, too." He takes a few deep composing breaths until he's able to sit upright again. "I've been known to break a sweat during rush hour, but you didn't think I considered working at Starbucks an active lifestyle, did you?"

I shake my head and smile. "Well, no, not really, but your response sounded so natural, I wasn't sure what to think. And there's nothing wrong with mastering the fine art of coffee making, you know. Honestly, I think it should qualify as a necessary life skill." I smirk at him.

He chuckles. "A necessary life skill, huh? I suppose you aren't wrong there. But as far as what I'm passionate about, what wakes me up every morning and what I dream about every night, well, it isn't coffee. I love to travel. Visiting a new place, exploring a different landscape—that's what I live for." I see the excitement etched in his face. It's alive in the creases at the corners of his eyes. He's lost in thought, staring just past my shoulder. It's as if he's dreaming awake. His mouth is slightly open and his lips are curved into a crescent moon. His eyes have a wistful look, as though he's in one of those far away locations at this very moment. I consider snapping him out of his reverie. I could clear my throat, feign a sneeze, or slap my hands on the counter, but he looks so content. I decide to let him have this moment. After all, peace is often hard to come by. I'm all too familiar with that harsh reality.

When the rare opportunity arises, he should be allowed to bask in it.

He blinks his way back to the present, and his head twitches to clear the fog. When his eyes find mine, there's no embarrassment. He makes no excuses for his momentary daydream. He just sits in contemplative silence for a beat longer, and I'm struck by the level of comfort I feel. Ordinarily, in a situation such as this one, I would be crawling out of my skin looking for an escape. Quiet makes me anxious, especially when it's shared. But with Jude, it's been several minutes since either of us has spoken, and I feel no need to dilute the tension because there isn't any. It's unexpected and refreshing. In fact, I'm so lost in the silence that I startle when he suddenly begins speaking.

"Coffee pays the bills, and I enjoy the social interactions that go along with the job. But it isn't where I see myself in five years—or even two years, for that matter. What I'd really like is to be able to travel for a living and get paid for it."

"Well, who wouldn't want that? It sounds like a dream job. But how would you even go about finding that kind of work?"

He smiles shyly, as if he's about to let me in on a secret. "That's the best part, Nellie. I didn't have to look for the job; it found me." He waggles his eyebrows, eliciting a chuckle out of me. "My college roommate and a buddy of his recently started up a company that produces gear for the adventurer. It's called Blue Blaze. They have an entire line of clothing meant for hiking, climbing, kayaking, you name it. If it's an outdoor activity, they've got you covered."

He's so animated with his descriptions; it's obvious this topic excites him. "It's awesome that your friend started up a company at such a young age. It's inspiring. But, I'm not sure I'm connecting all the dots. Are you a silent partner or something?"

He grins. "Not a partner, Nellie. An employee."

"An employee." I'm still not quite following and feeling denser by the minute.

He bobs his head. "Yep. See, in order to make the grand claims about how durable the fabric is and how well it holds up against the elements, they need to test it out. And not just on a short walk through the park. They need someone to travel to different locations and really run their products through the ringer. That's where I come in. We're still working out all the details, but the plan is for me to take a few trips a year on their dime. I'll wear their clothes while climbing mountains and hiking miles on trails. They want me to document my experiences using pictures which I'll be uploading directly to their company blog along with a journal entry. They're hoping the travel blog will entice people to want to try out their gear for themselves."

Jude speaks with passion and fervor. His enthusiasm is addictive, and I find myself itching to follow him on his journey. He clearly has what it takes to do a job like this and do it well. I have no doubt his adventures will elicit a huge following. This is definitely not a pipe dream for him, and I'm impressed with how much thought and effort he's already put into it. "Wow, Jude, that's fantastic. Good for you." The smile on my face is genuine. Whenever I meet someone filled with so much motivation, I'm always in awe of them. Given my current situation, I haven't been able to think much further than one or two days ahead, much less make a five-year plan. I'm not complaining. My mom needs me, and if the roles were reversed, she'd give up everything for me, as well. She already has. But I'd be lying if I said there wasn't a part of me that felt slightly envious of Jude's freedom. What would I do if there were nothing holding me back? Where would I go?

The screech of the metal legs on the stool as they scrape across the wood floor startles me out of my thoughts. Jude carries his empty glass over to my sink. He locates the dish soap in the cabinet underneath the sink. Reaching for the sponge, he gets to work cleaning his glass. He moves around my kitchen with such ease it's as if he's been here many times before. Once he's placed his cup on the drying rack, he turns to face me.

The question I ask next is one that's been bouncing around inside my head since the minute he showed up here. "Why are you here?" I blurt out the words as though I had no other choice, and really, I didn't. I've been trying to hold them back, but it's no use. It's like trying to plug a leaky water balloon with your finger over the hole. It's a temporary fix, but sooner or later, the liquid will still find a way to seep out.

He regards me with kind eyes and speaks softly. "Because you said, 'Something's come up.' In my experience, that excuse never leads to anything good. Just ask Marcia Brady." He pins me with a knowing look, and I find myself backpedaling.

"Yeah, well, something *did* come up, actually. Maybe not a date with a 'big man on campus,'—yes, I've seen that episode, too—but it was still something that threw me off my game. To be fair, I chose to cancel on you because I was sure I wouldn't be the best company." I don't take my eyes off of him. I want him to see the honesty reflected back at him. I wasn't ditching him for a better option. I was just trying to save him from having to deal with me in this state.

He gives me a half-smile and moves across the kitchen, closing the divide between us. He's standing right in front of me, and he's so close, I have to tip my head up to look at him. "Want to talk about it?"

It's only five words, but as soon as they leave his mouth, I realize they're exactly what I've been waiting to hear. With Meg constantly shutting me out and my mom unable to carry a conversation, I've been trapped inside my own head for so long. With nowhere to go, my thoughts swirl around and mix together until they're a jumbled mess of incoherent emotions. I've been suppressing my feelings for so long, I don't even know where to begin. I search Jude's eyes for understanding and find it immediately. It gives me the courage to find my voice. "I do."

He cups my jaw. "I'm here for you, Nellie. Tell me everything."

Chapter Eighteen

I'VE BEEN TALKING for so long, my voice has dropped an octave and my vocal fry is strong. We started out leaning against the kitchen counter, but as soon as it became apparent that I wasn't going to be able to stop anytime soon, we moved to my loveseat. Jude has stayed by my side, nodding when appropriate, and even taking my hand a few times. He hasn't said a thing since I began word vomiting all over him. Once I opened my mouth, I couldn't stop. I am water forcefully rushing out of a fire hydrant. I have no shut-off valve.

I tell him about growing up without a father. My and Meg's dad left when I was just a year old and Meg was six. I'm sure it must've been hard for our mom, but she never let us see her defeated. She always had so much fight in her. My poppy moved in with us when I was still very young. Poppy was my grandfather, but he was also my father, and he filled both roles so fully that I never felt the void of not having a dad. I explain what it felt like when I first heard my mom's diagnosis and the events that followed. I talk about how close I was with my sister when we were younger and how hurt I was when she chose to leave. I fill him in on every major detail of my life over the past twenty-seven years, leaving nothing out. The excitement I felt when I was accepted into a very prestigious college program for Photojournalism and the shame that overwhelmed me when I had to drop out. The immense sadness I endured when I had to assert my power of attorney over my mother and sign the paperwork on her room at Shady Villa. The worry I feel for my sister and her erratic lifestyle.

By the time I reach the part of my story that revolves around Claudette's illness, I'm crying. I don't even realize it at first. Jude lifts his finger to my cheek and catches a tear as it falls. I'm taking breaths so deep, I'm almost gasping. "So, you see, all of that?" I tap the side of my head. "That's my *something* that came up."

He doesn't speak. He just stares deeply into my eyes. At first, I assume he's just trying to take it all in. I unloaded so much on him, unpacked years of baggage and placed it right on his lap. Of course, he'd need time to process everything. But the more time that passes, the more uneasy I feel. I squirm under his intense scrutiny. "Why are you looking at me like that?"

He tilts his head and regards me with something resembling sad curiosity. "I'm trying to figure out where you put all of it."

My brows knit with confusion. "All of what?"

"Your grief. Where does it go?"

I think about his question for a minute. I've always associated grieving with mourning someone who has died, and I haven't openly expressed an emotion like that since I lost my poppy. But grief is more than just feeling tremendous sorrow when someone dies. Grieving is mental suffering. It's a visceral response to an overabundance of heartache. I see glimpses of it from time to time. When my mother can't remember her middle name and I feel my breath catch in my throat, or if I try calling Meg after an upsetting day and my call goes to voicemail after the first ring. It's fleeting, but it's always there, just below the surface. If I let even a bubble of anguish breach the barrier I've created, the armor that I've carefully built up around myself will crumble. So I do the only thing I can do. "I bury it."

He nods as though that's the answer he was expecting from me. And then he stretches his arm across the couch, grasping my shoulder and pulling me toward him. It's there, enveloped in his protective embrace, that I feel a sort of calm settle over me. Jude rests his chin on the top of my head. With my hand pressed against his chest, I can feel the rise and fall of his slow, rhythmic breathing.

"Oh, Nellie." He exhales the words in a soft murmur, and then he remains quiet for so long that I feel myself begin to nod off. Releasing years of suppressed emotions will do that to you.

As I drift in his arms, new thoughts begin to swirl with the torrent of old ones. I barely know this man, and yet, I can't remember the last time I felt so relaxed, so free. But I'm not free, not really. I'm still tethered to the people who need me, the ones who are counting on me to make the tough decisions. Still, maybe there's more to life than what I've been living. Jude might just be the answer to every question I've ever had. What does happiness feel like? Is it possible to be carefree? Can you forget the worst things and only remember the good?

My breathing is calm and even as I give in to the visions of happily ever after dancing around in my dreams. In my slumber, I am cocooned in warmth. At some point, I swear I feel the hint of a kiss on my cheek.

I awaken sometime later feeling disoriented, but also lighter than I've felt in years. The sun has almost disappeared, and dusk is setting in. The room is hazy, and my eyes are out of focus. I blink away the fog that blankets my vision and peer around my apartment, piecing together the events of the day. Jude. He was here. I told him everything, and then I must have fallen asleep. I scan my surroundings in search of him. My ears strain to catch a sound from the bathroom, but all I hear are the soft puffs of my own breath. I slide along the sofa and switch on the light on my end table. A warm glow fills the room, and my eyes catch sight of a blue Post-it note stuck to the top of the worn oak table. A few words in careful penmanship stare up at me.

I'm sorry to leave without saying goodbye. You looked so peaceful, I didn't want to wake you. Call or text me later and let me know how you're feeling. I'm always here for you.

I lift the edge of the paper, and it pulls away from the table with a little resistance. I press my finger along the sticky edge and study the last line of Jude's note.

I'm always here for you.

It's the same thing he said to me right before I divulged all of the inner turmoil I've been holding on to, only this time he added a word. *Always.* It's a tricky word. We toss it around so often, using it to describe the things we like or the habits we've formed. Oh, I *always* eat pepperoni on my pizza, or I *always* carry ChapStick in my purse. Being so casual with our use, we've taken the true meaning of the word for granted. In its simplest form, the word *always* means forever.

My eyes trail over the letters in Jude's handwriting, looking for clues. Did he mean he would always be here for me, just like he will always carry a pen in his left pocket? Or does he plan on serving as my shoulder to lean on for as long as I need him?

I'm prone to overthinking, and my thoughts are beginning to sprout legs. I shake my head to clear them away and reach for the TV remote. I toggle through the Netflix menu and select an episode of *Queer Eye*. As I settle back against the cushion, I notice the blanket sprawled over my lap. I usually keep it draped over the back of the loveseat. Jude must have covered me with it before he left. I smile as I imagine him tucking me in. My hand moves instinctively to my cheek as I faintly remember a kiss being left there. I remind myself that he plans to make a career out of traveling. It's better in the long run if I don't let myself get too attached to him. My mind makes a lot of sense, but I don't think my heart is paying much attention.

I set the note back on the table, pressing the sticky seam onto the wood. For now, I'm pausing the barrage of Jude thoughts and losing myself in my favorite show. I think the "Fab Five" should be required viewing. Every episode of this show tackles a relatable issue with an underlying theme of tolerance and love. We all want different things in life, but our end goal is always the same. Acceptance. All we really need is someone to love and support us. Everything else is just static.

There's a faint moaning sound in this episode that seems to be in every scene. It's odd and doesn't seem to fit with what's happening on the screen. I press a button on the remote to increase the volume, and the sound nearly disappears. That's strange. I try the reverse and lower the sound, and the distant noise is back, only now it's more of a wail and less of a moan. I pause the show, and now the sound is in stereo. It's coming from the other side of the wall I share with Claudette. I rise from my seat and tiptoe over toward it.

With my ear pressed against the wall, I can hear the cries of a woman whose life has been irreparably altered by devastating news. I recognize the sound. I've cried similar tears. It isn't the circumstances that bind us. My situation vastly differs from Claudette's. It's the feeling of complete and utter helplessness that I empathize with. She's facing something she cannot change. She can't will it away with happy thoughts and healthy eating. All she can do is accept her new normal and learn how to live with it.

I press the back of my head against the wall and slide down until I'm sitting on the floor. My legs splay out in front of me and my back presses against the drywall in search of support I'll never find.

As her cries become sobs, I contemplate going over to her apartment. It's nearly impossible for me not to do something to help, and I sit on my hands in a vain attempt at stilling them. That's not what she needs from me at this moment. She's alone with her thoughts, and those emotions are overwhelming her. But her tears are a necessary part of the process.

I'm reminded of Jude's question from earlier today. This is where Claudette puts her grief. If I go over to her apartment and breach her barrier with a knock on her door, she'll suck that sadness back inside of her and absorb it deep within her bones. That suppression will only do her harm. No, I can't invade her private moment. But I can share it. I can lessen the burden with my ears, even if she doesn't realize I can hear her. So I sit here perfectly still and I hold in my own sorrow. The lone tear that trickles down my cheek is the only break I allow myself to make. I hold everything else in and stay strong while Claudette gives her suffering a voice. Her pain is valid. Her anguish is human. She has earned the right to be mournful, and she deserves to be heard.

Chapter Nineteen

I WAKE to the sound of my phone ringing from its perch on my nightstand. My eyes feel puffy and my lids are weighted. It's an effort just to peel them open. My body feels as though I've gone ten rounds with a prizefighter. I vaguely remember falling asleep leaning against the wall in the living room. Waking sometime during the middle of the night only to stumble into my bedroom and collapse on my still-made bed. At some point during my slumber, I worked my way underneath the blankets, where I managed to swaddle myself. I'm still wrapped up like a mummy when I realize my phone is ringing. I snap up to sitting and curse the twinge in my back.

Reaching for my phone, I see Jude's name on the screen. I take notice of the time in the right-hand corner. 9:23 a.m. It's a little early for heartfelt conversations. Hopefully, he's just calling to talk about the weather. I shake my head at the ridiculous notion and clear the sleep out of my throat with a hearty cough.

"Hello?" I croak the word despite my attempt to sound more awake.

"Nellie! There you are. You never answered my texts."

"Your texts?" I slide the phone away from my ear and

swipe up to check my messages. Sure enough, there are four missed texts from Jude. The first one is a simple, *Just checking in. Are you okay?* Followed by the same message with increasing urgency until the final text left at 11:38 p.m., a single desperate plea, *Nellie??*

"Oh, I see them now. I'm so sorry. I fell asleep. Well, I guess you knew that..." I know why I never saw Jude's messages. Visions of Claudette's woeful sobs cause my lower lip to tremble. I could explain what happened, but it doesn't feel like my story to tell. It's a secret that I share with Claudette. One that I don't even intend to tell *her* about. "It was an emotional night, and I guess I just needed to unplug. I hope you can understand. I didn't mean to worry you."

I hear a deep sigh on the other end of the line. "Of course, I understand. And I'm sorry if I overreacted. When I left you, I thought it was for the best. You were exhausted and I wanted you to rest. But once I got home, I started worrying that I left you in a fragile state and when I couldn't reach you, I, well, I guess I freaked out a little."

I wave my hand, dismissing his apology. He can't see it, but I hope he hears it in my voice. "You don't need to apologize. Believe me. I know exactly what it's like to worry about someone. Being on the receiving end of that worry is new territory for me. I just need you to be patient with me while I figure it all out."

"Sure, I can do that." He pauses, and I hear him inhale. "You'll need to get used to it, you know."

"Used to what, exactly?"

"To someone caring about you, since I have no intention of turning these feelings off." And there it is. A grand admission if ever I've heard one. Now there's no doubt in my mind that Jude considered the true meaning of *always* when he wrote that note.

I steady myself as I brace for the impact of his words, but it never comes. At least not in the way I was expecting. The weight of his confession doesn't feel like a burden. It's not a cross to bear. It's a promise to hold on to. A vow that I can trust. A place to put my grief.

* * *

"IF YOU DON'T STOP HUMMING that song, I'm going to throw this bagel at your face, cream cheese side up." My threats are empty, of course. I would never mar Jude's perfect features with strawberry whipped cream cheese. Still, he hasn't let up on "Hot in Herre" since we sat down.

There's a wicked gleam in his eye. "Whoa, Nellie!" He draws out the "whoa" adding a vibrato while holding his hands up. His laugh fills the small cafe, and I'm powerless to the sound.

"Okay, spill. How long have you been waiting to say that?"

His laughter downgrades to a chuckle as he attempts to regain his composure. "The truth?"

I nod. "Of course."

"From the moment you told me your name for the coffee order." He gives me a sly smile. "But then you followed it up with that amazing story about Nelly, and I had to make a choice. And it was a tough one, let me tell you. Brutal even. I played a quick round of eeny meeny miney moe in my head, but in the end, 'Hot in Herre' won by a landslide. It was gold, and you handed it over on a silver platter." He gives me a pointed look as though this whole joke is my fault, and I guess, in a roundabout way, it is.

I feign irritation, but truthfully, I love the constant goading. Laughter is such an underrated physical reaction. You take it for granted when it's woven throughout your day, but when it disappears, snuffed away by sadness and strife, you long for it in the way a dog might yearn for a loving pat on the head. Jude's laughter is a gift. It's a loop of euphoria that connects us together, the first ingredient in a life-long friendship. Although, sitting here on this cold metal stool staring into Jude's bright sea blue eyes, it isn't friendship that I'm looking for. And the intensity of his gaze tells me he doesn't see me as friend material, either.

As if he can hear the thoughts resounding within my head, he picks that moment to reach across the table and take my hand in his. He threads our fingers together and kneads the fleshy spot between my thumb and index finger. I watch as he makes lazy circles on my skin with the pad of his thumb. My eyes fixate on the movement as I fight the urge to look up, afraid of what I might find looking back at me.

"Nellie?" Jude's voice is calm, but there's a lilt at the end. He's trying to sound composed, but his inflection is betraying him. The slight nervousness I detect in his tone gives me the strength to lift my head. There's a yearning in his eyes that's mixed with hesitation. His feelings for me have evolved, but he's unsure if I feel the same. I match his gaze, mirroring his emotions. A relieved smile blooms on his face and he opens his mouth to say more. But my phone beats him to it, breaking the moment with my mom's ringtone. Jude's face levels with concern. I bite my lower lip and give him an apologetic half shrug.

"Hi, Mama!" I attempt to make my voice sound upbeat, hoping to encourage her mood. It's never worked before and it doesn't work now, either.

"Nellie! I need you to stop at the store and get me more juice. I'm almost out of it." She sounds as if she's on the verge of panic, and it breaks me. Seemingly insignificant things upset her so easily. I hate that something as simple as cranberry juice has the power to send her into a frenzy.

"Listen to me, they have cranberry juice in the dining room, remember?"

"No, they don't!"

I breathe in deeply. "Yes, they do. Just go down and ask—"

"No! They ran out of it and I need it. Please, Belly!" Her pleading feels like hundreds of tiny needles piercing my heart. I'm sure they haven't run out of it. Shady Villa keeps a large stock of all the staples, and cranberry juice in a retirement home is like golf balls at a driving range. Still, there's nothing to be gained by arguing with her. When my mom has her mind made up, you can't change it no matter how hard you try. She's always been that way, and Alzheimer's has only increased her stubbornness.

My mind immediately launches into fixing mode. There's a mini-mart a block away from the bagel shop. It wouldn't be much trouble to stop there. I'm sure they have cranberry juice. Of course, then I'd have to drive it all the way over to her and I was just there yesterday, but it's not that big of a deal. A tiny hardship for me equals peace of mind for my mom. Doing this for her is a given.

"Okay, Mama. Okay. Calm down. I'll be over in a little while with some juice, all right?"

I hear her exhale. "Thank you, Belly. And hurry, please." She hangs up the phone, but I still keep mine pressed against my ear. My eyes find Jude's. He's heard my end of the conversation, so he knows what I'm going to say before the words even leave my mouth. He speaks first.

"Do you want to drive or should I?"

Chapter Twenty

I'M SITTING in the passenger seat of Jude's Honda CR-V twirling my fingers in the handle of the plastic shopping bag that holds my mom's juice. I spin my hand to the right until the plastic tightens around my finger and then I swirl it to the left and watch it uncoil and then wind back up again. I repeat the motion and keep my eyes focused on it, trying, in vain, to not let my mind wander. I don't want to think about what's about to happen now that we're on our way to Shady Villa.

"Thank you for driving." I say the words robotically, unable to inject any emotion into my voice.

My head is turned down toward the bag in my lap, but I see Jude glance over at me in my peripheral vision. He turns back to face the road. "It's not a problem, Nellie. I'm happy to help." His tone isn't quite as clinical as mine, but he doesn't sound all that happy, either.

I force myself to look at his profile. There's a slight tic in his jaw. He looks deep in concentration. I feel bad that I'm burdening him with my problems. "You didn't have to come with me. I appreciate the company, but I'm sure there are plenty of other things you'd rather be doing on a Sunday afternoon."

He peers over at me. The serious expression on his face stops me from looking away. "Don't do that. Don't give me an out when I'm not looking for one. I care about you, remember?"

He speaks with such finality, as if there were no other choice to be made. All I can do is nod.

I resume my twirling of the bag handles as we continue the drive in silence. The swirling of the frosted white bag matches the twisting in my gut. I'm clinging desperately to the small hope that today isn't one of my mom's bad days, but given the panicked phone call that led to this unplanned excursion, I don't have much faith in that.

* * *

I SLOG down the hallway like a housefly caught in molasses. Jude stays by my side, matching my impossibly slow stride. When we reach my mom's door, I hesitate, giving Jude a sideways glance. "Listen, Jude, my mom…well, what I mean is, the woman behind this door isn't my mom. Not as she was, anyway. The things she might say, the way she may act, it's not the version I wish you were meeting."

He rests his hand on my shoulder, giving it a gentle squeeze. "Nellie, you don't need to warn me. It's true, I don't have first-hand experience with your mom's disease, but what I do know is enough of an explanation."

I offer a small smile in response and mumble, "Here goes nothing." Summoning up all the courage I can muster, I raise my fist and knock on the door. There's very little lag time between me knocking and the door flinging wide open. Normally, my mom is much more guarded and routinely locks and unlocks the door before opening it. Throwing it open on the first knock is not an ordinary occurrence. But words like *normal* and *ordinary* no longer apply here.

My mom stands before me wearing dark blue jeans and a

pilled brown cardigan hanging loosely over a pink T-shirt. Her vacant eyes assess me with confusion. "Belly? Is it Saturday already? I thought you were just here…" Her eyebrows pull down with confusion and she tilts her head, staring off to the side just past my left ear. She's so deep in thought, she startles when I speak.

"Mama? You called me, remember?" I always do that. Say that word like it holds some kind of magic power. As if she'll suddenly recall what she's forgotten as soon as she hears the prompt. I can tell by the blankness in her expression that she has no idea what I'm talking about, so I just continue my explanation. "I brought you cranberry juice!" I hold up the bag in one hand and flash my other hand in a "ta-da" motion. I glance at Jude and amend my previous exclamation. "Actually, *we* brought you juice."

My mom's eyes flick to Jude and widen as she takes him in. He lifts his hand in a small wave. "Hi there. I'm Jude." His smile is kind, and his voice is soothing. When my mom doesn't reply, he adds another piece of information. "I'm a friend of Nellie's."

Friend. The word should bring me comfort. After all, I don't really have any friends. I had a few in college, but when I had to drop out, we lost touch. Or I pulled away. Either way you look at it, I don't have anyone to confide in. At least I didn't until Jude came along. Still, it's not the word I want to use when I describe what we are, but it's probably the most accurate. For now.

I give my head a shake. "Oh, I'm sorry. Where are my manners? Mom, this is my friend, Jude." I make a back-and-forth motion with my hand between the two of them. "And Jude, this is Charlotte. My mom." I offer him both names, punctuating each one in a careful attempt to keep them separate. When she was first diagnosed, I used to play a little game in my head to try to make sense of the changes in her personality. They were subtle at first, but they were still things I didn't recognize, so I would tell myself that her behavior or the words she used were something Charlotte would do or say. I never knew my mom as Charlotte, she was always just my mama, so it was easy to differentiate the two. I saw her as two halves making up a whole, but eventually the one half—the one I didn't recognize—started gaining momentum until eventually Charlotte had the upper hand and my mama was relegated to a much lesser fraction. In reality, I know that her behavior was unique to her disease and not another facet of her personality, but in the beginning, I was looking for anything to hold on to. Grasping at any fragment I could find until there was nothing left but the cold, harsh reality of this devastating illness.

Jude reaches his hand out toward my mom. "It's nice to meet you, Charlotte. Nellie's told me so much about you."

My mom looks down at Jude's outstretched hand and then up at my face, never making a move to lift her arm and return his shake. His hand hangs in the air for a beat before he pulls it back, letting his arm drape at his side. "You brought me juice, you said?" She eyes the bag in my hand.

Awkward tension fills the air like a dense fog. I feel like I'm lost, wandering aimlessly in some distant realm. An alternate universe in which my mother has been body-snatched or infected by a parasitic virus.

I let my gaze wash over her features. She's put on weight, but she still seems hollow. There's no essence underneath her skin and bones. She's an empty vessel.

I lift up the grocery bag of juice and hand it over to her. "Here, Mama. You were worried you would run out of cranberry juice so we made sure you were restocked."

She takes the bag from my hand, and a small smile plays on her lips. "Well, thank you, but you didn't have to come all this way just to bring me juice. They have plenty in the dining room, you know."

I lift my eyes to the ceiling and take a few calming breaths.

She doesn't want to be this way. She would hate this. This isn't her. The mantra repeats over and over on a loop inside my head, but today, in front of Jude, it's not enough.

As if sensing my internal struggle, Jude speaks up. "Nellie was showing me some of the pictures she's taken. She's quite the photographer. You must be very proud."

Mama's eyes flit over to Jude, and it's as if she's seeing him for the first time. I watch in wonder as a tiny fissure appears in her facade. The subtle crack is just wide enough to allow a memory to seep in. Her expression turns wistful and her smile widens. "Yes, my sweet girl is so talented. Always has been." She reaches a bony hand out and pats my cheek.

My lower lip starts to tremble, and I catch it with my teeth. Her words envelop me, wrapping me up in a warm embrace in a way I thought I would never feel again.

As quickly as the moment arrives, it passes. I watch as the curtain closes, dimming the light that was only just there. Whenever this happens, I'm overwhelmed with the feeling of mourning. It's like I've lost her all over again. The tiny glimpses are cruel and only serve to make this situation harder to bear. But not today. Today I feel grateful. A window opened, and for a few brief minutes, I saw my mama. Not the person she is now, living with this disease, but who she was, the woman who held my hand when I had to get stitches in third grade. The same person who arrived at school twenty minutes before the doors opened just so she could be the first to admire my photos in the art show.

I look over at Jude and find him beaming at me. He knows the significance of what just happened. A triumphant smile stretches across my face. I'm so glad he was able to meet my mama.

Chapter Twenty-One

JUDE HASN'T SAID MUCH since we left Shady Villa. I can't tell if he's upset or just lost in thought. He wears a pensive expression as he drives us back to my apartment.

Our visit with my mom ended abruptly. After that brief but incredible moment when the fog seemed to lift, I watched her blink a few times as if trying to hold on to the clarity, only to lose it again. The smile left her face, and in a monotone voice, she issued us a muted, "Thank you for the juice. Good-bye," before closing her door and shutting us out. But that's nothing new. It happens that way nearly every time I visit her. At least, this time we were able to catch a glimpse of the real person who's been lying dormant, trapped inside the confines of her disjointed mind. I'm used to things ending that way, but Jude isn't.

The quiet in the car feels stifling. I'm not normally one to fill silence with idle chitchat, but this stillness feels suffocating and my mind is beginning to create worst-case scenarios that all end with Jude dropping me off and then driving away without uttering a single word. Without any forethought, I hear myself blurt out, "So, read any good books lately?" My eyes roll back into my head, and I inwardly groan at my feeble attempt at conversation.

Jude turns his head and studies me like I'm a piece of abstract art in a museum. "Um, no, actually. I can't say that I have. Have you?"

I look down at my lap and filter through my mind in search of something, but I come up empty-handed. I used to love to lose myself in a good book, but aside from reviewing a few case studies online, I never seem to make time to read anymore. With a small shake of my head, I whisper, "No."

His eyes are back on the road, but I can tell his thoughts are elsewhere. Great. If he wasn't already having doubts about spending time with me, I'm sure he is now.

"Listen, Nellie. I've been thinking…"

Here it comes. Every classic breakup begins with those exact words. *Wait, breakup?* For us to do that, we would've had to have been dating in the first place. Is that what we've been doing?

Jude clears his throat, jolting me out of my mental spiral. "I know it's none of my business, but isn't there anyone else who could help you out with your mom? An aunt or uncle or maybe even a long-lost cousin? Does your mom have any friends nearby?"

It takes me a minute to realize that Jude isn't trying to brush me off. He's trying to help me. The questions he's asking are ones I've heard many times before. It's common for people on the outside to look in and try to fix things. I'm one of those people myself, and if the roles were reversed, I'd be offering the same suggestions.

Usually, when I'm asked those questions, I nod in agreement as though I've never thought of them before. And then I dole out rehearsed responses like, "She does have a few friends. Maybe I should give them a call. Thanks for the suggestion." I know they mean well, so I placate them with what they want to hear. It's easier that way. But with Jude, it's different. I don't want to lie to him.

On a sigh, I answer his question with the sad truth. "She has no one, but me." I glance over at him and find that we're wearing matching somber expressions. "My mom is an only child, so there are no siblings or cousins. And with a deadbeat for a father, I have no connection with any relatives on his side. As for friends, there are a few, but as far as I know, they haven't called or visited her in quite a while. The harsh reality is, Alzheimer's makes people uncomfortable. The person they used to know has been replaced with a stand-in who doesn't share their history and can't remember inside jokes or reminisce about 'the good ole days.' When you strip away those things, there's very little to talk about. And, for most people, it's just easier to pretend it isn't happening." I keep my head down and my gaze fixed on my hands resting on my lap, trying to hide the shame I feel. I'm not excusing her friends for abandoning her, but I can't pretend I don't understand why they have. "Her best friend, Liz, was the exception, but a few months ago, she moved to New Hampshire to be closer to her daughter. Living in a different time zone has made it more difficult to keep in touch, especially since my mom isn't a huge fan of talking on the phone. Liz calls me every so often to check in, and I appreciate that. I know she cares, but she has her own life and her own problems. I don't need to weigh her down with mine."

He regards me with kindness and not an ounce of pity. It feels like a hug, but he never touches me. I don't know how he does it. "That's a heavy load for one person to bear, Nellie. Do you ever feel overwhelmed by it all?"

I let out a humorless chuckle. "Only every day."

He reaches across the center console and places his hand on top of mine, giving it a soft squeeze. "Good thing you're not alone anymore."

I turn my head and catch his gaze. The sincerity of his

words is alive in his eyes and I soak it in. For the past few years, loneliness has become the sweater I never leave home without. I wrap it around myself, cocooned in misery and shut off from the outside world. For the first time in as long as I can remember, I feel warmth. Maybe it's time to take the sweater off.

Jude retracts his hand and places it back on the wheel where it belongs, giving me a wink before directing his attention back on the road. "So, Belly, huh? That's quite the nickname. Care to tell me how you got it?" Even though I can only see half of his face, there's no denying the broad grin he's wearing.

He's changing the subject and I'm so grateful, I have to sit on my hands to refrain from reaching across the car's interior and wrapping my arms around him. "Oh, you caught that, did you?" I say with an edge of sarcasm. I'm not at all surprised, seeing as how incredibly perceptive Jude is. I'm fairly certain there isn't much that gets past him.

He lets out a laugh. "Of course, I caught it, *Belly*! Now spill because looking at you, I can't figure out the connection." He eyes me knowingly, and I match his expression with a deliberate look of my own.

"Well, if you must know, it was a name given to me by my poppy. I was a rather burly toddler, so it actually suited me. And even though I eventually grew into that belly, or out of it, it's just one of those things that stuck." My gaze slides away from him and catches on the glare of streetlights passing over the windshield. "You know, I hadn't really thought of it until now, but it's pretty incredible that my mom still uses it. Despite the progression of her condition, she hasn't forgotten the nickname her dad gave me when I was just a kid."

"Tell me about her." His request pulls me out of contemplation. My eyes snap to him. He's focused on the road, but sensing my stare, he angles his head and gives me an encouraging nod.

This is one of the hardest parts about my mom's disease. It's changed her so drastically that sometimes I feel it threatening to change my memories of her, as well. At times, it's difficult to recall who she was before this vile diagnosis. It makes me sad to think of the sum of her whole life being reduced to the way she is now. I refuse to let that happen.

I lean back in the seat and feel the fabric give from the pressure. Letting out a wistful sigh, I turn my head and let my gaze drift to the side window. The outside world is a blur of concrete and brick with the occasional pedestrian sprinkled in. I close my eyes for a moment and think back to happier times.

Mom is in the kitchen. She's elbow deep in suds, washing dishes in the sink. The volume on the radio is at full blast. She sings a duet with John Fogerty and together they ask, "Have you ever seen the rain?" The cadence of her voice conflicts with his, but it doesn't matter. She's performing for an audience of glass and china as they bathe in detergent. They don't mind if she's slightly off-key. I'm standing in the doorway watching the show with a smile on my face. It's my default expression whenever I find her like this. Life hasn't been easy for my mom. I once asked her how she found the strength to keep going. She looked me deep in the eyes and told me, "The answer is simple, Belly, but, at times, it's also one of the hardest things to remember. On those days when you feel like giving up, turn up the music. Dance. Sing. Even if it only lasts for the few minutes while the song is playing, all of your problems will become background noise. And when that last chord ends, you'll feel a little lighter than you did before. Remember that."

As I watch her stocking-clad feet tap out a rhythm on the tattered carpet by the sink, I wonder if it's really that easy. She makes it look that way, at least, and maybe that's the key. If you fake it long enough, you start to believe it's the truth, and more importantly, everyone around you will believe it, too.

"Your mom sounds pretty incredible." Jude's voice breaks through my daydream, surprising me. I didn't even realize I was giving a voice to the memory playing out in my head.

"She was—is." I shake my head, berating myself. "This disease has made it far too easy to discredit the mom I knew, but that remarkable woman who sang her problems away is still in there, hidden some place I rarely see. But sometimes, like today, it feels like she can still hear the music."

He glances my way. The right corner of his lip lifts as he regards me for a moment. "That's beautiful, Nellie. And I'm sure you're right, your mom still hears the music. I think you hear it, too." His eyes flit across my face, making sure his words land. They do.

I'm momentarily stunned by this man sitting next to me. Not that long ago, he was a total stranger. He evolved from a guy I met at Starbucks to a true friend whom I've divulged many of my innermost secrets. I haven't known him long, but already I can't picture my life without him. That thought both excites and terrifies me.

When he looks at me the way he is right now, I feel myself falling. I'm desperate to know everything there is to know about him. It's time for me to shift the focus of the conversation. I rub my hands together. "Okay, enough of the 'Nellie Show.' It's your turn."

He pulls his chin back, looking a little perplexed. "My turn?"

"Uh-huh." I nod. "I've been taking center stage way too much, and the last thing I want is to be needy in a one-sided friendship. So tell me something about yourself. I want to know you the same way you know me." That last sentence hangs in the air. I want to grab it and stuff the words back into my mouth, but instead, I let them hover between us. It's how I feel. And Jude doesn't want us to hide from each other, so why start now?

His deep blue eyes seem to darken as he contemplates my

words. "Okay, here goes," he says as he clears his throat. "I love to eat oranges, but never orange *flavored* things. I think people movers are exactly what they say they are—an invention to *move* people. They are not meant as a resting spot for people to stand still. At the airport, it drives me crazy to see people on them just sagging like deflated balloons going for a ride. And I hate when I get a Christmas card from a couple and it's signed with an apostrophe before the s. The apostrophe shows possession so it's necessary if you're talking about the Smith's new car, but if you're just wishing me a Merry Christmas, there's nothing to possess. It's just 'The Smiths.' No apostrophe needed." He groans and shakes his head with frustration.

I let my head fall back against the seat and laugh. I can't help myself. I know what he's trying to do. Things were starting to get a little too intense, so in true Jude fashion, he lightened the mood. As I get my breathing back under control and wipe away a few rogue tears from my eyes, I realize I don't want him to ease the tension. I meant what I said. I want to know him. Taking a deep breath, I turn and face him.

"So, that's not exactly what I had in mind when I asked you to tell me about yourself, but I think you know that." I cock my head and give him the same look my mom used to give to me whenever I tried to evade her questions. "I mean it, Jude. I want your thoughts, your fears, your memories. I want to know what keeps you up at night. Give me everything. You can trust me." It's that final statement that gives Jude the push he needed to open up.

His throat moves with a swallow. Amusement leaves his face, and his expression turns serious. He doesn't turn to look my way, keeping his eyes glued to the road ahead. Several minutes pass, and I start to wonder if he'll ever speak. And then he does.

"Growing up with a twin was interesting. It was equal parts fun and irritating. Most of the time, I had a built-in best friend, but people always assume twins are carbon copies of each other, and we definitely were not. Dylan and I were fraternal twins, but even though we didn't look exactly alike, our voices made us sound like the same person, and we used that to our advantage many times." A wicked gleam sparkles in his eyes with the memory.

"When we were in eighth grade, Dylan had an enormous crush on Jennifer Combs. She's all he ever talked about and it drove me nuts. We shared a bedroom and I swear her name would be the last thing he said every night and the first word out of his mouth every morning. And judging by the way Jennifer would stare at Dylan during math class, I knew the feeling was mutual. The problem was, neither one of them ever built up the courage to talk to each other." He looks over at me and rolls his eyes as if the frustration he felt were still palpable. "There was never any follow through, and eventually, I had enough of all the talk and no action. So, on a random Saturday morning, I picked up the phone and called Jennifer." He starts to laugh as he recalls what happened. "I didn't tell Dylan what I was doing. I just did it. This was one of the many ways in which we were so different. I had confidence coming out of my ears."

This comes as no surprise to me. "You don't say? Hmm, I never would've pegged you for the confident type." I give him a playful wink, and he chuckles at my sarcasm.

"Yeah, that confidence comes in handy sometimes." He returns my wink. "But don't let it fool you. I talk a big game, but sometimes that's all it is. Just talk."

Somehow I don't believe that, but I remain quiet and let him finish his story.

"Anyway, Jennifer answered on the first ring. It was almost as if she was expecting the call. I pretended to be Dylan and asked her if she wanted to meet me/him at the movies that afternoon. Nellie, I'm telling you, I have never heard someone say, 'yes' quicker than Jennifer did that day.

Clearly, it was a question she'd been waiting for, but my brother was too terrified to ask."

I stare at him with total abandon. I'm utterly transfixed by the beauty of his smile as it fills his entire face.

"I set the whole thing up and then I told Dylan. I'll never forget the look on his face." His voice cracks with humor. "It was the perfect mixture of elation and pure horror. Within seconds, he became frantic; pulling every article of clothing he owned out of his dresser and flinging it onto his bed. He kept alternating between outfits, modeling them in front of the hallway mirror. But despite his nerves, he never considered canceling. I was so impressed with him for going through with it." He hums as the recollection plays in his mind, a dreamy look on his face.

Listening to Jude's animated tale, I feel invested in the story. "What happened after their first date? Did it go well?"

He slides his gaze over to me and grins. "It was terrible, actually. But it was also perfect. His soda cup slipped out of his hands and spilled all over her shoes, and she accidentally dropped an entire bucket of popcorn onto his lap. They were meant for each other. Their relationship was pure teenage bliss for nearly four months until Jennifer dumped him for Grant McDonald."

I let out a gasp. "She didn't!"

He nods solemnly. "She did, and he was crushed. But it all worked out for the better because Dylan was able to work out his awkward kinks with her. By the time he made it to high school, he was more self-assured. He no longer needed me to pretend to be him and call girls on his behalf. He could do it all on his own." A hint of pride flashes in his eyes, but just as quickly, it's gone, replaced with sorrow and regret. "He was oozing with tenacity, and ultimately, I think that's what led him to make the fatal mistake of getting behind the wheel that night. He thought he was untouchable until he wasn't."

I lean toward him and rest my head on his shoulder. It's

an awkward position with him driving, but I don't care. From the moment I let him in, he's been there for me. I need him to know the same goes for me. He tilts his head and rests his cheek on the top of my head for a moment.

When I speak, my voice is barely above a whisper. "I know he may not be here physically, but he lives on in your memories, and in that way, he'll always be with you."

He lifts his head and I start to slide back to my seat, but he takes hold of my arm, stilling my movements. His eyes bore into mine, cementing me in place. "The same is true for you, too, Nellie. No matter what happens, your memories of your mom can't ever be taken away from you."

I feel emotion start to build in my throat, but I swallow it down. All I can do is nod. Without realizing it, Jude has tapped into a fear that I've never put into words. Memories have been taken away from my mom, and buried away in my darkest thoughts is the fear that the same could be true for me someday.

Jude pulls into an empty space in the lot across from my apartment and turns his car off. He angles his body so that he's facing me and cups my chin. "I know what you're thinking. I can see it written all over your face. Yes, Alzheimer's can be hereditary, but Nellie, listen to me. You can't spend your days living in fear of the unknown. You'll only end up wasting the best parts of your life worrying about what could happen. And it might happen, but it also might not." His thumb glides back and forth along the side of my face and his eyes shine with candor. The frankness of his words and the way in which he seems to be able to see into my soul renders me speechless.

"Let me ask you something. If your mom had known this disease was a possibility for her, do you think she would've stopped fighting? Would she have just given up and given in? I know I don't know her well, not as she was, but from what you've told me, I think it's safe to say she would never stop fighting. She wouldn't give those thoughts any power over her life. And Nellie, neither should you. She wouldn't want that for you." He leans in until his face is flush with mine. When he speaks, his breath mixes with mine. I can smell the peppermint he popped into his mouth when we left Shady Villa. I've never been a fan of peppermint, but on Jude, it's my favorite scent in the world. His voice is barely audible when he whispers, "I don't want that for you either."

I barely have time to process his words before I feel his lips on mine. His kiss is slow at first. He knows he caught me off guard and he takes his time letting my brain play catch up. It only takes a second before I'm kissing him back. His hands slide into my hair and mine fist his shirt, pulling him closer and damning the divide that Jude's car has put between us.

This isn't my first kiss, but it may as well be because I've never felt anything like this before. Every kiss I've ever had has been a stepping stone to something else; a necessary step in a tedious process that ended with me lying horizontal and grappling with regret. With Jude, this kiss is not a prelude to bigger and better things. It *is* the bigger and better thing. It's filled with promise and hope—things I haven't let myself think about in so long.

My relationship with Jude is the only thing in my life that's just for me. It's beautiful and selfish, and now that I've experienced this side of it, I have no intention of ever letting him go.

WE MADE a vow that day in the car. Jude and I work best when we stop hiding from each other. The kiss we shared was a silent pact. In the weeks that follow, we manage to keep that promise—in the lobby of my building, on my sofa, in Jude's car, leaning over the counter at Starbucks. I feel like a lovesick teenager and I wouldn't trade it for anything.

I always thought that in order to make a relationship work, it would take a tremendous amount of effort on my part. Between taking care of my mom, working full time, fretting about my sister, and looking after my friends, I was already spread so thin. I shied away from commitment because I was certain I would fail, and to fail would mean that I would hurt someone. I couldn't bear that. Jude has proved me wrong.

He's been joining me every Saturday when I visit my mom. Sometimes he comes up to her room with me, and other times he sits outside on a chair talking to Gerry about the best places to visit in the world. As it turns out, Gerry and Mavis were quite the travelers. He's regaled Jude with many incredible stories, and Jude recently started a list on his phone of all the locations Gerry's told him about. He's pledged to visit every one and when he does, he's made a promise that he'll come see Gerry and tell him every detail.

I often leave my mom's room feeling drained, but when I reach the double doors that lead outside and spy Jude and Gerry through the glass window with their heads leaning toward each other in a conspiratorial exchange, it feels like life's way of realigning itself. Mavis' mental health has taken an unfortunate turn, and most days, it's an effort just to get Gerry to crack a smile. But when he's talking with Jude, his whole face is alive with a youthful joy. The power of memory is incredible. It allows Gerry to relive his past adventures while also inciting Jude to want to have some of his own. When I see the two of them together, it's as if I'm pressing a reset button on my emotions. I'm able to feel a sense of peace when only moments earlier I was in distress.

Jude's reach seems to extend to every facet of my life. He's helped Claudette with her weekly canned good drive, secretly depositing cans into her collection bag and even going so far as to help her carry it to the soup kitchen a few times. She's never accepted my offers to help, but I won't hold it against her. Jude's a charmer and he's pretty easy on the eyes. I've come to find out that he's a hard one to refuse.

He's also pretty skilled in the kitchen, and last week, he made what he called his "legendary mac and cheese." I have to admit, he was right about it. He made enough for Jodi and Annabelle, and Jodi actually thanked him.

He's even taken over feeding Swerve a few times and she's warmed to him even more. Just the other day, I found her sitting in his lap purring contentedly.

I've felt Jude's presence in my life in ways I never could have imagined. Without hesitation, he's lifted some of the burden from my shoulders and placed it on to his own. I never asked him for help, but that's the thing about Jude, I never needed to.

* * *

THURSDAY MORNINGS in the billing department are usually slow, but today seems exceptionally quiet. It's been nearly twenty minutes since my phone rang. The green light on my headset is still lit, and I've double-checked the cord on my phone, making sure it's still plugged in. A few of my coworkers are on calls, but for the most part, it's calm in the office, almost eerily so.

I lean back in my desk chair and push off the floor with my feet. The wheels send me backward until I'm in front of the opening of my cubicle. I peer across the aisle and spy on Shane. He's wearing his headset, but the light on the side is green, which means he's not on a call. His eyes are glued to his computer screen, and even though I can't see it from this angle, if I had to venture a guess, I'd say he's in the middle of a spirited game of FreeCell. His eyes move from side to side in a rapid motion and his lips jut forward and pull back in a steady rhythm, much in the same way a guppy fish might move its mouth. This is Shane's "concentration face." Believe it or not, we've had many lengthy discussions about it. It drives his wife, Carol, crazy, but he claims to have no control over it. He never knows he's doing it unless someone points it out to him.

I turn my head to the right and my eyes land on my glass candy jar filled with M&M's. Reaching inside, I scoop up a few and pitch one at Shane. I try to hit his arm, but I'm a terrible shot and the candy-coated chocolate sails behind him, pinging off the edge of his desk. Trying a second time, I over-throw and the M&M flies way over the top of Shane's cubicle. I hold my breath and brace myself for a shout from one of my coworkers, but it never comes. The candy must have avoided hitting someone and landed on the floor, the impact muffled by carpet. I close one eye and zero in on Shane's shoulder.

Holding a red M&M between the thumb and index finger of my right hand, I take aim and launch it at my target.

THWACK! Third time's the charm! He jolts a few inches out of his seat and his left hand instinctively raises to pat his right shoulder. His gaze falls to the floor where he eyes the candy culprit lying next to his shoe. His body immediately begins to shake with silent laughter as he realizes what I've tossed at him. He leans down to pick up the red M&M and glides his chair around to face me. He wears a disbelieving look on his face. Shane's always known me to follow the rules, but I'm learning that life is a little more fun when you test the boundaries.

I give him an innocent shrug, and he slides his headset off and lets it rest around his neck. His eyes lock on mine, narrowing in mock irritation. "Oh, it's on." He issues the threat as he pitches the candy back at me. It lands directly in my lap with an unsatisfying *PAT*.

I know what's coming next. I close my eyes and start counting. I only make it to two when I hear Shane's deep belly laugh bellowing out from his cubicle. The sound reverberates throughout the office, filling the space with his booming guffaw. The smack of his hand as it meets his knee only adds to the scene. All I can do is shake my head and join him. I swear, Shane's laugh is so contagious, he could take it to the stage. If he just stood there carrying on like this, he'd have the crowd in stitches. He'd be a highly successful comedian and he'd never have to utter a single word.

A few of our coworkers peer up out of their cubicles to watch the show, and within seconds, nearly everyone is laughing. Most don't even know why, but in the end, it doesn't matter. When it's your job to take calls from people who are unhappy about a bill they received, you take laughter anywhere you can get it. It's like manna, and we soak it up like a sponge.

I have another remedy for a blah day. Standing up, I ask, "Anyone up for coffee? I'm making a Starbucks run!"

* * *

IT'S 10:34 in the morning, and Starbucks is practically a ghost town. Pushing open the glass double doors, I'm met with the sounds of smooth jazz drifting out of the speaker system. One lone patron, a forty-something man, sits at a round table in the corner typing away on his laptop. My eyes scour the area behind the counter, but I don't see Jude. I considered sending him a text letting him know I'd be stopping by, but I thought it might be more fun to surprise him. Now that I'm here and he's nowhere to be found, I'm beginning to regret not giving him advance notice.

I start to turn my head in search of him when I hear a voice directly behind me. "Back for a little hair of the dog?"

I spin around and find Jude with his arms crossed and an impish grin on his face. My hand is pressed to my chest and I take a few deep breaths to control the erratic beating of my heart. I don't know why I even try. With Jude in such close proximity, my efforts are futile. "Jesus, you scared me! What, were you just lurking in a corner somewhere, lying in wait for the perfect opportunity to scare the shit out of me?" I try to make my voice sound irritated, but it's impossible. I'm not annoyed. Not even a little bit. And judging by the satisfied gleam in his eyes, he knows. Still, he holds up his hands in a pseudo apology.

"Sorry, Nellie. I was just right over there." He motions with his thumb toward a few tables to his right. "I was wiping down tables. I'm surprised you didn't notice me when you walked in." His tone is accusatory, but it's all in jest. His eyes are alight with humor. He's enjoying the banter between us.

I recognize his feeble attempt to shift the blame and decide on a different tactic. Keeping my eyes trained on his, I tug on a wayward curl. It wraps around my finger in a tight spiral and springs back when I release it. I suck in the bottom right corner of my lip and hold it in place with my teeth. Jude's gaze follows the movement. I release my lip and watch his eyes widen ever so slightly when they catch sight of my tongue as it darts out to moisten the spot I had pinched between my teeth.

Shaking his head, he lets out a defeated groan. "You don't play fair, do you?"

I respond with a smirk and a flick of my wrist on the ends of my hair. I've never been much of a flirt, so this side of myself is surprising me. I never even knew I had it in me. What's even more astounding is how effective it is. Jude is standing across from me, practically panting from a few simple movements. It's almost too easy.

He lets out a long exhale that ends with a chuckle. "So tell me, Nellie, to what do I owe the pleasure? Are you here for coffee or me?" He raises his eyebrow playfully, eliciting a laugh out of me. He doesn't play fair, either.

"Both, but really, it's more like you first and coffee second." I smile coyly.

Jude looks pleased with my answer. "Wow, you ranked me above coffee! I have to admit, I feel unworthy of the honor." He reaches out and takes my hand in his. I feel shy all of a sudden and steal a quick glance at the guy in the corner. He's still feverishly typing and doesn't seem to notice us. Jude leans in so that his mouth is inches away from my ear. When he whispers, his warm breath sends a shiver down my spine. "Don't worry about him. He's been working on his OKCupid profile for the last hour."

I angle my head and try to be stealthy as I peek at him. He's taken a break from typing and is currently pretending to sip his coffee while holding his phone out in front of him in an attempt to snap a photo. It's a cliché picture, but it's also pretty endearing. I hope all of his efforts lead him to his soul mate. At that thought, I look up at Jude. His stormy eyes pierce mine and make me wonder if maybe I've found my soul mate.

Emotion overwhelms me and I take a step back, putting a little distance between us. "So, about that coffee I mentioned earlier…"

Jude narrows his eyes ever so slightly. If we weren't standing so close to each other, I might have missed it.

"You always do that, you know?" There's a hint of an edge to his voice, but he sounds more frustrated than annoyed.

"Know what? What do I always do?" I feign ignorance, but I know exactly what he means. He's on to me.

He steps forward, closing the gap between us. "Redirect the conversation. Change the subject. Break the connection." His hands move to either side of my neck, just below my ears. His fingertips slide into my hair and his thumbs graze the skin above my jawline. "You pour water on the flames when you should be fanning them." He leans in and presses his lips to mine. Unlike the first time, he doesn't wait for me to keep up. He isn't careful. He's not worried that he'll break me; he knows I'm already broken. It's kisses like this one that are slowly putting me back together.

He's right. When things start to get a little too intense between us, I'm always quick to defuse the situation. The truth is, I'm falling too fast and even though I think he feels the same, there's a part of me that's positive he doesn't. And it's those doubts that trigger my flight reaction. But as I stand here kissing him in the middle of Starbucks, pulling away never occurs to me. And that should tell me something.

A deep cough startles us apart. We follow the sound and see the OKCupid guy grinning at us. He holds up his cup and tips it in our direction as though he's clinking against an imaginary glass, and then he turns his head back to his computer screen.

Jude and I shake our heads in unison, sharing a laugh. He leans forward, resting his forehead against mine. "I've wanted to do that the minute I saw you walk in here. You have no idea what you do to me, Nellie."

His words settle around me. My doubts were a chill in the air only a moment ago, but now I feel nothing but warmth. I press my forehead against his and close my eyes, letting out a small hum.

We stay that way a little longer, cocooned in each other, until Jude pulls back and slips his arm around my shoulder, tugging me toward the counter. "Come on, Nellie. Let's get you that coffee."

I hand him the order and take my spot underneath the *pick up order here* sign. Leaning against the counter, I have the perfect vantage point for watching Jude. His movements are fluid as he glides between the espresso machine and the blender. He steams milk and froths it into soft peaks. It isn't something I would normally consider sexy, but watching the cords of Jude's muscles pull taut beneath his shirt as he refills the canister with coffee beans just might be the sexiest thing I've ever seen. I'm openly admiring him, and I don't even try to hide my appraisal as he sidles up to the counter to deposit the drinks in front of me.

"Did you enjoy the show?" he says with a smug grin.

I feel no shame and nod emphatically. "Uh-huh. Sure did."

He leans over the counter, and I find myself pulled toward him, meeting him halfway. Our faces are inches apart. His eyes assess mine. "So, Nellie, are you doing anything Saturday afternoon?"

"I don't know, Jude. You tell me." I bite at my lower lip to contain my excitement, but a tiny giggle squeaks out. I have no game.

He reaches out and taps the tip of my nose. "You're

adorable. And I was thinking maybe you might like to join me on a short hike on one of the trails in Quillan Park. My friend Scott asked me to test out a new pair of hiking boots they've been working on. I thought it might be more fun if I had some company." He wags his eyebrows, and I chuckle.

"Hiking, huh? Well, I suppose I could give it a try, although I have to warn you. I haven't been hiking in quite some time and I'm probably just going to slow you down."

He's shaking his head before the words even finish leaving my mouth. "You? Slow me down? Impossible."

He seems so sure, but I'm still not convinced. Despite my reservations, I find myself unable to turn him down. "Okay, then. Looks like we're going hiking."

Chapter Twenty-Three

I HAVE no idea why I agreed to this. The closest I've come to exercise in the past year has been the short walk to and from work every day. That hardly qualifies as a workout and it definitely hasn't prepared me for hiking with Jude.

I'm pacing in front of my bed in a lame attempt to build stamina while also trying to mentally assemble the perfect outfit. I need something I can move easily in. Clothing that isn't too restrictive and maybe just the right amount of revealing. No matter what I do, I'm coming up empty-handed. I need advice, but I'm not sure where to turn for this type of help. And then it hits me. I stop moving and groan as I roll my eyes up toward the ceiling. I snatch my phone from my bed and dial Meg's number before reason catches up with me and I talk myself out of it.

It rings three times, and I wonder why I'm such a glutton for punishment when it comes to my sister. I keep giving her chances and she keeps letting me down. This is the way things always are between us. Why would I expect them to suddenly be different now?

Just as I'm about to give up hope and hang up, she answers. "Belly! How's it going, little sister?"

"Hi, Megs. It's okay. Listen, I, well, this is kind of uncharted territory for us, but I could use some advice." I close my eyes and shake my head. I sound so desperate, and I suppose I am if my long-lost sister is my only hope.

"Oh, advice, huh? About what? Nellie, do you have a boyfriend you haven't told me about? I can't believe you've been holding out on me!"

I don't miss how she called me by my actual name, but I decide not to pay it too much attention. If I allow myself to get too caught up in something that was probably just a slipup on her part, I'll lose my nerve. I blink away the emotion that was threatening to bubble over. "Well, yeah, I guess you could call Jude my boyfriend. We haven't really had that discussion exactly, but I'm pretty sure that's where we're at."

She tsks into the phone. "Belly, Belly, Belly. I have failed you as a sister." *Gee, Megs, you think?* "You have to have that conversation. It's important to know where you stand because if this—Jude? Is that his name?"

She knows that's his name, but I'm desperate, so I'll play her game. "Yep, that's his name."

"Cute! Okay, so as I was saying, if Jude doesn't think of you as his girlfriend, but you think of him as your boyfriend…do you see how messy things could become?"

Great, have I been completely misreading things with, Jude? I didn't think it was so off base to think of him as my boyfriend, but maybe I'm wrong. "Um, yeah, I guess I could see how that could happen."

She hums into the phone like she's comforting an injured animal. "Oh, Belly, listen, you might be right. He might be your boyfriend. Tell me this, have the two of you kissed?"

"We have. Several times." It feels weird to be admitting that out loud. Like telling my sister somehow diminishes the intimacy in a way.

I can hear her clapping over the line, and I bite down on

my lip to stifle a groan. "Oh good! That's an excellent indicator. Now, how about anything else?"

I swallow. I don't like where this conversation is going. "Anything else?"

"Uh-huh. Has he felt you up? Have any clothes come off? Was a bed involved or the back of a car, perhaps?" That last word leaves her mouth with a suggestive lilt on the end.

I should have known she'd go there. Meg doesn't know how to have a relationship that doesn't involve giving her body away to the first guy who notices. She hasn't always been this way, but ever since she's moved to Hawaii, she's developed a skewed idea of what a healthy relationship looks like. I know I'm going to kick myself for this, but I answer her anyway. "No. Nothing more than kissing has happened yet. It's all still new and we're taking our time getting to know each other."

She sighs, and I hate her for it. I don't want to hear pity in her voice. I don't need it, nor do I deserve it. Jude and I have something real, but she doesn't know what that looks like. And for that, I pity her. "Oh, my dear sweet sister." It's an endearment that should be laced with love, but it tastes sour coming from her. "I can tell you like this guy, so let me give you some advice. I know it sounds crass, but you need to unlock your knees. How else do you expect to hold on to him?"

And there it is. The total sum of Meg's existence all tied up in a disgusting bow of crippling self-doubt. The only way to get a man is to give yourself to him. I may be the younger sister, but clearly, I'm the one who should be dispensing the advice here. And I have, repeatedly, but it always falls on deaf ears. So I'm saving my breath and my dignity and ending this call.

"Well, you've definitely given me a lot to think about, Megs. Thanks for taking my call."

She laughs as though the idea were utter nonsense. "Of

course, I'd take your call, silly. You're my sister!" I'm reminded of all the other times I've tried to contact her to no avail, but there's no point in bringing any of that up. She'd either deny it or explain it away, and somehow I'd end up being the villain.

"Well, I appreciate that. I'll talk to you soon."

"Sure thing, Belly. And remember what I said!"

"Oh, trust me, Megs, I won't forget it." Even if I wish I could.

I end the call and feel a deep sense of loss for the sister I used to have.

* * *

JUDE SENT me a text last night telling me he'd be by at 1:00 p.m. and that I should be "ready for adventure." I'm not exactly sure how to prepare for that, but looking down at my tight-fitting yoga capri pants and snug T-shirt, I think I'm about as ready as I can be. My hair has been tamed with a bandana and I've limited my makeup to light brows and mascara.

I glance at my watch for the fifty-millionth time. 12:43 p.m., only two minutes since the last time I checked. I groan. I feel like I'm crawling out of my skin. This is ridiculous. It's just Jude and it's only a hike. What's the worst thing that could happen? I could trip on a rock and fall flat on my face, splitting my nose open and needing twelve stitches right down the center of my face. I cringe. Yep, that's definitely a scenario I hope to avoid today.

I'm not sure why I'm so nervous. It isn't like I'm completely incapable. I think it's probably more that Jude looks like a walking advertisement for a men's fitness maga-zine, and I'm more likely to be the before picture for any hair product that promises sleek results. I'm just not someone who oozes fitness. I may be on the slender side, but thin doesn't equal fit.

My phone chimes with an incoming text and I pluck it from the pocket of my pants. How I managed to find yoga pants with pockets is beyond me. I feel like I won the lady lottery! A photo of Jude grinning widely on the front stoop of my apartment building fills my screen along with the text, *Adventure awaits, my lady!* He's so corny. I laugh and feel the bundle of nerves in my stomach begin to uncoil.

I grab my water bottle off the counter and plunk it into my bag. When I lock my door, I mentally picture my anxiety on the other side. I'm sure it'll be all too happy to wait for me when I get back, but for now, I'm happy to shrug it off of my shoulders.

There's a bounce in my step as I bound down the stairs toward the front door. Jude waits for me on the other side, and when I tug at the door, he pushes on it, both of us frantic to get to the other. When there's nothing between us, he pulls me to him and plants a kiss on my lips. He doesn't linger, but I can tell it pains him to back away. With a bit of distance between us, his eyes roam the length of me. "Jesus. I think you may need to lead the way on this hike."

I feel a bit of panic surface at that thought. "What? Why?"

He laughs at my instant reaction. "Relax, Nellie. What I meant was, if you walk in front of me, it'll give me motivation to pick up my pace and put these boots to the test." He lifts up the toe of his right foot and taps it against his left.

I let my gaze slide up as I admire the fit of his khaki pants slung low on his hips. He's paired them with a simple gray T-shirt, but there's nothing ordinary in the way it clings to his biceps. I have no idea how he manages to make workout clothing look practically edible, but he does it with ease. He'll be perfect at this job.

I shrug off his compliment and give him a shy smile. "Well, should we get this over with?"

He barks out a laugh. "Try not to sound so excited!" But he sobers up quickly and his face contorts with concern. "Hey, listen, if you're not into this, I can go on my own. It's really not a problem."

Great, now he thinks I don't want to spend time with him. I quickly backpedal. "No, no, it's not that. I'm just worried that I'll be out of shape and embarrass myself somehow."

He reaches out and takes my hand in his. "You won't embarrass yourself, I promise." He cocks his head as if he's considering something, and then he adds, "Unless you fall flat on your face and need to go to the ER for stitches." He grimaces. "That would be SO embarrassing!"

I playfully smack him on the shoulder. "Get out of my head, will you?" Laughing, I tug his arm toward the parking lot across the street. "Let's just go before I change my mind."

"Careful, Nellie, you might be reaching to new levels of excitement! I wouldn't want you to pull a muscle or anything." He chuckles as he pops open the passenger door for me.

Chapter Twenty-Four

QUILLAN PARK IS NESTLED in the center of Columbia Heights. It's a tiny oasis of pine trees with a rolling open meadow and a network of trails. I haven't visited the park in years, but once we're there, it's clear that I've been over-thinking the extent of the hike we'll be doing today. Most of the trails weave throughout the trees with a bed of soft pine needles blanketing the path.

Jude chooses the farthest one to the left of the park entrance since it has a few short inclines and a bit of gravel. He's hoping to capture Blue Blaze's boots in a few different terrains, and this path has the most to offer.

Speaking of capturing, Jude decided to spring a little surprise on me in the car on the way over. Turns out, he had an ulterior motive for inviting me along. He's hoping I'll come out of retirement for the afternoon and take a few photos for him. I don't have any of my equipment with me, but truthfully, smartphones have come so far over the years, the pixels on my tiny phone camera far exceed the ones on my formerly state-of-the-art DSLR camera.

I feel a little uneasy at the notion of taking pictures again. It's not that I'm worried I'll be rusty. It's more that I'm afraid

I'll fall back in love with it. I stopped taking pictures as a hobby or a possible career once everything changed with my mom. At first, it was too painful to get behind the lens. I felt like a failure in so many ways, and I just didn't see the point in torturing myself. After some time passed, I thought I might be able to pick it up again, even if it was just for fun, but I was always so exhausted from work and caring for my mom that I didn't have the energy.

When I brought it up in the car, Jude pointed out how easily I've been able to carve out time to be with him. He looked at me in that arresting way of his and said, "Nellie, if there's something in this life that you want, you need to nurture it. Keep adding parts of yourself to it so that it can continue to grow. And once it takes root, never ever let it go."

"Well, aren't you just ripe with the plant analogies today." I chuckled. "See what I did there?" He just shook his head at me, a small smile playing on his lips. I tossed that smart-ass comment at him in jest, but mostly I was deflecting. His words resonated with me, and I wasn't sure I could handle it.

As we make our way across the meadow to the start of the trail, I close my eyes and breathe in the sweet spring air. Cutting off my sight, I let my other senses take over. Birds chirp in harmony in the trees overhead. A group of teenagers to my right are playing a rowdy game of Ultimate Frisbee. At the foot of the path in the middle of the park, a mother is admonishing a young child for riding off on his bike without a helmet. The world is alive all around me. I peel open my eyelids slowly, allowing sunlight to filter in. As we approach the trail, there's a diffused glow behind the trees that line the path we're about to walk on.

The start of the trail is indicated by a tiny placard nailed to the first tree.

Hodes Trail
In loving memory of Christopher Hodes

Every trail in the park has been funded and aptly named by local families. I'm not familiar with Christopher or why he's being honored this way, but I still find myself pausing briefly to allow thoughts of him and his family to pass through my mind. It happens every time I encounter a sign like this one.

Jude clears his throat and I realize I've been staring at the sign. "Someone you knew?" He gestures toward the placard.

I shake my head. "No, I just always pay my respects when I see things like this. Christopher Hodes clearly made his mark if he's had a trail in this park named after him. It feels only right that I take a minute to acknowledge his memory."

His smile is warm as he takes both of my hands in his. Holding them up between us, he gazes at his thumbs as they sweep across my knuckles. "Of course, you'd do that. Just when I think I have you all figured out, you still manage to surprise me."

"Uh-oh, is that a good thing?" I glance at his face and my eyes flick back and forth between his.

Keeping his eyes fixed on mine, he brings my hands up to his mouth and places a soft kiss on the top of each of them. "It's a great thing."

We're jolted out of our little bubble by the ear-splitting shrill of a toddler delighting in watching her dad fly a kite. Her chubby legs pump up and down as she scampers around the meadow pointing vigorously up in the air.

Jude releases my hands, and I don't miss the sigh that passes through his lips. The glee that this little child seems to feel for a kite is no match for the tornado of emotions swirling between us. "Well, I guess we should get started. Stopping to take photos of the boots in action will make this hike take double the amount of time it normally would."

He slides his backpack off his shoulder and unzips the side pocket. He reaches inside and pulls out a small tripod with bendable legs. "Listen, I know you're a professional photographer and all, but have you ever used one of these before?" He gives me a playful wink.

I feign surprise and bring my hand to my chest. "Oh no, I'm afraid I've never seen one of those crazy things before in my life. Is it some sort of new age back scratching apparatus?"

He laughs and hands me the tripod. It occurs to me then that photos of his boots shouldn't require a tripod at all. "Um, Jude?"

"Nellie?"

"Why do we need a tripod if we're just taking pictures of your boots in action? Can't I just hold the camera for those?"

He looks at me with a thoughtful expression. "For the action shots, sure, you can just take those. But I thought it might be nice to stage a few pictures of the two of us. That is, if that's okay with you?"

My cheeks flush and my eyes dart to my shoes as I pretend to kick at an imaginary stone. I realize I'm a poster child for bashful behavior, but I can't seem to stop. "Uh, yeah. That's fine."

He touches my chin and raises my eyes to his. "Are you sure?"

I reach deep inside of myself and find the confidence I've buried. "More than sure. I'd love that."

He smiles and nods. "Good. All right, you have your phone, right?"

I slide my hand into my pocket and retrieve it. Holding it up between us, I answer, "Got it!"

We start off in silence as we allow the serene surroundings of the cluster of pine trees to envelop us. I haven't been out in nature in far too long. I've forgotten how peaceful it is and I tell Jude that.

"You need to make more time for it, Nellie. Being outside is what saved me after Dylan died. It's the only thing that brought me any comfort."

The path is wide enough to allow us to walk side by side. I steal a glance at him, but he keeps his eyes trained forward. I don't know much about Jude's home life. I decide that now is as good a time as any to ask him about it.

"What was life like for you and your family after it happened?"

He looks over at me and lets his eyes fall from mine and drift back down to the ground. We keep walking, and several minutes pass before he speaks. "It was the worst hell I've ever experienced. My whole family was in ruins for so long, and it took years for us to find some semblance of normalcy. And, in many ways, we're still searching for it. I think we always will be." He clears his throat and pauses his movement. I stop walking and turn to face him, unsure of what he's planning to do. He motions behind me to a cluster of large rocks. "I think if I place my foot on one of those lower rocks and my hands on one of the larger ones above, we can make it look as though I'm climbing. It might be a good shot. What do you think?"

What do I think? I think I may have whiplash from his sudden change of subject. Maybe Jude isn't ready to tell me more about himself. After all I've shared with him, I can't help the feeling of disappointment that overwhelms me. Despite the turmoil of emotions happening inside of me, I put on a brave face and pretend his sudden shift hasn't affected me. "Sure, that sounds good. How about you get into position and I'll start snapping away when you're ready."

We take several pictures and a few closeups. Once we agree that we've exhausted the poses in that particular setup, we make our way back to the path. Silence descends upon us again, but this time it isn't quite as comfortable. It doesn't last long.

"My mom stopped speaking after Dylan's funeral. The last thing she said to me was earlier that morning when she asked me where I found the tie I was wearing. I told her it belonged to Dylan. She gave me a nod and never said another word."

I stop walking, and it takes Jude a few seconds before he realizes I'm no longer next to him. He turns to face me. "She never spoke again? As in never, ever?" My voice sounds incredulous, but I can't help the shock I feel from Jude's admission. Even with her disease stealing her memories from her, my mother still speaks to me. It's odd, but I feel strangely lucky for that in this moment. Lucky, and also incredibly sad for Jude.

He takes a few steps in my direction, closing the gap between us. "Thankfully, no, not forever. She didn't speak again for three months, but they were the three longest months of my life. My family…we're not from around here. I grew up in a microscopic town called Braswell, smack dab in the middle of Iowa. Dylan, Sam, and I moved out here to California for college. We wanted a change from small-town life." He chuckles. "And now here I am, two thousand miles away from home and I've still managed to find myself in yet another small town. Life is funny like that."

A slight breeze whips through the trees and catches a few of my curls, scattering them aimlessly into a heap on top of my head. Jude reaches out, taking a hold of each disheveled ringlet, and carefully rearranges them. His movements are instinctual. It's incredibly intimate and I blink my eyes closed, momentarily soaking in the feeling of being cared for. The palms of his hands smooth down the sides of my head and land on my shoulders where he lets them linger for a moment. His arms fall down at his sides and his eyes glaze over with recollection.

"After Dylan died, Sam and I went home for a while. We stayed in our childhood bedrooms and tried, in vain, to keep our family together. But it all felt wrong. It felt wrong because it was wrong. Our family was more than fractured. A part of our soul was missing. My dad threw himself into his work.

He'd be up at dawn and out of the house until late at night. We hardly saw him. My mother was a voiceless, empty shell who wandered the house with unbrushed hair and a soiled bathrobe. Sam and I quickly took on the role of parents to our mom. We made sure she ate and forced her to bathe and get dressed. Eventually, we convinced her to join a support group for bereaved parents of children. Those people saved her. In a manner of speaking, they brought her back from the dead, made her see that her life still had meaning. There was still a purpose for her. It wasn't an overnight transformation, but slowly we started to get our mom back. In bits and pieces, at first, but eventually, she was almost whole. I say 'almost' because she'll never be fully whole again. Just like the rest of us, there's a big gaping hole in our lives where Dylan once was."

I can't handle the separation between us while he's baring his soul in this way, so I reach out and wrap my hand around his forearm. Giving it a squeeze, I look up into his eyes and make sure I have his full attention. "You know something, Jude? You're right, that support group did help your mom, but it wasn't what saved her."

He squints at me as though he's trying to see my words more clearly.

"It was you and Sam. You pushed your own grief aside and rescued your mother from a fate worse than death. She was sliding into an abyss of darkness and you both pulled her out of it. From where I'm standing, that makes you both heroes." I rise up on my tiptoes and place a soft kiss on the right corner of his mouth. His eyes close and I watch his chest rise and fall with a deep breath.

He shakes his head slightly. "I guess I never thought of it that way. We were just helping our mom the same way we know she would've helped us, if she could." He eyes me knowingly. "But I suppose you know a little something about that, don't you?"

I nod. "I do."

We're still standing in the middle of the path when we hear a voice call from a short distance. "Bike on your right!" We glide out of the trail and watch as a man and woman riding a tandem bike come into view from around the corner. They pedal in unison, their bodies swaying side to side with the motion. When they reach us, they angle their heads to look our way. The man in front taps the side of his hand against his helmet in a salute.

Jude and I both call out, "Hello!" And we watch as they continue on their way, following the trail through the woods.

Once they've passed us, we give each other a fleeting look and then make our way back to the path. Jude doesn't say more about his family, and I don't ask him to. We keep the conversation light, discussing the family of squirrels we pass and joking about how hard that poor mama must work to keep that wild little baby of hers in line.

I continue snapping pictures, some planned, others impromptu. I'm feeling a bit of that familiar fire in my veins with every click of the shutter. I don't tell Jude, but from the looks he's been giving me, I'm pretty sure it's written all over my face. I've missed this. I've missed being me. In all of the chaos of life, I've forgotten who I was. I imagine taking pictures of Jude modeling these boots feels the same to me as a watercolor artist might feel painting a landscape. It's about the creation of art more than it is about the art itself. I can't believe I had all but given up on this part of myself.

We reach a small clearing where the sunlight has filtered down through the trees to create a perfect backdrop for our first picture together. We're in complete agreement, even though we haven't said a word. Jude motions toward a low hanging tree branch across the path. I whip out the bendy tripod from my bag and wrap it around the limb. Affixing my phone to it, I move back into the sun-drenched spot to pose with Jude. I tap the screen on my watch every time we're ready for a new picture. We start out in the classic prom pose: my back to Jude's front, his hands precariously balanced on my waist while mine rest folded at the base of my rib cage holding a twig bouquet. We reenact the famous "lift" scene from *Dirty Dancing*, and Jude hoists me overhead with ease. We're laughing at how ridiculous we're acting and I snap the most pictures in that moment. I won't know until I look at them, but I'm pretty sure these will be my favorite.

Our laughter tapers off and our eyes remain fixed on each other. His search mine and I catch a glimpse of a life so different from the one I've been living. It dangles like a carrot in front of my face. The more time we spend together, the more I let myself indulge in the idea, and the less it feels like a fantasy that's just out of reach.

Jude takes my hand and tugs me toward him. My arms snake around his waist, and his hands slide into my hair. He tips my head back and guides me up to meet his waiting lips. When we kiss, it's like breathing underwater; we never come up for air. We are each other's oxygen. It's as if I haven't taken a breath in two years, but since I met Jude, I'm breathing freely again.

We take one final picture, and I realize I was wrong before. This one is definitely my favorite.

Chapter Twenty-Five

JUDE STARTS HIS CAR, and Glen Hansard croons out of the stereo speakers. He's singing a soulful song about a woman who's been beaten down by life, but through it all, he vows to be there to remind her that she's better than everyone trying to tear her down. It's beautiful and the words resonate with me. It feels like Jude could be singing this very song about the two of us. He keeps showing up for me day after day. The scale is definitely tipped in my favor, which reminds me—he never finished his story from earlier. Without pausing to get my thoughts in order, I open my mouth and ask the first thing that comes to mind—"So, whatever happened to your dad?"

My question seems to startle him and he looks over out of the corner of his eye, regarding me for a moment. "My dad?"

"Yeah, you said your dad threw himself in to work after your brother died. Is that still the case?"

He nods solemnly. "Sadly, it is. He's gotten a little better over the years, but he's still mostly gone. Even when he's home, he's not really there. My mom hasn't given up on him, though. She's even managed to get him to join her at a few of her support group meetings. She said he hasn't opened up yet, but he's definitely taking it all in when he's there."

Now that I know things haven't improved, I regret having brought it up. "I'm sorry, Jude. That must be so hard for all of you."

He reaches over and gives my hand a quick squeeze. "It is, but you know, there's still hope for him. There's hope for all of us. You just have to want things to change before they can. I say that like it's simple, and it is, but it's also the hardest thing you'll ever do. If change was easy, all of the therapists would be out of business." He laughs and I join him.

"You make a lot of sense, Jude. Have you ever thought about being a therapist? You'd make a great one."

Now he really laughs. "Oh, Nellie, I'm just good at repeating what I've been taught. My therapist is a great teacher. He helped me process everything I went through leading up to and after Dylan's death. He's still helping me. I see him once every few months just to check in. I think of it like recharging my batteries when they're getting low."

"I love that for you. Maybe I should think about getting myself one of those battery charger therapists."

"You should." His voice is so sincere, it's almost pleading.

I give him a nod. It's a promise, even if I never say it out loud. I know he's right. It's something I should've done years ago. It just never occurred to me to make myself a priority.

I let my hands fall against my thighs with a light smack and slide them down toward my knees. "So, Jude, you said you and your brother weren't identical twins?"

He shakes his head. "No. You could tell we were related, but most people didn't believe us when we would tell them we were twins. Everyone has this idea in their heads that twins always look exactly alike. What they don't realize is, it's actually less likely for twins to be identical than it is for them to be fraternal."

"Huh. I never knew that." I sit with this new information and let it swirl around in my head. I give a voice to the next thought I have. "I would love to see a picture of the two of you sometime." I peek at him, hoping that I didn't breach a fine line, but if what I said upset him, he isn't showing it. In fact, a thoughtful expression crosses his face.

"There's a picture of us in the glove box. It was taken a few months before he died." He points over to the compartment. "Go ahead and take a look, but I have to warn you, it's a bit of a disaster in there." He rubs at the back of his neck. He looks embarrassed and it's completely adorable.

I reach out and pop open the latch on the box. The door hinges down and with it comes several envelopes, at least a dozen balled-up receipts, and two half-empty tins of mints. He wasn't kidding. This is a mess. I peer into the blackness and wonder where the little interior light is.

As if he can read my mind, he says, "Oh, sorry, the bulb burned out in there a while back and, uh, I guess I never replaced it." He shrugs and looks as though he wants to crawl under a rock.

I've been to Jude's apartment a few times, but only briefly. In the short amount of time I spent there, though, I thought his place was pretty tidy. I'd even go so far as to call it stark. With very little furniture and even less hanging on the walls, it looked as though he had just moved in. Of course, I never opened any drawers or closet doors while I was there, and judging by the looks of this glove compartment, I'm guessing I'd find them in utter disarray. There's something about this side of Jude that I find so endearing. He's seemed almost perfect, and I like that I've found a flaw. It evens the playing field a little.

I reach into my bag and pull out my small flashlight. As I'm shining it into the glove box, my eyes flit back over to the light in my hand. The one I stole from Home Depot. Shame fills the pit of my stomach and coils around my insides. I feel physically ill. I switch off the light and toss it back into my bag. Pushing the glove compartment closed, I half-heartedly mumble, "I'll just look at it some other time." And then I angle my body toward the passenger door. My forehead rests on the cool glass of the window and I close my eyes. I know Jude's looking at me. I can feel his eyes on me, but I don't turn my head. I can't let him see me this way. He'd be so disappointed in me. *I'm* disappointed in me.

I feel his finger as it lightly presses the skin above my knee. "Hey, Nellie? Will you please look at me?"

I inhale deeply, trying to suck back the remorse and bury it deep where I've kept it hidden, but when I turn and face him, I can tell by his reaction that I've failed miserably. A look of surprise passes over his face and is quickly replaced with worry. "What's wrong?"

I shake my head and answer the way anyone would in this situation. I lie. "Nothing." It feels like a copout, and it is, but I still feel the need to pad the lie, to give it more weight, so I add, "I just didn't want to snoop around in your personal space. I figured you could show me another time when you have a chance to search for it yourself."

His eyes narrow slightly before returning to the road. He lets out a quiet hum and I feel it reverberate inside of me, settling next to the shame I tried to bury. "You know, it doesn't count as snooping if I told you to look."

I hate lying to him, so I don't reply. I just shrug and let my eyes drift back to the window. I think back to what he said a few minutes ago about change and how it can happen for anyone as long as you want it. I hate the way stealing makes me feel almost as soon as I do it. After the rush wears off, I'm left with nothing but guilt and shame. Sitting here in this car with Jude, I want nothing more than to shed this humiliation I've been wearing like a second skin. So, with determination coursing through my veins, I turn and face Jude.

Taking a deep breath, I mentally count to three. I don't wait for another question. If I really want to change, then I think it's important for me to offer an explanation on my own. I reach into my bag and pull out the pocket-sized flashlight. Holding it up, I say, "They sell these flashlights at the Home Depot. I was looking at them the night I ran into you and Sam."

Jude glances over at me and gives me a short nod. His eyes draw down with confusion. I'm sure he's wondering where I'm going with this, but he doesn't try to interrupt me.

"They aren't expensive. I think the sign said they were like ten bucks, but I wouldn't know because, well…see, I didn't pay for it."

His eyes snap to mine and understanding passes between us. I keep talking because I'm afraid if I stop to take a breath, I'll never get through this. "I take things. Things that don't belong to me. Tiny things that fit into the palm of my hand and slide easily into a pocket in my purse. I don't steal things because I can't afford to pay for them. I take them because it's the only time I feel anything at all. Or at least that's how it used to be. I was going through the motions day after day. Running errands, taking care of my mom, checking on my sister. I was always coloring inside the lines and taking things like this"—I let the flashlight slide over my fingers and catch it in my palm—"well, I guess you could say my crayon went rogue and made a few over strokes. Color seeped out past the point I usually allowed it and it gave me a jolt." I shake my head. "It's stupid and reckless, believe me, I know. And I hate myself for it. But you once told me you didn't want me to hide from you, so this is me, standing out in the open, waving my crazy around in the air."

He's quiet. Too quiet. I can see his chest rise and fall in a calm succession, so if I've shocked him, it hasn't sent him into cardiac arrest. He's probably terrified of me and he should be. What sort of person steals things they can afford just to feel alive?

"When was the last time you took something, Nellie?" His voice is solid. There's no waver and his words don't falter. He doesn't sound afraid. He sounds like he's building a case.

I answer him easily. "This flashlight. I haven't taken anything else since that night. I've hardly even felt the urge, come to think of it." That last thought lingers. It hadn't even occurred to me until I said it out loud, but it's been over a month since I've stolen anything. I usually can't go more than a few days, and I'm definitely tempted every time I go into a store, but after that last time when I nearly stole a pen from the grocery store, I haven't even thought about taking anything. Not since I started spending so much time with Jude. I haven't needed a cheap thrill to feel something real. I feel it every time I'm with him.

Jude continues. "Have you ever told anyone about this before?"

I shake my head vehemently. "Nope. Never. You're the first person I've ever felt I could admit it to."

He keeps staring straight ahead as he takes us down my street and turns his car into the parking lot across from my building. He puts the car in park and pulls up the hand brake, but he doesn't turn off the ignition. He just sits there, eyes facing forward, not saying a word, and I start to get the feeling that maybe this is my cue to leave. He's probably so disgusted with me, he can't even bear to look at me. I nod with resignation. I'm an awful person. I deserve this. I unfasten my seatbelt and pluck my bag from the floor. My hand reaches out to grasp the door handle, but before I can open it, Jude speaks.

"I don't blame you for stealing, Nellie. I may not agree with your tactic, but I do understand it." He looks over at me. His eyes shine with compassion.

His words stun me. "You do?"

He nods. "Of course. You've been taking care of everyone around you for so long. I think it's only natural for you to let loose. It makes sense, and if I'm honest, I'm surprised that's all you've done."

"Really?"

"Uh-huh. Think about it. Most people would be far more reckless than you've been and probably not even feel a fraction of the guilt you've been living with. And for the record, you're not crazy." He levels me with a look that tells me that last part isn't up for discussion.

My eyes fill with emotion. I angle my body to face his and lean my head against the seat. My cheek rests on the cool leather. I can't believe how accepting he is. I just bared my deepest darkest secret, one I was sure I would take with me to my grave, but instead of running for the hills, he's still here. And he's trying to make *me* feel better. "Where did you come from? Who are you?"

He sighs and reaches out to tuck a lock of hair behind my ear. His palm rests on my cheek. "I'm exactly who you needed at the exact time you needed me."

I breathe out a quiet chuckle. He's not wrong. "How did you know?"

He smiles. "Well, that's easy. Because, my dear Nellie with an -*ie*, you were exactly who I needed at exactly the right time I needed you." He leans in, and his lips find mine. And I wonder how I ever existed without him.

* * *

"AHH," I moan as I slip under the covers. After a long day, there isn't much that tops that feeling. I lift my phone off of the wireless charger and the screen comes to life. There's a notification alerting me that I have two missed calls and one voicemail, all from my mom. Looks like she must have called while Jude and I were on our way home and my phone was in drive mode.

I bring up her message and hit play. "Oh, um, this is Mom calling. I'm almost out of tissues, so could you bring some the next time you come? Love you. Bye."

I'm glad it wasn't an emergency, but it rarely ever is. I still feel a pang of guilt for missing the call. There isn't much I can do for her, but taking her phone calls and alleviating her worry is one way I can help. Not being there to answer the phone feels a bit like breaking a promise.

My head lolls back against the pillow, pressing in deep enough to leave an indent in the fabric. I know I'm being unnecessarily hard on myself, but I hate feeling like I've let her down.

I curl my legs up into a fetal position and lean onto my side. This missed call serves as a reminder. It's easy to let go of my worries when I'm with Jude, but I can't ignore them completely. As my eyes begin to close, I make a mental note to stay grounded in the present.

Chapter Twenty-Six

SUNDAYS ARE MADE for sleep and loungewear. Every Saturday night, I'm practically giddy at the thought of not having to set an alarm for the next morning. I wake up when it suits me and spend most of the day in various degrees of relaxation. And I never, *ever* wear pants that don't have an elastic waistline.

Today is no exception. When I finally peel my eyes open, I do it with a huge smile plastered on my face. A night full of vivid dreams starring Jude will do that.

The conversation we had yesterday was emotionally charged and we definitely crossed over into new relationship territory. I've only been awake for a few minutes, but I already feel like I'm looking at our relationship through a crystal clear lens. I have no lingering doubts, no leftover questions. I feel free to just be who I am with Jude and it's incredibly liberating.

I slide out of bed and brush my teeth. My hair is a disaster so I twist random sections and secure them with bobby pins. Curls are pretty forgiving that way.

I haven't seen Swerve in a couple of days, so I decide to take a peek out front and see if she's there. I'm still wearing my sweatpants and T-shirt when I crack open my apartment door. Claudette is in the hallway locking up her door, and when she sees me, her smile is so wide, it takes up more than half of her face. "Nellie, hunny! Just look at you! Are you finally coming down to the gym with me?" She gives me a wink followed by a hearty laugh.

I chuckle and shake my head. "Hey, Claudette! Nope, sorry to disappoint you, but I'm not planning to go anywhere near a gym today. I was just on my way to the front door to check on Swerve. Have you seen her lately?"

She tilts her head up and taps on her chin. "Hmm, you know, come to think of it, I can't say that I have. It's probably been at least a week or so. I'm pretty sure your Jude was taking her a bowl of food, and that was the last time I saw her. But don't you worry, Nellie. Strays are like that, you know? She'll be back."

I nod along with her, but I don't quite share her certainty. It isn't like Swerve to disappear for so long.

"Hey, speaking of that tall drink of water of yours. How is Jude?" She giggles and I join in. I'm not the only one he's won over.

"Oh, he's pretty perfect, but you already knew that, didn't you?" I wink at her.

"Nellie, girl, I'm so happy for you. I've been so worried about you." She threads her fingers together as if she's partaking in a silent prayer.

"Worried about *me*?" I place my palm on my chest. I don't like the thought of her spending any of her time fretting over me. Especially when she has her own health to be concerned about. She's assured me that the new medicine she's been taking has her feeling almost as good as before, and she does seem more like her old self lately.

She sidles over to me and takes my hand in hers. Giving it a squeeze, she gazes deep into my eyes. "Sweetie, listen to me, you are always worrying yourself about everyone else. I can see you in your head doin' just that very thing right now! You take on everyone's problems and it's too much for one person. You're trying to save the world, hunny, but who's gonna save you?"

She may as well have plunged a dagger into my chest because her words split me wide open. I want to tell her that I'm strong and I don't need saving, but the truth is, we all need to be rescued. Finding a savior doesn't mean you aren't enough for yourself, it just means you don't want to do all of life's heavy lifting alone.

When Claudette asks me who will save me, one name immediately comes to mind. *Jude.* His name is on the tip of my tongue, but I hold back. Being my person is a hefty burden. Even though he says he'll always be here for me, I wonder if he really grasps what that means.

Claudette puts a finger underneath my chin and tilts my head up so that I'm looking her in the eyes. "Hunny, I know it seems like the whole world is on your shoulders sometimes. I've seen it. I know what you put yourself through. Just remember, you aren't alone. I'm always here for you and so is Jude. I think he came to you exactly when you needed him most."

I'm struck by how similar her words are to what Jude said yesterday. I've never been one to put much faith in fate. I've always believed you get what you get and it's how you handle it that matters. I still believe that, but I'm also starting to wonder if there may be more to life than that. In the short time I've known him, Jude has been such a positive influence on me. He's helped me put some of my focus back on myself. I had always put my needs second to those around me. For the first time in years, I've started to entertain thoughts on what might bring me happiness. It still feels foreign to think that way, but with each new day I spend with Jude, it's beginning to feel more and more normal to want to be happy. It's a simple concept, but it's one that's eluded me for so long.

I grin up at her. "I think you're pretty wise, Claudette. I'm so glad I have you in my corner."

She pats my cheek. "I'll always be in your corner, Nellie. Just like I know you'll always be in mine. You're good people, as my mama would say." She glances down at her watch. "Oh dear, I'd better get a move on or else Alfonse will have me doing extra burpees as payment for being late!" Her mouth opens in an O and her hand covers it as she tries to contain a chuckle. She likes to pretend that would be a punishment, but the truth is, she loves the extra work, and we both know it.

I shake my head and laugh. "Well, then, I guess you better get going! Wouldn't want to keep Alfonse waiting." I wink at her. She's never admitted it out loud, but I'm certain she has a not-so-secret crush on her trainer.

She gives me a quick wave and turns to leave. When she's right by the stairwell, she calls back over her shoulder, "Now, you remember what I said, you hear me? There ain't no shame in needing someone. That boy wants to be a part of your life. Let him."

I nod in agreement even though she can't see me. She knows I'd never argue with her, and this time I know she's right.

* * *

I'M on my front stoop, but Swerve is nowhere to be found. Claudette said that strays come and go like this, but I still can't help but worry that something may have happened to her. I decide to head back to my apartment and fix her a dish of food. Maybe she's somewhere nearby and the smell will entice her to eat.

I'm halfway up the stairs when I hear my phone ringing in my pocket. Jude. My entire body warms when I see his name on the screen. Texts are usually his method of communication, but it isn't out of the ordinary for him to call me instead. I tap the screen to accept his call.

"Well, if it isn't the man who makes the sad songs better!" I say on a laugh.

He sighs dramatically. "There it is. You know, I was beginning to wonder if you'd ever bring up that connection. Especially with all of my incessant 'Hot In Herre' teasing. It sure took you long enough!"

I hum a few notes of the iconic song. "I was just waiting to see if the name suited you."

"And?"

"And I think it couldn't be more perfect if it were written expressly for you." I mean it. That song was one of my mom's favorites. I used to dissect the lyrics when I was a kid, before I knew that Paul wrote it for John's son. I loved the idea of someone being made for someone else. It's such a basic, beautiful concept. And it fits Jude completely.

"What a coincidence, Nellie with an -*ie*. I think your song suits you just as impeccably." His voice is smooth and dripping with innuendo. And it feels like someone must have turned the temperature up in here because the warmth I was feeling is quickly morphing into an intense heat.

Clearing my throat, I attempt to keep the desire from leeching into my voice. "Um, so what can I do for you?"

I hear his quick intake of breath over the line. *Wrong question, Nellie.* "Well, when you put it like that..."

"I just, uh, I meant why, are you calling? Did you need something?" I try to regulate the conversation. Try and fail. That last question provides exactly the lead-in Jude was hoping for, and he pounces on it.

"I do, in fact, *need* something, Nellie. Want to take a guess what that is?" Jesus, he isn't holding back here. Aside from kissing, our relationship hasn't progressed physically, and we've both been acutely aware of that. I'd be lying if I said I wasn't ready for us to take that next step.

I try another tactic. "Okay, all kidding aside, is there a reason for your call or are you just trying to see how many shades of red you can make me turn with one conversation?"

His laugh is deep and gravelly. "Oh Nellie, Nellie, Nellie. First of all, I'm far from joking, and that's just it—if you're turning shades of any color, I'd much rather see that with my own eyes. Which brings me back to why I'm calling, I have news. Pretty fucking fantastic news, as a matter of fact. But it isn't anything I want to tell you over the phone. Can I come over?"

"Yep!" I don't even hesitate. I've never been great at playing hard to get, and honestly, what's the point? I think his intentions are pretty clear and so are mine. I have enough uncertainty in my life. I don't need my relationship with Jude to be filled with it, too.

"Perfect." I hear the smile in his voice. "I'll be over in a few minutes."

"Oh, hey, Jude?" I giggle at my intentional phrasing.

"This is going to be a *thing* now, isn't it?" There's a playful lilt in his voice.

"You knew it would be. Turnabout is fair play."

He concedes. "I suppose you are right about that. It *is* only fair."

"I just wanted to let you know that I'm not really dressed for going out. I'm not even wearing pants—"

"Say no more. I'll be right over!"

Shaking my head and laughing, I finish my sentence. "— with a zipper! My pants have elastic. There are no buttons and no zipper."

"Is that supposed to be a problem, Nellie? Because, from where I'm sitting, that's just code for easy access."

"Oh my God, you're relentless!"

"And you love every minute of it." He sounds so sure himself, and he should be because he's one hundred percent right.

"Whatever. I'll see you in a little while. I'll be the one wearing grungy sweatpants."

"Still not a problem, Nellie!" he yells out as I end the call.

Something tells me things are about to change for us today.

Chapter Twenty-Seven

IN THE FEW minutes after our phone call ends, I keep myself busy by prepping food for Swerve and filling up a fresh bowl of water. I'm placing them outside when I see Jude round the corner. He's wearing navy sweatpants and a fitted white T-shirt, and I wonder how the hell it's possible for him to look that good in such basic clothing.

He catches me checking him out and his lips curve into a cocky grin. He glances down at Swerve's bowls. "I just saw her down the street. She was looking a little extra scraggly, but it looked like she was headed your way."

I breathe a huge sigh of relief. "Oh good! I hadn't seen her in a little while and I was starting to worry. I'll pop down and check on the bowls in a few minutes. Hopefully, I'll find her eating."

We stand a few feet apart, awkwardly staring at each other. This is weird. We've never had a problem filling the void with conversation before. It must be the anticipation of what we both know is coming.

"So, what did—"

"I just—"

We laugh.

Jude leans in. "This is strange, right?"

I nod. "Very."

"So, then, let's not do this with each other."

Well, now, let's not be too hasty. My face contorts with concern, and Jude holds up his hands. "What I meant was, things have always been easy between us. I don't want that to change, and I don't think it has to just because things between us are evolving."

What he's saying makes sense and I find myself nodding in agreement, but I can't help the unease I feel. I liked where things were going during our phone conversation earlier, and I'm afraid he's planning to put the brakes on it. I'm definitely not okay with that.

He gives me an easy smile and I feel my fear begin to thaw ever so slightly. "Are you going to invite me in, or should I just give you my news right here on your doorstep?"

My cheeks flush with embarrassment. "Oh, right. Sorry. Sure, let's go up to my apartment."

He touches my elbow. "Relax, Nellie. I was just teasing you." He leans forward and places a chaste kiss on the tip of my nose. Taking me by the hand, he leads me up the stairs toward my door. He seems anxious, and it's infectious. My body hums with nervous energy.

Once we're inside, he pulls out one of my kitchen stools and motions for me to sit down. I assume he's going to take the other one, but he doesn't. He starts pacing back and forth, and I feel like I'm going to explode from pent-up anxiety.

Just when I'm about ready to shout at him to spit it out, he starts talking. "This news I have, Nellie…it's incredible. I'm torn between wanting to just blurt it out or hold it in just to prolong the anticipation a bit more."

Is he insane? I can barely contain myself. I have to know what he's planning to tell me and I have to know now!

He's studying my face, and I watch as his lights up with a Cheshire cat grin. "I can tell by your expression that I'm about two seconds away from being strangled so I'll just start talking. I heard from my friend, Scott, this morning. You know, the one who owns Blue Blaze?" He waits for me to acknowledge him, and I shake my head up and down with more force than necessary. "Right, well, he and Dave, his partner, were looking over the images from our hike yesterday and—" He glances over at the framed pictures on my wall.

"Oh my God, Jude, and what? Please, I'm dying over here!"

He laughs and I can't believe it. I'm on the verge of losing my mind and he's laughing. He stalks toward me and lowers himself to a squat. Placing his hands over mine to still them from fidgeting, he leans in and whispers, "Nellie, they fucking loved them. No, that's not even accurate. They more than loved them. Scott called them 'a work of art.' He said he wanted to meet the artist who managed to capture the 'essence of his vision.' Those were his exact words."

I squint my eyes in an attempt to follow along, but I'm coming up short. "I'm sorry, Jude. It's awesome that Scott was so happy with the photos and all, but I'm afraid I'm missing something. You seem way too excited about this."

He shakes his head. "Nellie, don't you see? You're so damn talented, and finally, someone with the ability to do something about it has recognized that."

"Do something about it?"

"He wants to hire you, Nellie. In fact, he and Dave wanted me to take a trip up to Yosemite in a few weeks and they want you to come with me."

I feel my body tingle with excitement, but also with dread. How can I go anywhere? "Jude, I…this is great news, but I don't see how I can go with you. I can't be away from my mom for that long."

He gives my hands a squeeze. "I know that, Nellie, which is why this trip is perfect. It's only six days. We could leave on

Saturday afternoon once you've visited your mom and we'd be back in plenty of time before your next visit."

I feel the excitement radiating off of him and I hate that I have to be the one to take that away. "Listen, Jude, I know this feels like the perfect arrangement, but what about those six days in between my visits? My mom calls me out of the blue sometimes and I always take those calls." My mind drifts to the one I missed last night. That can't happen again. "I can't be out on a trail somewhere with no cell service. And what if there's an emergency? Yosemite is far enough away that it would take some time for us to drive back." I shake my head with sad resignation. "I just don't think this will work. I'm sorry."

He's watching me so intently and the smile hasn't left his face. I'm beginning to worry that he's not listening to what I'm saying. "I know you feel like you can't leave your mom. I may not know exactly what you're going through, but I can imagine, and it's a lot, Nellie. Way more than one person should ever have to handle on their own. I told Scott about your mom and he said to tell you that if there's an emergency of any kind, he will put you a plane back home on his dime. And I know you're concerned that your mom won't be able to reach you while we're deep in the park, but there's cell service in over fifty percent of Yosemite, so even if we're out of range for a little while, we won't be far from it. Sure, you may miss a call, but you'll be able to return it quickly." He leans in close, so close that his lips graze my ear when he speaks. "When was the last time you took a vacation? This is an opportunity of a lifetime. You'll actually be paid to travel. And the best part? You'll be with me. Think about it, Nellie."

I close my eyes, and I do think about it. What he's saying is true. I haven't been away from this town in so long; I can't even remember the last trip I took. It still feels a little strange to think about leaving my mom, but he's right. She'd only be a phone call away, and if I have service most of the time, it means she'd be able to reach me whenever she needed me. I don't love the idea of missing one of her calls, but her emergencies are never true emergencies. Plus, I know she's in good hands at Shady Villa; we pay an exorbitant amount of money each month just to ensure that. And then there's Jude. Thoughts of the two of us sleeping in close proximity in a tiny tent make me feel lightheaded. I lean over and place my head in my hands. I feel the movement of my lips on the palms of my hands as they pull back into a smile. I want to do this. I *can* do this.

I open my eyes and find Jude still crouched down in front of me. He waits for my answer with bated breath and when he sees my smile, he knows he has me. I don't even have to say the words, but I want to. I want him to hear me say it, but mostly I want to hear myself speak up on my own behalf. I'm putting myself first and it feels incredible. "Okay, Jude, I'm in." It's just four words, but they hold so much hope.

Jude wastes no time. He's on his feet, pulling me up until our bodies are flush with one another. He strokes the side of my face with the back of his hand, and I lean into his touch. In a hushed voice, he says something I wasn't expecting. "I'm so proud of you."

My bottom lip trembles with emotion. I haven't heard those words from anyone in years, and I thought I had grown accustomed to it. I blend in on purpose. I haven't wanted to stand out because there are so many other people who have way more going on in their lives, people who need me, people who count on me. I stopped putting any real effort into bettering myself, and I never let myself think about it until now. It became a habit to avoid thinking about anything I might want, what might make happy. I can't believe I discredited myself for so long. With Jude's encouragement, I'm finally pulling myself out of the shadows, and it feels good in the sun.

I stare into his eyes and try to silently communicate how

I'm feeling. But something about the depth of emotion that I'm experiencing makes me think it would be better if I showed him. I lean in and touch my lips to his. It's sweet at first, but that only lasts a few seconds. All it takes is a sweep of my tongue, and Jude is gripping the backs of my thighs and lifting me up. My legs wrap instinctively around his waist and I press my body against him, feeling his taut muscles flex as he holds on to me.

Our kisses become frantic as he walks me backward until my back hits the wall. He holds me there as his lips continue their intense pursuit. We break apart, both of us breathless, and he rests his forehead against mine. His eyes implore me. He's looking for permission and I give it to him. Holding his gaze, I nod my head ever so slightly.

He doesn't miss the movement, and he responds quickly, tightening his grip on me as he moves us down the hall to my bedroom. He places me on the bed with reverence, never breaking eye contact as he reaches for the hem of my shirt. I lift my arms above my head, encouraging him to continue, and he lifts my T-shirt slowly up my body. I hear him gasp when he realizes I'm not wearing a bra. My shirt is tossed somewhere across the room. His fingertips skim along the waistband of my sweatpants. He's wearing a confident grin as he grips the top of my pants and slides them down. "See, what did I tell you? Easy access."

I give my head a slight shake and softly chuckle as my hands grasp the top of his pants. "Same goes for you," I say, pulling them down. He springs free, and I hear my own gasp. I wasn't expecting that.

He shrugs. "Underwear can be so restricting, Nellie. Wouldn't you agree?" He reaches behind his back and tugs off his shirt. "I guess these aren't so bad," he says as he palms the black lace on the front of my panties. His fingers slip under the elastic around my leg, and I feel my pulse quicken as my heart begins to pump faster. "Still, they do make what

I'd like to do to you a bit difficult." He glides his hand in farther and my head lolls back. A small moan escapes my lips, and when I lift my head, I see Jude's eyes burn with desire. "Yep, they definitely need to go." He rolls them down slowly, slipping them off one leg at a time. I lie back on the bed feeling confidant in a way that I never have before. Jude's eyes roam over my body. "So beautiful."

His hands lower to the bed and he inches toward me. My legs part in response and he settles between them. His forearms nestle on either side of my head as he hovers above me. The look in his eyes as he stares down at me is unmatched. No one has ever looked at me this way before. I want to commit it to memory and play it on repeat every night as I fall asleep.

When I gaze up at him, one thought is louder than the rest, pushing all other thoughts aside. I love him.

I reach up between us and cup his chin. "Jude, I—" I suck in a breath, the words precariously balance on the tip of my tongue.

"I know, Nellie. Me, too." His eyes flit back and forth between mine.

My hands grip the back of his head, and I pull him down to me. He moves carefully as he follows my lead. I give myself over to him freely, but that isn't anything new. I give of myself every day. But this is the first time that I take something in return. I give to Jude and he gives to me. We give and we take and I feel—everything.

Chapter Twenty-Eight

THE TRAIL IS muddy and full of debris from a storm that passed through last night, but the views in Yosemite are unparalleled. Jude is a few feet ahead of me, dressed head to toe in Blue Blaze gear. His khaki pants are full of zippers and pockets capable of holding enough snacks for a few hours of nonstop hiking. At least, those are the product claims and part of what we're putting to the test today. I'm snapping away, capturing images of Jude modeling the apparel and accessories. He's in his element, looking completely at ease among the harsh terrain.

We march along, and I stop to take a few pictures of the lolling water in a beautiful little creek that feeds into an enormous lake. "Wow. Look at how the sun reflects off the water. It's like nature is posing just for me." Jude doesn't respond, and when I look away from the creek, I see him much farther up the trail. Too far to hear me speak. I lift my leg to start walking, but it's stuck. Without realizing it, I stepped in a puddle and am now ankle deep in mud. In this moment, I'm grateful that Blue Blaze supplied me with their knee-high waterproof boots. I try to force my foot out of the mud, but it won't budge. I feel panic begin to creep in and I take a few deep breaths to calm my nerves. It's just mud. I won't be stuck here forever.

I call out to Jude, "Hey! I could use a little help here!" He turns around and it's hard to make out the features of his face, but it looks like he's grinning. His arms are moving animatedly, as though he's telling me a story. I watch as he points up in the sky. I follow his finger and see a hawk flying overhead. That's great, but this is hardly the time to be bird watching. I cup my hands along the sides of my mouth. "Jude! I need help!" But his feet keep moving, taking him farther away from me. He looks back at me and motions for me to follow him. In one last desperate attempt, I scream, "HELP!"

He's too far away. I can barely make him out on the trail ahead. And then I feel it. The ground seems to shake and my feet slip deeper into the mud. I'm sinking. This is bad. My whole body quakes as the earth moves under me. In the distance, I can hear the faint sound of a ringing alarm. It's nothing like the earthquake sirens I'm used to, but maybe this is what they sound like in the park. The shaking is so intense that I start to lose my balance. My body tips forward and I fall.

I launch myself upright and blink my eyes rapidly, trying to decipher how Yosemite suddenly looks like my bedroom in my apartment. Jude's hands are on my shoulders, shaking me as he softly rouses me from the foggy haze of sleep. The ringing is still blaring and it takes me a minute to realize where it's coming from. "Nellie, wake up. Your phone keeps ringing. I think you should answer it."

I follow the sound to my nightstand. It's the middle of the night, and calls at this hour are never good. The words *Shady Villa* flash on the illuminated screen. I snatch the phone and press the button. "Hello?" My voice sounds shallow.

"Nellie?"

I'm nodding as I speak, "Yes, this is she. Is my mom okay?"

The woman exhales before she answers my question. I want to tell her to save her words. Her breath was all the answer I need. Something has happened. "I'm afraid your mom is in the hospital—"

"What? When?"

"Well, we aren't exactly sure what happened. She pressed her call button and when the aide came into her room, she was clutching her hand to her heart. We believe she may have had a heart attack. An ambulance took her to Hope Community a few minutes ago. I don't want to worry you, but I think you should head over there."

I barely make out the words she said. The thoughts in my head are so loud, they're drowning out her voice. I managed to hear heart attack and hospital, and that was enough. "Sure. Thank you for calling."

"Of course. You and your mom are in our thoughts. Please let us know if there's anything we can do." I thank her one last time, and then I bolt out of bed and fly around my room.

"Nellie? What happened?"

Jude. I can't believe I almost forgot he was here. My mind was too preoccupied with thoughts of my mom lying in a hospital bed with tubes and wires probing into her skin. I stop moving long enough to fill him in.

"Okay, take a deep breath and just focus on getting dressed. I'll drive us over there."

He's coming with me? "Oh, Jude, I'm sure I'll probably be there all night. You don't need to come with me."

He strides over to me, taking my hands in his. "You and me, we're a team, remember? You aren't alone anymore and you never have to be again. I'm coming with you and whatever happens, we'll face it together."

Emotion overwhelms me. I give him a solemn nod and continue putting on my clothes.

Less than fifteen minutes later, we're out the door and in Jude's car.

* * *

THE STARK WHITE bed engulfs my mom as she lies there,

gaunt and still. The sound of beeping monitors echo in the sterile room. They still aren't sure what caused her accelerated heartbeat, but they've moved her to Intensive Care for "observation." A nurse comes in every half hour to check my mom's vitals and to press a few buttons on one of the monitors, but other than that, I haven't seen much observing.

Tiny white discs are scattered on my mom's body, stuck in place by tacky padding. There's one on each temple, a few around her collarbone, and more along her chest underneath her gown. Each one is affixed with a wire that leads to one of the monitors. Red lines rise and lower on the screen like miniature mountain ranges.

There are two metal chairs in the room, each fitted with a material that's pretending to be padding. I've pulled one up to the side of my mom's bed. They said she was agitated when they brought her in, so they gave her a sedative. She still hasn't regained consciousness. I perch on the edge of the seat and lean in, watching her eyes move beneath her closed eyelids. They flit back and forth like a tennis ball in an intense match.

A doctor came in once in the last two hours, and I can tell her condition must be serious by the hushed tone of his voice as he whispered to the attending nurse. Aside from a curt "hello," he offered me no explanation, no words of comfort.

I called Meg from the car on the way over here. My voice was clipped as I told her that our mom was in the hospital. I could tell from the anguish in her voice that she was worried, but I couldn't find it in myself to comfort her. I don't want to make this easier on her. She should be here with me. I shouldn't have to go through this on my own. I told her I would let her know more once I spoke with the doctor, but I feel like I know less since I got here. No one wants to offer me false hope, but in a way, I wish they would. Anything would be better than this.

I take a hold of my mom's hand. It lies limp in mine as I study the folds of her skin, the way it glides easily over her knuckles. It's slack and pliable, but despite that, there's a familiarity. These are the same hands that held mine on our walks to the playground. These hands wrapped around my back and pulled me in for hugs. These fingers tucked curls behind my ears and swiped tears from my cheeks. They made countless school lunches and prepared thousands of dinners. I lay her hand back on the bed and press mine into the sheet next to it. I've never noticed it before, but my hands look like a younger version of hers. It's been said over the years that I favor my dad's side of the family and growing up without his influence, I've had to take the word of others. But now, as I look down at our hands side by side, I feel like I came only from this woman. She created me; she molded me. I am hers and she is mine. And this is my fault. Were there warning signs that something was wrong? There must have been. I should have been paying more attention. I should have been there with her.

How long has it been since someone came in to check on her? I tilt my wrist, but the screen on my watch doesn't light up. I tap it and still nothing. Great. The battery must be dead. I snatch my purse off of the floor and fish through it in search of my phone. When I tap the screen, I don't even notice the time. My eyes immediately focus on the missed call and voicemail alerts. My mom tried to call me four times last night and she left two messages. With a shaky hand, I swipe open my voicemail and hit play.

"Belly? I don't feel very well. They had meatloaf in the dining room tonight and I think maybe it made me sick. Call me back, okay? Love you, bye."

"Nellie? Where are you? You said to call you if I needed anything and I think something is wrong. I

don't know what to do. Please call me as soon as you
get this, okay?"

I let my phone fall to my lap. My chin quivers, but I press
a hand to it. *You let her down. You don't get to cry. This isn't
about you. It never was, but you forgot that and now look at her.*

She's so frail and brittle looking, and she needed me. But I
was too busy giving in to my own selfish desires. Jude was
playing music on his phone last night and the sound must've
drowned out my mom's ring tone. I can't believe this
happened again.

For now, only immediate family is allowed back here so
Jude has been patiently standing by in the waiting room. I
think about him out there, putting his life on hold for me. I
can't let him do that. I don't have room in my life to recipro-
cate. It brought me a bit of comfort just knowing that he's
here. But that's just it. I shouldn't be thinking about what
makes *me* feel better. I should be focused on my mom. I've
been so selfish. I've lost sight of my purpose. I'm all my mom
has and I've made such a mess of things. It's time to fix it.

* * *

JUDE LEANS FORWARD in a chair that looks like it was made
by the same company that manufactured the chairs in my
mom's room. His elbows rest above his knees and his hands
cradle his head. I've been standing in this same spot,
watching him for the last few minutes, and aside from the
small rise and fall of his back from breathing, he hasn't
moved.

I take a few tentative steps toward him and clear my
throat. It's rougher than I meant for it to be, and his body jolts
a bit as he wakes up. His eyes are heavy with sleep as he
squints up at me. When his eyes find mine, he gives me a sad
smile and reaches out his hand. I take it and flop into the seat

next to him, sighing as I lean back. I scrub the front of my face with my free hand, hoping that I'll wake up from this nightmare. But when I glance around, I'm still here in the hospital waiting room of the ICU.

Jude gives my hand a light squeeze. "How's your mom? Any change?"

I shake my head solemnly. "She's still under sedation and they haven't told me anything."

"I'm so sorry, Nellie. She's in good hands. I'm sure the doctors and nurses are doing everything they can. They'll tell you more as soon as they have information."

I peer over at him. He sounds so certain. I want to ask him how he does that—stays so positive all the time.

The true problem here is one that I'll never say out loud. No matter what the outcome, nothing positive will come from this. If my mom pulls through, she'll go back to Shady Villa, where Alzheimer's will slowly rob her of her life. And if she succumbs to this, then my mama—the parts of her that remain—will be gone.

"Thanks for saying that. Things are at a standstill for now while we wait."

"That's all you can do, but Nellie, whatever happens, I'll be here." He regards me with love in his eyes.

I can feel my heart begin to splinter at the thought of what I'm about to do. "Yeah, um, about that..." He's nodding his head, fully engaged in what I'm about to say. "I'm going to stay here, at least until my mom wakes up, and we know what we're up against."

"Of course. We'll stay here as long as we need to." His hand lands on mine and his index finger strokes the top of my hand. He's not making this easy on me.

"Well, actually, I was thinking *I* would just stay here on my own. You can't come back to my mom's room and I'm going to be camped out in there. It doesn't make sense for you to wait out here."

The smooth skin between his eyebrows wrinkles with confusion. "It doesn't make sense for me to be here to support you? I'm not sure I follow."

I try to make my voice sound upbeat. "Jude, you can support me from the comfort of your apartment just as easily as you can do it here. We won't be together so it doesn't make a difference where you are."

He's shaking his head. "It definitely makes a difference." He angles his body to face mine, and our knees softly collide. "Nellie, listen, I know you're used to doing everything alone. I understand why you might think this is an inconvenience for me, but believe me when I tell you, there isn't anywhere else I'd rather be right now. You need me whether you can admit that or not. And I'm staying." There's a finality in his voice that's hard to argue with, but I know what I need to do.

"No, that's where you're wrong. I need to focus on my mom and I can't do that knowing you're out here waiting for me. You being here makes it harder on me." I know the second my words land. The smile melts off his face and his eyes narrow. I wish I could take back what I said, but it's the only way to repair this disaster I've created. I pulled him into this chaos, and I owe it to him to set him free.

His expression hardens and his jaw tics. "You really want me to leave?"

I nod slightly. "I do, but only because I'd feel worse knowing you were out here wasting your time."

"Wasting my time." He says the words under his breath, and out of his mouth, I hear how cold I must sound. It's not how I meant it, but I don't bother correcting him. The truth is, I love having him here, but I won't be selfish. It's not fair to ask him to wait around and do nothing. And I won't tell him about the missed calls, either. He'll just tell me that I can't blame myself, but I need to. After all, it's my fault that I never heard my phone and it's my fault that I wasn't there when she needed me.

He looks resigned. "If that's what you want, then I'll go." His hand slips off mine and the warmth is gone. All I feel is numb.

He stands up and slowly slogs away from me like he's wading through water. When there's a few feet between us, he turns to face me. My breath catches when I see the devastation on his face. He offers me a sad smile, and it's the final splinter in my heart. I want to tell him I take it all back. I want him here with me. I can feel the words pushing their way up my throat, but I hold them there, keeping the truth hostage.

"Just, please, text me when you know anything." His eyes plead with mine.

I can't speak. I'm too afraid of what I'll say, of what I'll admit. I give him a quick nod and then watch as he walks away from me.

I'm sending him home, but it feels like much more than that. If I'm honest, I just set the wheels in motion for my life to go back to the way it was, before I met Jude. I tried my hand at juggling having a life of my own while taking care of my mom, and it almost worked. But I think I've always known I couldn't have it both ways. It was fun to pretend for a while.

Chapter Twenty-Nine

IT'S BEEN three hours and fourteen minutes since Jude left. No, that makes it sound like I gave him a choice. He didn't leave. I pushed him away.

When the hallway door closed behind him, putting a barrier between us, I stayed frozen in my seat in the waiting room. I was paralyzed with grief, mourning the life I almost had.

You know, they say that a person's life flashes before their eyes before they die, but when I sent Jude away, my mind was flooded with images of what could have been. I pictured the two of us on amazing trips for Blue Blaze—climbing mountains, scaling rocks, hang-gliding off of cliffs, swimming in oceans. Our lives filled with adventure and promise. In my mind, I saw Jude ask me to marry him at the base of Denali, the vastness of the snow-encapsulated mountain dwarfing us. We said our vows in front of Mauna Loa, the active volcano providing the perfect backdrop for the incredible future ahead of us. We had two children—a boy with ocean blue eyes and a passion for thrill seeking, and a pure hearted little girl with a fury of fiery red curls. I closed my eyes and sat there, soaking in the enormity of what I gave up. When I finally opened my eyes, I felt different, irrevocably changed by my decision.

I'm standing vigil next to my mom's bed. Aside from the time I was with Jude, I haven't left her side.

She woke up briefly about an hour ago and asked me to change the channel on the TV. There's no television in here. She was referring to the screen monitoring her heart rate. I just shook my head and tried to find a smile. "It's okay, Mama. Just get some more rest." She looked up at me and I saw it, the hint of confusion behind her eyes. It took a moment for recognition to find her. As much as it pains me to admit it, that's been happening a lot more often lately. One day the memory will never come, and no matter how hard she squints, she won't recognize me. I know I'm on borrowed time.

She fell back into a fitful sleep, and she's been resting ever since. They tell me what she had wasn't a heart attack. Instead, they're referring to it as a heart "episode."

The pithy doctor who was whispering to the nurse earlier came in a little while ago. He spoke in short succinct sentences, his voice punctuating each one with a slight lilt. "Your mother didn't have a heart attack? It was an episode?" Maybe I'm not being fair here, but it's hard to have faith in his abilities when everything he says sounds like it ends in a question mark.

Despite his brusque behavior, he managed to explain to me that what happened to my mom is called supraventricular tachycardia, or SVT. It's an episode in which the heart rate elevates to an abnormally rapid rate. It can be triggered by stress or medications, but often there's no cause. It's only dangerous if it becomes a regular occurrence. Still, "Dr. Surly" wants to keep her here for one more day just to be sure.

I wish I could say I felt relieved by the news. I'm not upset. I'm not hopeful. I'm not resigned. I just am.

A hand falls on my shoulder, startling me. My head jolts to

the right. A petite nurse with graying hair fastened into a bun at the nape of her neck and round flushed cheeks is gazing down at me. She has kind eyes and tiny red lips, which seem to be moving. It takes me a minute to realize she's talking to me.

I bite at my lower lip. "I'm so sorry. What were you saying?"

She pats my shoulder, and it's such a maternal gesture, it takes everything in me not to lean in and nuzzle her hand. "Oh my dear, you poor thing. You've been sitting here for so long. Why don't you go on outside for a minute. Get some fresh air and stretch your legs."

I shake my head. "As nice as that sounds, I can't leave my mom. What if she wakes up and I'm not here?"

Her round cheeks look like two plums as she smiles down at me. "Sweetie, listen, how about I stay here with your mom? Then she won't be by herself."

"I couldn't ask you to do that."

She chuckles. "Nonsense. I have a twenty-minute break coming to me and I would like nothing more than to sit here while you take a much-needed break of your own. Now go on." She tilts her head toward the door. "The sun is just starting to come up. You don't want to miss the show." She winks at me.

Her kindness overwhelms me. I glance up at the window and sure enough, I can see the golden hue in the sky from the waking sun. She's right. I think the change of scenery would be good for me. It'll help me gain some perspective in a situation that feels bleak from all angles.

I rise out of my seat and take her hand, giving it a shake. "Thank you so much. I'm Nellie, by the way. I didn't catch your name?"

She clasps her free hand over our joined hands. "It's nice to meet you, Nellie. My name is Mary." She gives our clasped hands a pat and then eases out of my grasp. "Go ahead, dear. I'll be right here when you get back."

* * *

THERE'S a small wooden bench just outside the exit. I wonder if Jude took notice of it on his way out. On a sigh, I plop down on the seat, tucking my leg underneath me. I've really made a mess of things. I didn't mean for any of this to happen, but no one ever does.

Being with Jude was like standing on top of a mountain—one that took me a lifetime to climb. I was so busy soaking in the reward that I failed to recognize the struggle I had yet to face on the climb down. My descent began when I saw the missed phone calls from my mom. I had to leave Jude at the summit where he belongs.

A small, but mighty chirp brings my attention to the trash can a few feet in front of me. It's overflowing mostly with discarded coffee cups. At its base sits a cardboard container. The familiar cone shape once housed a full order of French fries, but when its owner carelessly missed the trash receptacle, they also missed a few fries still inside. A tiny brightly colored yellow bird is delighting in the discovery.

I glare at the little bird. "I remember you." I spew the words with disdain. "You're the same bird I saw a few years ago outside of the flower shop. Did you come back here to rub my face in the shit storm that is my life?"

Sitting here on this bench, looking down at the tiny creature in front of me, I notice the fervor in which he devours the bits of French fry. Someone else's trash is his treasure. He gorges on scraps, knowing it might be a while before he finds his next meal. Sure, he can fly and that's amazing, but it's also his only means of transportation. I imagine it must be disorienting at times, flying so far into the unknown, taking a chance on a new location. What if he chooses wrong or what if he's struck down by a predator? His life isn't better than mine; it's just different. "I guess you don't have it all that easy either, do you?"

"Uh-oh, you're talking to birds now, Belly? It looks like things are worse than I thought." A shrill laugh fills the air.

Whipping my head up, I see a woman standing on the walkway to my right. She looks a bit like my sister and she sounds like her, too, but the rays of sun behind her make her appear otherworldly. She must be a mirage. God, I need more sleep.

I rub at my eyes and blink a few times, but when my gaze returns to the path, she's still there. She strides over to me and flips her hands out at her sides. "What? No warm welcome for your sister? Where's my hug?"

Yep, it's Meg, all right. To look at her, you would never know we're related. Her stick-straight blond hair has been lightened to almost white from the sun. Her designer jeans and cropped yellow T-shirt are skin tight, making me wonder how she takes a breath. And the heels on her Jimmy Choo booties raise her up to an unnatural height. She's only been home to visit a handful of times since moving to Hawaii, but I'd recognize that "look at me" pose anywhere.

I could dig all day and I don't think I'd ever find anything resembling true happiness to see her. Her presence confuses me more than anything. So I just spit out the first question that pops into my head. "Meg, what are you doing here?"

My question slaps her in the face, and her head rears back from the impact. "What do you mean? Our mom is in the hospital, Nellie. I couldn't let you deal with this alone."

What is she talking about? Alone is how I've handled everything since she abandoned me. "I don't get it, Meg. Mom hasn't been well for years. Why the sudden interest?" It must be the exhaustion talking because everything that's coming out of my mouth is completely unfiltered. But I can't find it in me to care. I think it's way past time for her to see things for how they really are.

"Okay, I deserve that. And listen, Nellie, I want to have this conversation with you. It's long overdue, but first, can you tell me how Mom's doing?" Her eyes search mine like they're seeking relief, and I'm the only one that can help. I feel my resolve soften a tiny bit. She seems sincere, and if she came here out of concern, I can't prolong her worry.

"She's fine, Megs. I was actually going to give you a call. It was just a rapid heartbeat. It scared her. It scared me, too, but she's okay. She's just inside resting." I jerk my thumb toward the door behind me.

Meg glances in that direction and then she peers back down at me. "Can you take me to her? Please?"

I nod and place my hands on either side of my legs, hoisting myself up. Standing face-to-face with my sister, I don't know whether to hug her or shove her. Every possible reaction feels foreign to me. We're sisters, but we barely know each other. I settle for a light pat on her arm and then I tug on the sleeve of her coat, pulling her toward the doors.

Chapter Thirty

MARY IS STILL SITTING at her post when Meg and I enter the room. She's holding a well-loved copy of *In the Fields* by Willow Aster and is reading aloud to my mom. Her tranquil voice fills the air and settles over me, washing away the complex train of emotions I was feeling toward my sister.

It isn't about us. It hasn't been for years. I'm here for my mom, and now, so is Meg. We have a mountain of problems to work through, but I'm glad she's here. I glance up at her and am surprised to see tears in her eyes. She swipes at her face and gruffly chuckles. "Yeah, yeah, I know. Shocking, isn't it?"

Mary pauses her reading and beams up at my sister and me. "You're back." She dog-ears the page in her book before closing it and places it on the table by the bed. "I'll leave this with you in case you'd like to continue reading to her. She hasn't woken up since you left, but she has let out a few contented sighs. I think she was enjoying the story."

I smile at her. "Mary, thank you so much for spending your break with my mom." I crane my neck and look over at my sister, holding her gaze when I say, "As it turns out, you were right. Stepping outside was exactly what I needed."

She claps her hands together, and a look of sheer delight fills her face. "I'm so happy to hear that, dear." She stands and glides over to us. "Is this your sister?" She looks between Meg and me and places a hand on each of our cheeks. We nod in unison. "It's so good that you have each other. Nothing is more valuable than family. Especially when things look bleak. You lean on each other and you'll soon find that you're both stronger than you give yourselves credit for." She lightly pats our faces, and then she breezes out the door.

Meg looks at me with wide eyes. "Who was that magical woman?"

The right corner of my mouth lifts and I shrug. "I'm pretty sure that was our fairy godmother, Megs." I jut my chin toward the bed. "Go ahead over and say hi to Mom. I'll give you some privacy."

Meg grabs my hand, and I feel it quake in her grasp. "You're not leaving, are you?"

I shake my head. "No, Meg. That's your move, remember?"

Hurt brews in her eyes, and she bows her head to look down at her feet.

Okay, that was a little harsh. I give her hand a squeeze. "I'm sorry. I shouldn't have said that."

She lifts her head slightly and peeks up at me. Her cheeks glisten with tears, and even though I'm still hurt by the choices she's made, I can't ignore how hard this all is for her. We're both burdened by this cruel circumstance; we've just had vastly different ways of dealing with that.

I lean in and catch her eyes with mine. "I'm going to send a quick text to a friend." The word tastes bitter in my mouth, but I don't let myself think about that. "I'll just be out in the hallway. Come and get me when you're ready." She nods and casts a nervous glance toward mom. "It's okay, Megs. I promise she won't bite. At least, it hasn't happened yet." I pretend to gulp and she giggles, grateful for the joke. When I leave her, she's slowly lowering herself into the chair next to Mom, and my fractured heart heals a tiny bit.

The hallway of the ICU isn't alive with a flurry of movement. It's barely awake. A trio of nurses sits behind a station staring bleary-eyed at computer screens while one lone nurse exits a patient's room pausing just outside the door to make a few notes in a chart. The only activity comes from a well-meaning janitor mopping up a spill near the exit. He's bopping to the music pouring out of his headphones, blissfully unaware of the struggles going on inside the rooms of this unit.

I take a deep breath and fill my nose with the antiseptic scent of the hospital. On an exhale, I reach my hand inside my pocket and pull out my phone. I should've sent this text an hour ago when I first heard that my mom would be okay, but the truth is, I wasn't sure what to say. Which is a strange turn of events since I've never had a problem talking to Jude. But that was before I dismissed him, sending him away like an old shirt that I no longer had use for. It's a lie, of course. All of it is. Jude is all that I ever need in life, but look where that got me? No, even though it kills me to know that I hurt him, I have to let him go.

I tap open my messages and shoot off a quick text.

Me: My mom is going to be okay. It wasn't a heart attack, just a rapid heartbeat.

His reply comes immediately, making it seem like he was just staring at his phone willing it to ring.

Jude: That's great news, Nellie. I'm so happy to hear it. Thank you for letting me know.

No cute emojis decorate his words. They're simple. Final. I did this. I only have myself to blame, but it's what I wanted.

That's not true. It's the last thing I wanted. Still, it's what had to happen. I could respond. I could keep things going back and forth between us, but where would that lead? It would give him false hope and it wouldn't be fair. So I slide my phone back into the pocket of my jeans and I push back the curtain to my mom's room.

Meg has Mom's hand in hers and she's leaning her body over the bed, resting her chin a few inches from mom's ear. I can hear the soft murmuring of Meg's voice as she speaks to Mom. I still my movements and allow her to finish. She came a long way to say whatever it is she's whispering to our mom. It seems only right that she's able to get it all out.

I take this time to observe my sister. When we were kids, I looked up to Meg. She was always so fashion forward with her wardrobe choices. When she would leave the house to go out with friends, I would sit on the little white stool in front of the vanity in her room and pretend to be her. I'd use her brush on my hair and imagine that it would magically smooth out the frizz and leave me with shiny sleek hair like my sister's. I'd glide open the drawers under the counter and sift through her lipstick collection. My fingers would land on one of the dozens of red hues and I would pluck it from the bin. I never wanted her to know I used her things without asking so I would dot the color onto my lips and use my index finger to smooth it out. Turning my head this way and that, I'd pose in front of the mirror and try to make my voice sound like hers. Where mine was shrill and scratchy, hers was feminine and velvety. I'd place my hand over my heart pretending to be surprised by all of the male attention I was receiving. "Why, yes, I would love to go out with you." "Oh, aren't you just so sweet." Batting my eyelashes, I tried to be the one person I always looked up to. But now, as I stand here watching my sister struggling to keep her composure as she pours her heart out to our mom, I realize I'm no longer that little girl sliding into Meg's big shoes hoping to fill them.

Sensing my presence, Meg turns, offering me a solemn smile. I plod into the room and take the seat on the opposite side of the bed. I watch as Mom's eyes dance behind her lids. "She still hasn't woken up. They must have some serious stuff pumping through here." Meg lifts her hand to thwack her nail against the IV tubing streaming clear liquid into Mom's veins.

I bob my head. "Yeah, the nurse told me she was pretty inconsolable when they first brought her in here. I imagine the confusion from her disease makes situations like this much scarier than they might normally be." Normal. I love and hate that word in equal measure. Once upon a time, I had normal. I sometimes felt bored by it, wishing I could trade it in for something more exciting. Now, as I sit across from the sister I hardly know staring at the mom who barely knows me, I'd give anything for another shot at normal.

Meg's voice pulls me out of the downward spiral my mind was about to go on. "Belly?" She clears her throat. "I mean, Nellie?"

I keep my eyes on my mom's face as I answer, "Hmm?"

"Um, it's just, well, what I wanted to say was, I'm sorry." It's two words, but the weight in them is so heavy I'm afraid the bed might buckle. My eyes snap to Meg's face in search of truth, and I find it instantly.

When a person lies, you can spot it easily if you know what to look for. It took a bit of studying, but I got pretty good at detecting when Meg was being truthful or not. When she lies, her eyes get as big as saucers ,and she barely blinks. It's as if she's afraid that blinking might reset her face and reveal the truth she's so desperately trying to hide. She told a lot of lies when she was a teenager, but on the rare occasion when she was telling the truth, Meg's entire body would relax as though it were taking a giant exhale. Her limbs would be loose and mobile, holding no rigidity. But the one telltale sign that Meg was being truthful was her nose. It sounds odd, but when she's telling the truth, Meg flexes her nostrils. They flare in and out as she speaks.

Looking at her across the divide of our mother's slumbering body, her nose dances as she repeats the words I've been waiting years to hear. "I'm so sorry, Nellie."

I close my eyes as I absorb the gravity of this moment. I've never understood Meg's decision to skip town right after we learned of mom's disease. I can't pretend that it ever made sense to me, but that's just it—it never had to make sense to me. It wasn't my journey. But it still affected my journey. Meg moved away and I took over. I never had a person to bounce ideas or plans off of. I never knew if any of the decisions I was making were right or not, but I had to trust my instincts. I had no other choice. I only had myself. It forced me to be strong, but it also forced me to never depend on anyone else for support. I think of Jude and how incredible it felt to have someone to lean on. I squeeze my eyelids tighter and push away those thoughts.

When I blink my eyes open, I find Meg looking at me with earnest sincerity. Her words can't fix everything that's happened, but they're a start. I give her a reassuring smile. "I know you are, Meg. Thank you for saying that. I didn't realize how badly I needed to hear those words."

She pushes out a short, breathy laugh. "Oh, believe me, Nellie, as much as you needed to hear them, I've needed to say them even more." She reaches across the bed, and I meet her in the middle, taking her hand in mine. Her bottom lip trembles. "I can't believe I just left, Nellie. You were all alone and you never should have been. I took myself out of the equation, making you an only child. I don't even think I have a right to ask you this, but can you ever forgive me?" Tears flow silently down her cheeks in thick streams, soaking the bed sheet. The thin white material darkens to a deep gray from the wetness.

"There's nothing to forgive, Megs. You handled things the only way you knew how at the time."

She's shaking her head fiercely. "But I was wrong, Nellie. So wrong. I'm the big sister. I'm supposed to be the one who takes charge, but instead, I ran away like the coward that I am. When the going gets tough, Meg bails." She rolls her eyes. "What kind of person does that?"

I give her a sad smile. "A confused and scared person."

"You were both of those things, too, Nellie, but you didn't leave. You stuck by Mom and took care of her, and you never gave up on me, either. No matter how horrible I was to you, you still kept calling and texting me, trying to keep me included." Her words leave her mouth in choked sobs. "You are the only good and pure thing in my life, and I walked away from you."

Rising up out of my seat, I round the bed and squat down in front of her. I take her face in my hands and sweep my thumbs under her eyes, wiping away her tears the way our mom used to do when we were kids. "Listen, Meg, you did what you thought you had to do. Maybe you wish you had chosen differently, maybe I wish that, too, but it doesn't matter. It's in the past and neither one of us can change that. You're here now and all is forgiven. Let's not waste any more time dwelling on what could have been. Okay?"

She gazes down at me through red-rimmed eyes. "How'd you get to be so wise, huh?"

I look up at her and deadpan, "Jeopardy."

She laughs and wraps her arms around my neck, pulling me in for a hug. Her head rests on top of mine as she takes in deep calming breaths. It dawns on me that it's the first time we've hugged since the day she left for Hawaii. She had reached across the center console of my car and gave me a half hug, half pat, and then she breezed out the door, melting into the crowd at the airport. It was a tepid goodbye that felt final in a way that I couldn't admit to myself. This hug in our mother's hospital room is nothing like that day. It holds a renewed promise between two sisters. It's not a goodbye. It's a reunion.

"Meggy? Bells? Why aren't you two dressed? We need to leave right now if we want to make it to the beach in time." Mom's voice fills the room in a way that only hers ever could.

Meg and I pull apart and stare up at her. She's confused, but for a few minutes, neither one of us corrects her. Our eyes fill with wonder as her words take us briefly back in time. Back to when things were normal.

Chapter Thirty-One

IT TOOK Meg and I all morning to get Mom readjusted back to life at Shady Villa. She had only been in the hospital for a few days, but it was enough to completely throw off her whole routine. Meg is still there with her, a decision that surprised me. She insisted on staying with Mom until after dinner. She told me she had missed too much and I couldn't argue with her there. She wanted to get a true sense of how much her disease has progressed.

The ICU doctor told us he didn't see any further complications from the scans they had done. He sent Mom home with strict orders to take it easy for the next few days. That shouldn't be too hard for her to follow, considering she spends most of her time parked on her sofa watching game shows.

As I lumber up the stairs to my apartment, I feel the taxing weight of the last few days settle on my shoulders. Exhaustion doesn't even come close to how this feels. All I can think about right now is how great it will feel to slip off my shoes and let my entire body flop onto my sofa.

When I reach the upstairs hallway, Claudette is coming

out of her apartment. Air pods plug her ears and her body sways freely. I stand still, marveling at how great she looks. She jolts with a start when she spots me out of the corner of her eye. Yanking her air pods from her ears, she settles her fist on her hip and tilts her head. "There you are, hunny! Haven't seen you in a while!"

I fill her in on my mom, telling her about Meg, as well. I've mentioned my sister to her a few times, leaving out the part about how she left me alone. Claudette is sharp and I'm fairly certain she figured that out all on her own.

"Oh, Nellie, I'm so sorry, dear. How's your mama now? Better, I hope."

I nod. "She is. Meg is with her now."

Claudette looks pleased. "Well, I'm sure glad to hear that. 'Bout time that sister of yours pitched in."

I chuckle. Nothing much gets past that woman.

"Say, now, what's that over there in front of your door?" She cocks her head and her eyes come alive with mischief.

I peer out around her and notice a small rectangular box with a red satin bow sitting on the brown tweed carpet in front of my door. I look back at Claudette with a raised eyebrow, but she just shrugs and says, "Don't look at me, hunny. Santa Claus must have put it there." Her laugh tells me she knows more than she's letting on, but she isn't giving up any more details. She pops up her hand in a quick wave and then saunters down the hall toward the stairs. Her giggle follows her the whole way.

The box is wrapped in a rich bronze coating that feels smooth in my hands, and when I lift the bow from the top, the lid comes off with it. Waves of white tissue paper conceal the inside, and a simple gray envelope rests on top. My name is written in careful print across the front. I'd recognize that handwriting anywhere. It's the same familiar penmanship that's graced my Starbucks cups over the past few months.

My entire body tingles with anticipation as I lift the envelope from the box. The air is heady with the scent of bergamot and citrus as I reach inside and find a small folded sheet of paper tucked away.

> Nellie,
> I fixed the light in the glove box of my car and found this inside. It's yours now. When you look at it, I want you to remember that no matter how much things have changed, the past will always remain exactly how it was. The memories we've made are a part of us. They help make us who we are now. No matter what happens, no one can take your mother away from you. Not even her disease. Her essence is woven all throughout you, the same way Dylan is inside of me. I'm here for you when and if you'll have me. I hope you'll let me in. I'll be waiting.
> All my love,
> Jude

Hidden beneath the tissue paper is a photograph of Jude and his brother Dylan. I remember Jude's story about how it had been taken a few months before Dylan died, so they must have been around twenty-six years old. It isn't a posed image. They were captured mid-laugh by someone candidly snapping their picture without them knowing. Those are my favorite kind. Organic images tell a story. They give you a sense of who people really are. All a posed picture does is show you that a group of people all stood together in one spot and smiled at a camera once. This picture told me so much about the relationship Jude had with his twin brother. They aren't identical, but Jude was right, there's no denying they're related. It's apparent more in their facial expressions than anything else. The way they both have their heads thrown back at the same right angle, their mouths are open wide with straight glimmering white teeth on full display. If I had to guess, I'd say this picture was taken in Iowa, probably by a family member who knew them well.

Dylan is leaning back against an old wooden fence. His hands grip the weathered wood on either side of his body. His hair is much shorter than Jude's, closely cropped and gelled to perfection. I can tell from his choice of clothes that Dylan was more formal. He's wearing jeans, but they're a dark black denim that appears stiff. His gray and white striped button-down shirt is tucked into his waistband and buttoned up to his chin. Sleek black boots complete the ensemble. Jude is far more casual in both his pose and his outfit choice. He's leaning to the side and has his right hand resting on Dylan's shoulder. His jeans look worn and comfortable; his hair is free and wild; and his faded blue Converse and relaxed T-shirt make him look more like the boy next door. Despite their obvious physical differences, they are clearly at ease with each other, sharing in a laugh that is now forever immortalized.

When I flip the picture over, I'm surprised to find a message on the back. It says, *Brother, laughing looks good on you. Remember to do it every day.* It isn't Jude's handwriting. The staggering realization that Jude gave me such a priceless gift hits me square in the gut. I yank my phone from the back pocket of my jeans. My fingers are clumsy and frantic as I shoot off a text to him.

Me: Thank you for the picture. It's incredible, but I can't keep it.

He doesn't reply right away, and I start to worry. I've been so used to Jude's responses coming at lightning speed, and now, more than ever, I'm desperate to hear from him. The picture is like a burning ember in my hand and I need to extinguish it. I appreciate the sentiment, but it's far too valuable for me to have in my possession. I don't deserve it.

His reply comes nearly a half hour later.

Jude: Sorry. I'm at work and had a huge crowd. You're welcome. And, of course, you can keep the picture.
Like I said in my note, it's yours now.
Me: But your brother wrote on the back. Don't you think you should hold on to it?
Jude: I feel better knowing that it's with you. You need it more than I do.

I struggle to understand what he means. This is the last picture ever taken of Jude and Dylan. Why would I need it more than he does? Glancing up at my gallery wall, I can't imagine not having these images of happier times.

I'm sitting on a stool in the kitchen—the same place I was sitting that day when Jude asked me to go to Yosemite with him. I wish I could go back in time and relive that moment. Everything seemed possible, and then with one phone call, it was all wiped away.

My fingers probe the corner of the picture as Meg barrels in through the front door. Her mouth is already moving a mile a minute and she hasn't even entered the room.

Her hands flap around wildly as she struggles to hold on to her shopping bag, her purse, and the food bowl. "Oh my God, Nellie, if that little Swirl of yours—"

"Swerve."

She flips her hand, dismissing my correction, and nearly drops the food bowl. "Same thing. If she keeps bringing more friends to dinner, we're going to need to start buying cat food by the case. I swear—" Her words freeze in her mouth. "What's that?" She sidles up beside me and peers down at the picture. Realization hits her fast, and she tilts her head up so that she's looking directly at me. Her eyes narrow and she levels me with a look that makes me want to duck for cover. I know my sister, and she only ever looks at me that way when she's about to spew some harsh truth. "Okay, Nellie, listen to me because I'm only going to say this once." *Somehow I doubt that.* "You need to stop gazing at that boy's picture and call him already! I understand you needed space, but it's obvious how much you miss him. Don't think I haven't noticed you bringing up his name every chance you get. Mom is much better and she's out of the hospital now. Call him. Seriously, what are you waiting for?"

I slide the picture onto the counter next to me. "It's not that simple, Megs." I haven't told her about the missed calls from Mom. I know she wouldn't see it the same way I do. Meg has come a long way since she's been here, but she hasn't come that far.

"But it is, though! You just pick up your phone and press his cute little face in your contacts. You don't even have to dial his number. Technology has made it so easy for you!" She lets her purse fall to the ground and it clanks in response. She has so much loose change in there, it's like she's an old lady ready to take on the nickel machines at the casino.

My eyes flit back to the photo. Jude's frozen laugh makes me wish I was in on the joke. Since he gave me this picture, I've been dying to know what was so funny. I guess I could call and ask him. It's a good place to start. I hold my hands up in surrender. "All right, fine. I'll call him." I reach for Swerve's bowl and pluck it out of my sister's hands. "But first, I'll feed our little bevy of cats."

* * *

WOW, Meg wasn't kidding. I've counted six cats prancing

around outside the front door. Swerve sits in the center quietly preening herself while the other five parade around her. I glance down at the two bowls of food in my hands and am glad I decided to fill a second one. I just hope it's enough.

I angle my body and shove open the door with my hip. Swerve's disciples scatter with my presence, but my old friend never moves. "Are you and your friends hungry, sweet girl?" I place a bowl in front of her and she nuzzles the side of my hand with her cheek, mewing softly. I peek up at the other cats and find them watching me with interest. "I hope you all like salmon!" I say as I set the other bowl a few feet away from Swerve. Then I scurry back inside, knowing that if Swerve won't eat in front of me, the chances of these other strays doing it is slim to none. I dart to the side of the vestibule and take cover among the shadows. It's the perfect place to spy on the action. Swerve wastes no time. The minute I'm inside, she descends upon the bowl in front of her. The other cats are more tentative, but after a few minutes, they've all found a place at their dinner table outside. They look like a little family, and with as much stealth as I can muster, I squat down and snap a photo of them through the glass.

Jude would get such a kick out of this. Without thinking, I tap a few buttons and fire it off in a text. The magnitude of what I've just done doesn't dawn on me until I'm halfway up the stairs. I quickly open up my messages and find his at the top. When I open it, I'm greeted with his last text to me—You need it more than I do—followed by the picture I just took of six stray cats eating on my porch. *Great work, Nellie. He sent you a sincere text and you left it hanging only to answer him with a photo of cats.* I smack my forehead. I'm such an idiot.

Maybe I can fix this. I start to type out the words, *Oops, wrong person*, but I nix them immediately. That's a lie and it's lame. No, the best thing I can do here is be honest. I tap my finger inside the message bar and watch the cursor blink a few times, trying to decide exactly how honest I intend to be. I settle on a short explanation.

Me: I think I may have a little kitty soup kitchen on my hands! Swerve has been spreading the word! Ha-ha!

It's a little cringe-worthy, but I send it anyway. It's the type of text I would've sent to him *before*. Before I broke his heart and mine. The lump in my throat is strong and almost rises to the surface. I can feel the prickling of tears in the corners of my eyes, but I shake my head and will them away.

When I reach the door to my apartment, my phone chimes with an incoming text.

Jude: You should probably think about hiring a security guard before things get out of hand. I'd go with a German Shepherd *dog emoji*

I chuckle, and it feels good to be laughing at Jude's ridiculous humor again. My fingers work over the keys, and I send him a reply.

Me: Good point. I could name him Furcules!
Jude: Eh, it's not bad, but what about Fido Castro?
Me: I like it! Or maybe James Earl Bones?
Jude: Hmm, Lick Jagger?
Me: You know, these are great, but what if the dog is a girl?
Jude: True, if that's the case, I think there's only one possible name.
Me: Oh, really? And what's that?
Jude: Molly Ringworm

My laughter echoes throughout the hallway. This is just like Jude, making me feel instantly at ease. I'm being ridiculous here. Maybe we don't have to be apart. I'm going to call him.

I flick my finger across the screen and tap on the green icon. But before I can find Jude's name, my phone rings in my hands. The familiar drum tone reverberates off of the empty walls pounding into my ears like a truth bomb. On a sad huff, I accept the call. "Hi, Mama. What's up?"

Chapter Thirty-Two

AS IT TURNS OUT, my mom has called to ask me to have my sister call her, which just means she's forgotten Meg's number again. Meg and I have been toying with the idea of upgrading Mom's phone to one with pre-programmed numbers. I think it may be time to make that happen.

While we are talking, I hear another text come through.

Jude: Uh-oh. You don't like it?

It takes me a minute to figure out what he's referring to, but then I remember our silly pun game. After another frustrating phone call with my mom, it seems more absurd than funny and I no longer have it in me to conjure up a witty reply.

Meg and I are washing dishes from the dinner she made. We've formed an assembly line in which she submerges the dirty plates and silverware into sudsy water and sponges them off, then she hands them to me for a quick rinse and then a rest in the drying rack. It's such a simple domestic task, but there's something profoundly beautiful about it. I'm standing next to the sister I thought I lost, listening to an early seventies rock station on Pandora, washing the remains of one of our mom's recipes off of my dishes.

The familiar strumming of "Have You Ever Seen the Rain?" comes through my Bluetooth speaker. Meg and I turn to each other and grin. We set down the dishes and start dancing, shaking our bodies in time with the music. Our hips sway and our limbs move with wild abandon. When John Fogerty begins singing, so do we. We don't skip a word; we know every one by heart. This song is the anthem of our childhood, and we sing the lyrics at the top of our lungs.

Until Meg suddenly stops in her tracks, putting her hand on my arm to still my movements. She cranes her neck and tips her head toward the door. "Did you hear that?" She has to yell to be heard over the drums and tambourine.

I lean over the counter and press the volume button on the speaker, lowering the music. "Hear what?"

A few light knocks on the door answer my question.

Meg smiles slyly. "That." She arcs her thumb toward the door.

I swat her on the butt with my towel and she jumps. "I'll get the door. You keep washing."

"Aye, aye, cap'n!" she calls out as she saunters back to the sink.

I wipe some residual dish water from my hand onto the leg of my jeans and then grasp the knob of my door, pulling it open.

Jude stands on the other side. His left hand is thrust into the pocket of his olive green pants. The cotton fibers of his navy-blue T-shirt pull taut when he shifts his body, angling his hip away from me. He looks as though he's poised to leave at any moment. He wears a guarded expression on his face, and I'm to blame for that. I put it there.

I'm sucked into the vastness of his deep blue eyes and rendered speechless. Neither one of us says a thing for several seconds. It's the first time we've seen each other since I pushed him away, and we're both too caught up in the moment. Jude breaks the silence with a cough that almost sounds genuine.

"Hey." He smiles. "It's good to see you."

His words settle over me and I smile in return. "You, too."

His body is facing me and his hand has left his pocket and is relaxed at his side. His eyes are etched with hope, but his forehead creases with worry. His emotions are a jumbled mess of contradiction, and it's written all over him. I want nothing more than to reach out and soothe the anguish that I inflicted on him, but then what? Do I just let him back into my life and damn the consequences? My heart is at war with my head, and the loss is inevitable, no matter what the outcome.

My brow furrows as I realize that Jude is inside my apartment building and he never pressed the buzzer. "Wait a minute. How'd you get in here?"

His smile turns sheepish. "Claudette let me in. She's a card-carrying member of the Jude and Nellie fan club, you know?"

I giggle and his body instantly reacts. He takes a few steps closer and his hands open and close at his sides as though he's fighting the desire to reach out to me. I want to walk the rest of the way and put an end to this distance between us, but I ignore the feeling and swallow, forcing myself to answer him. "Yeah, I've definitely gotten that impression from her."

He glances over at the closed door to Claudette's apartment. "She seems like she's doing well."

I let out a relieved sigh, and his gaze slides over my face. "She's thriving, actually. The medicine she's taking appears to be agreeing with her, and it makes me so happy."

The smile on his face is sincere. "It makes me happy, too, Nellie."

I bite at my lower lip and nod.

Meg picks that moment to clear her throat loudly behind me. I spin around and find her leaning to the side trying to catch a glimpse of Jude. When she spots him, she lifts her hand in a small wave. "Hi, I'm Nellie's sister, Meg."

"It's nice to meet you, Meg. I'm Jude."

She nods. "I kind of figured." She turns and faces me with a conspiratorial gleam in her eyes. "I'm sorry to interrupt. I just wanted to let you know that I've finished the dishes and I'm going to go hang out in my room. With my door closed. And my headphones on." With a wink, she saunters toward the guest room, leaving me alone with Jude.

I'm shaking my head as I turn toward him. His eyebrow is raised, and he's wearing a presumptuous grin. "I like her."

I bark out a laugh. "Yeah, she's something, all right."

My eyes flit over his face, taking in all the features that I've missed. I'm not sure how much longer I can stand in such close proximity to him and not touch him. My hands are fisted at my sides and I keep my body rigid, but the pull I feel is becoming harder to fight, and I'm beginning to wonder why I ever fought it in the first place.

As if sensing my internal struggle, Jude speaks up. "So, you're probably wondering why I'm here."

I tip my head, acknowledging that he's right.

He continues. "I was wondering if maybe we could talk. Would that be okay?"

I don't let myself overthink. I let my heart answer. "Sure. Come on in." I pull open the door and walk toward the kitchen, calling over my shoulder, "I'm going to grab some water. Do you want anything?"

"Water sounds good, thanks." His voice comes from behind me as he pulls out one of the stools and perches on it. The soles of his black low top Converse hook onto the cross bars at the base of the seat. He leans his elbows onto the counter and looks so casually relaxed, it gives me pause. It feels so familiar. Despite all that's happened, in this moment,

I can almost pretend that everything is how it was. My heart aches with the realization that nothing could be further from the truth.

I'm afraid of where this conversation will take us. I'm taking my worry out on everything I touch, wrestling with the glasses in the overhead cabinet and flinging open the refrigerator door with too much force. I keep myself busy in an effort to avoid the conversation, but it looms like an intruder hiding away in the shadows of a darkened room, ready to pounce when the moment is right.

With two glasses of water poured to the brim, there's nothing more for me to do except turn and face him and whatever it is he wants to tell me. I spin around and lumber toward him with tentative steps. "So, what is it you wanted to talk about?" I try to sound strong and confident, but my voice betrays me, breaking with the last word.

As though he just wants to put me out of my misery, Jude takes aim and fires. "I'm leaving tomorrow." *Bam*. He must be an expert marksman because his words slice straight through my heart. My knees wobble, threatening to take me to the ground. I grip the counter and steady myself.

I can hardly hear a thing over the roaring in my ears, but somehow I manage to speak. "You're leaving? Tomorrow? Why? Where are you going?" I launch my questions in quick succession.

A look of bewilderment followed by sorrow settles on Jude's face. "Tomorrow is the trip to Yosemite, Nellie."

That hardly seems possible. It feels like only yesterday that he was asking me to go with him? My brain works in overtime, cataloguing the days. It all adds up. "You're right, sorry. With everything that's happened, I guess I lost track of time."

His hand reaches out and rests on top of mine. His touch is like a warm breeze on a chilly day, and I close my eyes, reveling in the feeling. The smooth timbre of his voice fills me with comfort. "You've been through a lot lately. It only makes sense that your days would blend together." He's quiet for a moment, but when he speaks again, I'm struck by the desolation in his voice. "Time is funny that way, funny and cruel."

I lift my eyes to his face, but his gaze is fixed on our hands. I watch him take in a breath before he continues. "So, listen, I'm sure I already know the answer, but I have to ask anyway. Will you come with me?" He looks up at me and searches my face for the response he's hoping for. His voice is pleading, and I feel my resolve start to bend. But then I picture my mom swallowed up by her hospital bed and my head begins shaking fervently.

"Jude, I'm sorry, but I just can't leave my mom. There are too many things that could happen. I need to be here, *for her*." I place extra emphasis on those words so that he understands that my decision has nothing to do with him and everything to do with my mom.

"I get it. After what happened, I'm sure you're even more on edge than you were before, but the doctor said your mom was okay, right?" I nod, but remain silent as he continues. "And Meg is here now so if something happens, she could hold down the fort until you come home."

I shake my head. "I know it sounds like an exaggeration, but *I'm* the one my mom needs. I'm the one she calls when she needs help."

"But that's what I'm saying, Nellie. With Meg home, your mom could call her—"

"She called me that night!" His face registers with surprise. "Jude, the night she was taken to the hospital, she tried to call me four times, and she left two messages. Only I never heard the phone ring because ..."

"Because you were with me." His throat bobs as he swallows my confession. He leans in close, his gaze searching mine. "Nellie, you can't take on all of that guilt. It isn't fair.

Your mom would want you to have your own life—one that's separate from her."

"Rationally, I know what you're saying is right, but I can't ignore the way it felt to know that she reached out to me when she needed me most and I wasn't there." I suck in a breath, but it's no use. There's no way to prepare for what I need to say. "That's why I need to let you go." I choke.

He holds up his free hand. "Wait, hold on. If you can't go with me on this trip, it's okay. That doesn't mean we can't still be together. This isn't goodbye, Nellie. It's just a see you later."

Tears pool in my eyes, and with a blink, I send them cascading down my face. "If only that were true, but I tried putting myself first and look what happened. I should've been there for her, Jude. I should've picked up the phone. I know my mom is okay now, but what if she's not so lucky next time? I could never forgive myself if something happened to her and I wasn't there. I can't let that happen again. I know you might not agree with me, but I hope you can understand where I'm coming from," I say as I search his eyes for confirmation.

A defeated expression settles on his face. "I do understand, but I'll never stop hoping that you change your mind." He gives my hand a soft squeeze and then he lets it go. In that one motion, I feel it. I've lost him. His eyes flick back and forth between mine. He looks as though he wants to say more, but instead, he lifts himself off the stool and slides it back into place.

He stares at me with an intensity that makes me feel bare. He's studying my face like he's trying to sear it into his brain. His lips curve into a sad smile. "I love you, Nellie." Four words are all it takes for the ground to open up and swallow me whole. I want him to take them back, while at the same time, I want to hear him say them again and again. I should be running to him, but instead, I'm standing still, watching his back as he retreats.

My brain is a fury of activity, and my thoughts are disjointed. But above all, the activity raging inside of me, one thought is glaringly clear, and I know it's exactly what I need to say. "I love you, too, Jude."

He presses his hand against the door and turns. His face softens. "I know you do, Nellie. That's the problem."

My hand covers my mouth, stifling a gasp. His response fills me with shock and confusion. "I don't understand. How could loving someone ever be a problem?"

"For most people, it isn't. But you aren't most people, Nellie." He's looking at me like I'm a delicate glass vase balancing precariously on the edge of a table. "You love me. You love your mom, your sister, your neighbors, the residents at Shady Villa. Everyone is worthy of your love, except *you*. When are you going to stop living for other people and start living for you? Love yourself first, Nellie. Just for once."

He strides over to me and cradles the side of my face in his hand. "I know I asked you to never hide from me, but don't hide from yourself, either." He presses his lips against my forehead and places a trail of soft kisses down the center on my face, pausing briefly when he reaches my mouth. The air around us seems to crackle. He leans in until his mouth is inches from mine and then he closes the distance. He doesn't hold back. He puts the full weight of his love in his kiss.

Some kisses are full of promise. Some are full of desire. Some leave you breathless and wanting more. Some are just a prelude of things to come. This kiss is all and none of the above. This kiss is goodbye.

Jude pulls away, breaking our connection. He peers down at me. The heartache in his eyes is on full display, and I feel my own heart shatter. The pain radiates throughout my body. He sweeps his thumb across my cheek, swiping at the tears I didn't realize had fallen. "Take care of yourself, Nellie." He backs away, moving toward the door without ever turning around. He knows that once he does, he'll be walking away from me and out of my life.

I stand by wordlessly as he reaches for the doorknob. With one last look over his shoulder, he lumbers into the hallway. The door clicks softly behind him and then he's gone.

Chapter Thirty-Three

I'M STILL STANDING in the same spot between my kitchen and my front door. Letting him go was the right thing to do. I just wish it didn't feel so wrong.

"Hey, sis?"

Meg's voice jolts me out of my waking nightmare. I turn my head in the direction of her voice and find her leaning against the wall in the hallway.

My hand raises to rest over my heart, and I feel the muscle working in overdrive. It's amazing to me how I can feel dead inside, and yet my heart still beats. It's as if it's working extra hard despite my grief, or maybe in spite of it.

"What's up, Meg?"

Her eyes widen in shock. "What's up? Well, why don't you start by telling me what the hell is up with you letting such an incredible guy walk out the door?"

I sift my hands through my hair and cradle my head in exhaustion. "It's complicated, Megs."

"So, un-complicate it, then." She rests her fists on her waist and cocks her hip. "I know you're upset that you missed Mom's call that night, but you're not responsible for everything that ever happens to her."

I narrow my eyes at my sister. "Just how long were you lurking in the hallway? Hmm?"

She bites at her lip. "Long enough to hear you refuse to go to Yosemite with Jude and then send him on his not so merry way," she says with a shrug. "Hey, in my defense, you weren't exactly whispering."

I roll my eyes and brace myself for more unwanted advice. My hands are twisted together in front of my chest. She glides over and wraps her hands around mine, pulling them down to rest at my sides. Placing her finger on my chin, she lifts my head so that we're looking at each other eye to eye. "You've been everything to everyone for so long, Nellie. How do you do it?"

The answer comes easy. "I haven't had a choice."

She smiles sadly. "Well, you do now."

I let my eyes fall closed and shake my head. "Meg, Mom needs me. She's the only right choice here."

She takes my hands in hers, pulling them between us. "Correction. Mom *needed* help and you gave that to her, Nellie. It's because of you that she's receiving the best care. But here's the thing, it's actually possible for you to take care of yourself, too."

I tug at our joined hands until she releases them. "I wish people would stop saying that like it's such a simple thing to do."

"Nellie, no one said it was simple. Nothing worthwhile ever is. But that's why I'm here. Listen, I know you're afraid to leave Mom, but it's a short trip and I'll be here with her the whole time."

She's speaking so earnestly and I wish I could believe her, but a part of me—the part that remembers how she abandoned me when I needed her most—still has doubts. I don't say that out loud, but judging by the way Meg's head bows with shame, I think she gets the message. "I know I let you down. I was an asshole with a capital ASS. But these past couple of weeks have changed me, and I'd like to think you've noticed. You have, haven't you?"

I nod. She's right. She's been so attentive and helpful. In a lot of ways, it's like I have the old Meg back, except this one is the new and improved 2.0 model.

"I know I wasn't here for you before, but I'm here now. And if you'll let me, I'd like to be the big sister and take care of you, for a change."

I appreciate all that she's saying, I do, but there's nothing she can do to stop this incessant pang in my heart. There's nothing anyone can do. "Meg, thank you for saying that. You have no idea how much I needed to hear that."

"But…" She eyes me expectantly. She knows there's more that I'm not saying.

With a trembling lip and tears threatening to spill over, I continue. "But, what if she forgets who I am while I'm gone? I'm so afraid that I'll go off and have an amazing trip only to come back to a mom who doesn't remember my name, or worse—my face. I can't handle that, Meg. It would break me."

She sighs and wraps her arms around me, pulling me in for a hug. Speaking into my hair, she says, "Oh Nellie, that's a fear I know all too well. It's the reason I ran away back when Mom was diagnosed. When I thought about losing her piece by piece, I couldn't get away fast enough. But you stayed so you could soak in the bits of her that remained, knowing that it would all end eventually. Sadly, one day that will happen, and there's nothing you or I or anyone can do to stop it. It's part of the ugly beast that is this disease." She loosens her grip and places her hands on my biceps, holding me out in front of her. "But, Nellie, I promise you, every single day that you're gone, I'll show her your picture. I'll mention your name. I'll remind her of stories from when we were little. I will do *everything* within my power to make sure that when you come back, she still knows exactly who you are."

My sister drives a hard bargain. I want nothing more than to give in, but even though my hesitation is shrinking, it's still there. "I don't know, Meg."

She shoves me away with a huff and stalks into the living room, snatching a tissue out of the box on the wine barrel table. Tearing it into tiny shreds, she traipses my way, holding the bits of tissue in her hand. Once she's standing a few feet away from me, she plucks one of the snippets out of her hand and hurls it at me. It flutters through the air, landing a couple inches from my feet. "Meg? What are you doing?"

She steps closer and closer, continuing to pelt me with microscopic balls of tissue. Her face begins to redden with frustration, but she doesn't relent. I've gotta hand it do her, when she commits to something, she doesn't give up easily. Even when it's something as crazy as tossing tissue bits at her totally perplexed sister. She pauses mid throw with her arm hovering in the air. "Remember in high school when we used to watch those cheesy romance movies on Life-time?" I'm not quite connecting the dots between those movies and the tissue littering my floor, but I nod for her to continue.

She tosses another chunk of tissue. "We used to get so irritated when stupidity kept the characters apart. We'd shout at the TV in frustration, but do you remember what else we did?" She looks at me pointedly and waits for the lightbulb to turn on. It only takes a second.

I give her a sheepish grin. "Uh, we threw popcorn at the screen?" I say it like I'm asking for confirmation, but I don't need it. Watching those ridiculous movies with Meg is one of my favorite memories from my teenage years.

A piece of tissue is smashed between the thumb and index finger of her right hand. She pulls her arm back and lets it loose with a snap of her wrist. It whizzes in the air, making contact with my nose. We both start laughing, and Meg declares, "Bingo! So, let's pretend that tissue was a piece of popcorn and you're the female lead in the movie who needs to take her head out of her ass."

I shake my head in exasperation. "Oh, Meg. You're relentless, you know that?"

"Of course, I know that! Now, listen to your big sister, and go find that boy."

"Now?"

She bobs her head up and down. "Uh-huh. Right now." She smacks her forehead with the heel of her hand. "Oh my God, would you listen to me? You're turning me in to Duckie at the end of *Pretty in Pink*. Which, now that I mention it, he sure got a raw deal, didn't he? I mean, what was with that ending? Andy clearly needed a big sister to steer her away from lame Blaine." She rolls her eyes up to the ceiling.

I chuckle and pull her in for a hug. "Thanks, Megs. I love you." I give her a quick peck on the cheek.

She grabs my shoulders and turns me around to face the door, giving me a push. "I love you, too. Now, get out of here!"

* * *

I STRIDE down the hall with purpose, taking the stairs two at a time. But when I reach the front door of my building, my hands still when they touch the handle. What am I doing? I don't even have a game plan here. I've been unyielding in my refusal to be with Jude, and now I've done a one-eighty and I'm expecting him to just accept that? But then I think about Jude, and I know, without a doubt, that yes, he'll definitely accept that. That's just the sort of person he is. I mentally berate myself for almost tossing him aside.

My conviction is back as I shove open the door and bound down the concrete steps. I cross the street and head toward the parking lot. I shove my hand into the pocket of my jeans, and my fingers probe in search of my keys. It's only when my finger makes contact with the metal keyring that I see him.

Jude is leaning against the passenger door of his car, which is parked in the space beside mine. The glow from the streetlight overhead casts a warm hue on his face. His arms are crossed and his expression is sober and unreadable.

Oh my God, this is so much like Pretty in Pink—I can't wait to tell Meg!

I raise my hand and flutter each of my fingers one by one while mouthing, "Hi."

And then I want to die because *what the hell was that?* I'd say I've completely lost my game, but I'm pretty sure I never had game to begin with. I don't think any of that matters because Jude is grinning mischievously like he's in on a private joke. After my feeble attempt at a seductive wave, I'm pretty certain the joke is me.

I stalk toward him until we're standing toe to toe. His right eyebrow lifts slightly and he cocks his head trying to get a read on me.

I take a deep breath and catch a whiff of bergamot from his cologne. Standing this close to him and not touching him is agony, and honestly, I can't come up with a single reason why I should stay away. I nudge the side of his shoe with mine, and he readjusts his stance, widening his legs. I've wasted enough time apart from him, so the minute he moves, I step in, sliding my hands around his waist and molding my body against his. He doesn't hesitate, immediately wrapping his arms around me and pulling me close.

"You didn't leave," I say into his chest.

I hear the smile in his voice when he speaks. "I told you I would always be here for you, didn't I?"

I press my chin to his chest and angle my head to look up at him. "How long were you planning on staying out here?"

He tilts his head and kisses the tip of my nose. "As long as you needed."

"But what if it took me days?"

"Then I would've waited days." He speaks without hesitation. His words warm me from the inside out. He always seems to know exactly what to do or say to make me feel perfectly at ease. It makes me think of the picture he gave me. He told me he hoped it would remind me that the past is permanent and that the memories we've made are a part of what makes us who we are today. And as usual, he was right.

"So, there's something I've been meaning to ask you," I say as I gaze up at him.

"Go ahead. Ask away."

"That picture of you and your brother?"

He nods for me to continue.

"You both appeared to be sharing in some sort of joke. What were the two of you laughing about?"

His expression turns introspective as he stares off into the dark night. He's rifling through the catalog of memories in his mind, trying to pull up the one that was immortalized in the picture. I keep my eyes trained on his so I won't miss a thing. Sometimes the most important parts of a story are the ones that are never spoken out loud.

I can tell the moment he remembers. His eyelids pull down, shutting out everything around him. A hint of a smile plays on his lips. It steadily grows, spreading its wings like a butterfly about to take flight. He begins speaking, slowly at first, but the tempo of his voice continues to increase as the memory flows freely from his lips.

"Our mom never went anywhere without her camera. It was always attached to her like an extra set of eyes. She wasn't a skilled photographer, not like you." He taps me on my nose. My mouth curves in a smile. "Still, she wanted to capture everything. She used to say they got it all wrong. 'Memories fade, but a picture lasts forever!'" He chuckles at the memory. "She loved to pose us, manipulating our arms and legs like we were marionettes. Dylan and I couldn't resist messing with her. She'd have us arranged exactly how she wanted us, and the second she'd turn her back, we'd reposition ourselves. It would always end the same way. Mom would get mad and Dylan and I would laugh and she'd take the picture anyway. It became a game. Over the years, Mom took hundreds of pictures, just like the one I gave you, with the two of us in various states of hysterics. We were in our mid-twenties in that last picture, yet mom was still trying to pose us like dolls." He shakes his head and his laughter slowly fades. "You know, now that I think of it, I'm pretty sure she knew what she was doing. She'd get so angry with us for goofing off after she'd made such an effort to get us to stand in the perfect position, but it was all an act. We'd bust up laughing and the shutter would snap. We gave her the picture she really wanted after all." The nostalgia brings an easy smile on his face.

I run my finger along his lower lip. "That's beautiful, Jude." When he gave that picture to me, I thought it was a sweet gesture, but now when I hear the story that's attached to it, it holds an even deeper meaning. I think of the photo albums in my apartment filled with images of my mom, Meg, and Poppy over the years. I took most of those photos, treating them like practice—a means to improve my skill. But they held so much more. They are an array of pixels, making up the sum of everything that's ever meant anything to me. I took them for granted. Every time I lifted my camera and peered through the lens, I was capturing a moment, but on some level in my subconscious mind, I was also recognizing the importance of what I had. Even though some of the people in those images are lost, either physically or mentally, they still played a significant role in molding the person that I am, here and now. And I will forever be grateful to them.

Jude grasps a rebellious curl and tucks it behind my ear, leaving his hand to rest on the side of my head. He surveys my face, witnessing the vast array of emotions cresting the surface. His stormy eyes hold me captive. "It's your turn, Nellie."

"My turn for what, exactly?"

His arms encircle my waist and he spins us around, pressing my back against the cool metal of the door. He bends his neck and brings his face so close to mine our noses touch. "To live."

When his lips capture mine, they're demanding. There's an urgency to this kiss that has us gasping for air. I match his desperation with my own, assailing his mouth like it's necessary for my survival. And right now, it is. Food, water, shelter —none of that matters quite as much as my need to be held in his arms, to capture this memory. He feels like my literal lifeline. Without him, my life ceases to exist, but with him, the clouds lift, the birds sing, my heart soars, and every single facet of those cheesy romance movies Meg and I used to watch comes to life. Because this main character finally made her choice.

And I choose me.

Chapter Thirty-Four

JUDE IS a pillar and I'm leaning all of my weight on him. I'm staring at our clasped hands, trying to muster up the strength for what I'm about to do.

Last night, I told him that I would join him on the trip to Yosemite. We leave this afternoon, and I didn't want to go without saying goodbye to my mom.

We're standing outside the door to her apartment and I can't seem to summon the courage to knock. The thing that has my feet cemented to the brown tweed carpet is fear. It's one word with four letters, but in that particular arrangement, they are a powerful force. But there's another word that's even more sinister, goodbye.

When you leave on a trip, saying goodbye to a parent or loved one is really more like "see you later." Sure, there's a chance that something may happen while you're gone, but more than likely, you'll be back and everything will be just as it was when you left. With my mom, it's different. For us, goodbye could very well be exactly what it means. Every time I leave my mom, I know when I say that word, it may be the last time. The last time she knows I'm her daughter. The last time she knows me at all.

Jude lifts our joined hands to his mouth and feathers soft kisses along my knuckles. "Are you ready?" He tips his head toward the door.

I answer quickly and honestly. "No." I force myself to stare at the closed door. It's similar to how Alzheimer's feels—like a door that's slowly drifting shut until it's closed off forever. Never to be opened again. I look up at Jude and find the confidence I need. I give him a reassuring smile. "But I'm going to do it anyway."

I raise my fist and rap it on the door in quick succession. Within a few minutes, I hear the locks disengaging, re-engaging, and then disengaging again. My mom cracks open the door until she sees me on the other side. Then she glides it wide open, greeting me with a warm smile that has my heart beating in my throat. "Belly! This is a surprise!"

It shouldn't be. I come every Saturday, but she knows who I am, and she seems genuinely happy to see me, so I let it slide. "Hi, Mama. I hope we're not disturbing you." I steal a glance inside and find her TV paused on Florence Henderson. Her face is frozen in a scrunched expression that she's probably wearing in relation to whatever comical answer she's giving on *Hollywood Squares*.

My mom follows my eyes to her television. "Oh, well, maybe just a little. But it's okay. I always have time for my little girl." The sentiment is like a trigger directly linked to my heart. My eyes well up and my chin quivers slightly, but I dig my fingernails into the palm of my hand to keep my emotions in check.

"I'm so happy to hear that, Mama. We're here because, Jude and I—" I nudge him with my elbow and my mom's eyes roam over him, the same way an overprotective parent might assess the date their teenager brought home. She smiles with satisfaction and her gaze drifts back to me. "We're going on a little trip." I hold my hands up to stop her from launching into a full-blown panic attack and am shocked to find her still smiling at me. I speak slowly to ensure that she's hearing what I'm saying. "We won't be gone long. And Meg will be here to help you with anything you need."

Her eyes shine in a way that tells me she's reliving a past memory. I may be standing here speaking to her, but the version of me that she sees and hears is not the one in front of her. She reaches her arm out, and the loose-fitting sleeve of her pink cardigan slides away from her wrist, revealing translucent skin thinly veiling the blue and purple veins underneath. She pats at my cheek with haphazard movements. "Okay, Bells, but remember your curfew? You're wearing your watch, right?"

I tilt my arm toward my face and the screen of my Apple watch lights up, displaying the time. This isn't the watch she's referring to, though. I know she's remembering the Guess watch she bought me for Christmas when I was sixteen. I don't acknowledge any of that. It's not necessary, and besides, it would only confuse her. I just nod. "Yep, I've got it."

"Good." She sounds content with my response. "All right, you two kids have fun. I'm going to go watch my show now." She starts closing the door, but I reach up to stop it.

"Hey, Mama?"

"Hmm?" She looks from me to the TV like she's a runner in a marathon and I'm the roadblock keeping her from the finish line.

I know this little bubble we're in is going to pop soon, so I quickly I wrap my arms around her neck and hug her. She doesn't feel like my mom, but yet, she does. That would only make sense to someone in my same situation, but it's as though there are two versions of my mom. One before the disease and one after. The one before remains fixed in my memory. The one after is always changing, but if you look hard enough, you can still find pieces of the one before buried deep inside. Maybe it's in the way the right corner of her lip lifts a little higher than the left when she smiles. Or maybe it's the way she waves her hands when she's describing something she doesn't like. I've had a lot of experience trying to siphon out the parts of her that feel like home. As time goes on, they're getting harder to find, but they aren't gone. Not yet.

"Goodbye, Mama."

She smooths her hand across my shoulders. "Bye bye, Nellie." And then the door closes with her on the other side. I shut my eyes and hope it'll open again when I come back.

* * *

THE DISTANCE between us and my mom's room grows as our legs take us away from it. We barely speak as we lumber down the hall. I think Jude knows I'm internally processing everything that just happened, and, if I'm honest, I appreciate the silence. The ride down in the elevator is quiet and introspective, but Jude never lets go of my hand, keeping me grounded in the present.

When we reach the lobby, it's a flurry of activity. There are four improv comedians performing a skit for a small crowd of residents. One of the entertainers asks for suggestions on an action, and I hear a familiar voice call out, "He should rub Bengay on her shoulder!" I'd recognize that booming lieutenant anywhere, and my face erupts in a smile.

I look at Jude and hold up my finger signaling for him to wait, and he nods. I scan the crowd and find Gerry and Mavis nestled together on a loveseat. They're seated off to the side, and from this vantage point, it's hard to tell if they're even watching. I'm sure that's on purpose. Gerry would never want to give the impression that he's fully invested, yet he's far too nosy to ignore the action altogether.

I stroll over to them, and it's Mavis who spots me first. She gives me a toothy smile and elbows Gerry hard in the ribs. He makes an "Oof!" sound and presses his hand to his side. "Oh, for cryin' out loud, Mavis! These old bones are brittle. You can't go digging your elbow into my side or you'll bust a rib! Now, what is it you needed?" Severe lines crisscross along his forehead, but he can't hold the annoyed expression long. Within seconds of staring down at Mavis, his face begins to soften, and the creases are less rigid. Mavis hasn't been speaking much lately. She mostly communicates by pointing at what she wants. She raises a gnarled finger and aims it at me. Gerry follows the direction, and when his eyes land on my face, any residual irritation he'd been feeling melts away. His skin is smoother and his eyes gleam.

"Why if it isn't my Nellie girl!" He stretches his arm out, and I take his hand in mine, covertly sliding a 3 Musketeers bar into his palm. His smile is wide when he sees the candy. He peels off the wrapper and breaks the chocolate bar in two, handing half to Mavis and popping the other half into his mouth. He chews and swallows it in five-seconds flat while Mavis takes tiny bird-like bites. She'll be working on it for the next twenty minutes. "Your mama looked real good today. Have you seen her?"

"I have!" I grin. "And you're right. Today was a good day."

He narrows his gaze, and I can almost see the cogs turning behind his eyes. "Something different about you, kiddo." He squints as though this change is something he can see on the outside. And who knows? Maybe it is. "I can't quite put my finger on it, but you've changed. Are you parting your hair on the other side?"

I giggle and shake my head.

"Huh. Yeah, didn't think so. How 'bout your outfit? Is it new?"

I look down at my worn jeans. The hole in the knee stares up at me. Ripped jeans are on trend, but this pair didn't come pre-torn. That happened organically when I tripped up the stairs carrying too many grocery bags.

"Nope. These old jeans have been in my closet for years."

Jude sidles up behind me. His arms slide around my waist and tug me so that my back rests against his front. The warmth from his body radiates throughout mine. He rests his chin on the top of my head.

"How's it going, Gerry? Hiya, Mavis!"

Mavis giggles and gives Jude her best princess wave. Gerry reclines his head against the back of the loveseat. From that angle, he can see Jude's face, and I watch as his eyes bounce between us. His body shoots up until he's sitting ramrod straight, and he snaps his fingers. Mavis startles at his sudden movement, and he pats her hand in a silent apology. "I know what it is! He finally got through to you, didn't he?"

My face pinches in confusion. "Got through to me?"

His head bounces like a bobblehead and his jowls shake from the force. "Yep! I've been watching the two of you and I've seen the way that one looks at you." He extends his finger, directing it at Jude. "Nellie, that boy has been in love with you from the word go, but I knew you wouldn't be an easy one to win. You're too focused on everyone else around you, and I knew it would take an awful lot of convincing to get you to turn that attention onto yourself. But I had faith, didn't I, Mavis?" Gerry looks over at his wife with pure adoration in his eyes. She bobs her head feverishly in agreement. Satisfied with the backup, he continues. "I'm just so happy you finally did something for yourself. No one else deserves it more'n you do."

He's right. I know that now. Jude, Claudette, and more recently, Meg, have been saying the same thing, but what can I say? I'm clueless when it comes to my own needs. It took quite a bit of prodding to convince me, but the remnants of the tiny wall I had built around my heart finally came crashing down. I see it now—the value of my own happiness.

Gerry can tell that his words hit their mark and he looks utterly pleased with himself.

Jude's deep chuckle reverberates down my spine, sending a tingle that I feel from the base of my neck down to my heels. "I think you'll appreciate this, Gerry. I'm taking my girl here on an adventure."

Gerry raises his eyebrow and leans forward, placing his hands on his knees. "You don't say! Where to?"

"We're heading up to Yosemite for a week. We leave this afternoon."

He nods in approval. "Well, that sounds like a perfect plan. And don't forget, I want to hear all about it when you get back."

"You got it!" Jude and I speak in unison and then share a laugh at how in sync we are.

"Uh-oh, Mavis. Did ya hear that?" Gerry eyes his wife with mock concern, and a small "Teehee" escapes her mouth before she covers it with her hands. "Only together a short while and they're already talkin' alike." When he looks up at us, the smile on his face stretches from ear to ear. "Just you wait, someday you won't be able to tell where one of you ends and the other begins." He sets his hand on top of Mavis' knee. "I'm just so glad I was here to witness the beginning."

* * *

ONCE I'M SAFELY INSIDE, Jude shuts the passenger door of his car. When he rounds the back, I find my phone in my purse and notice a text from Meg.

> **Meg:** Hope it went well with mom today. I'll see you when you get back and remember, you won't be good for anyone if you don't take care of yourself first.

I roll my eyes and shoot off a quick response.

Me: Yes, ma'am! Since when did you get to be so philo-
sophical?
Meg: Who me? I've always been full of good advice!
Remember the time I told you to make sure you took
the thumbtacks out of your back pocket before you
sat down?
Me: I do, but that was only because the day before you
plopped down on the chair in the dining room forget-
ting you had put mom's extra push pins in your
pocket. You stood up so fast I thought you had been
bitten. Which, I guess, in a way, you were.
laugh/cry emoji
Meg: Well, that may be true, but that never would've
happened if someone had given me the same valuable
advice I gave to you.

I snort out a laugh. I've missed this side of my sister. I'm
so glad she's back.

Me: I love you, Megs.
Meg: Love you, too, Nellie Belly. Go have fun with
Jude in that tiny tent! *man and woman kissing emoji*

I'm still laughing when Jude slides into his seat. He grins
at me and leans over the center console. His palm rests
against my cheek, and his fingers comb into my hair. He
brushes his lips against mine, and when he pulls back, he
looks at me like I'm something he thought he lost and finally
found. "You're pretty remarkable, you know that?"

I scrunch up my nose. "I am?"

He nods. "You are, and I'm going to keep telling you until
you believe me, no matter how long it takes."

My face warms with his words. "Well, you're pretty
remarkable yourself."

"Oh, I know." He grins. "But you can keep telling me, if you want." He lifts his shoulder in a confident shrug.

I give his arm a playful smack and throw my head back against the seat in a fit of laughter.

Jude turns his key in the ignition and reaches over to press the button on the stereo. Gliding his finger along the screen of his phone, he doesn't look up when he speaks. "Did I tell you I put together a playlist for our road trip?"

"Oh, did you now? And let me guess, both Nelly and The Beatles make an appearance on that list."

He chuckles, and the skin around his eyes creases. "Well, of course, they do! They're our theme songs, after all."

I shake my head, and he taps his finger on the screen, making his selection. In seconds, the first few chords of a guitar riff flow through the speakers. I recognize the strumming and thwacking on the guitar instantly as the melody of Van Morrison's "Into the Mystic" fills the small space. I've always loved this song. I let my eyes fall closed as I soak in the lyrics.

This is one of those songs where the music and lyrics are one cohesive entity. One can't exist without the other. I've always heard this song one way. I thought it was the story of a man who misses his love and wants to come home to her. But now, as I let the words flow into my ears, I hear a different song. This one is about the journey we take into the great unknown. The mystic is what lies ahead, and even though we can't see where we're going, we can't stop the boat from moving. So we just hold on to our loved ones and float into the vastness together.

I turn to Jude with tears in my eyes. "I have a theme song and so do you, but this song? This is *our* theme song." I grasp the dial on Jude's stereo and turn the volume up.

Chapter Thirty-Five

WHACK!

I slap the side of my neck the second I feel the pinch, but it's too late. I feel the burning itch as the mosquito's saliva enters my body. A small, raised bump is already beginning to form. When I pull my hand back, I see the tiny insect's body mashed against my hand like a flower that's been pressed in a book. Plunging my hand into my pocket, I retrieve a tissue and unceremoniously wipe the poor bug's remains off my palm.

We're on day three of our Yosemite trip, and so far, mosquitos have been the only negative aspect I've been able to find. And I've been looking. I know I should just let myself be carefree and relaxed, but old habits are hard to break sometimes.

My mom called once during our drive. She was in a panic over her remote control. She kept repeating that her "clicker" wouldn't work, no matter how hard she pressed the buttons. I was sure it just needed new batteries, but it was impossible to convince her. She was certain it was broken and nothing could be done to repair it. I saw Jude glance over at me with worried eyes, but I just flipped my hand back and forth, waving away his concern. Problems like this are so common, I rarely get upset over them anymore. The key in situations like that is repetition. I acknowledge her concern, and then I assure her we'll take care of it. Over and over, I say those words to her until she finally relaxes enough to let me hang up and call Meg.

Meg. We still have some work to do, but we're slowly repairing our damaged relationship. She's only been back for a few weeks, but already, I can't imagine how I ever did any of this without her. She's been incredible these past few weeks. She's handled every crisis and put out every fire, and she's never bothered me once. I, on the other hand, was texting her every hour the day we left, but she quickly put a stop to that. She told me she would only reply to one text a day and she wouldn't answer it until after six p.m. Meg assured me she'd call me if there was an emergency, so I had no choice but to let her handle things. It hasn't been an easy adjustment, but I'm getting there.

And Jude has definitely been helping me with that. I would say he's the perfect distraction, but he can't be a distraction when he's the main focus. He's reminded me of how incredible the world can be. And I'm not just referring to the astounding scenery in Yosemite. Although it is indescribably beautiful here, that's not what convinced me that I made the right decision. That was all Jude.

Like me, he's been through trauma, but he's come out the other side and that's given him perspective. He knows about the struggle—the constant internal fight between keeping your chin up and your gaze ahead, or succumbing to the anguish that threatens to pull you under. He seems to know what I need before I do. He's been attentive and engaging, allowing me to direct conversations and challenging me to make myself a priority in my own life. He reminds me of that every chance he gets. Just yesterday, we were deciding on where to go for lunch. I lifted my shoulder in a half shrug. "It makes no difference to me. I'm happy to eat wherever you'd like."

Jude's eyes narrowed into slits and he shook his head dramatically. "Oh, no, you don't. Stop deferring to other people. Your opinion matters, Nellie."

I let out a frustrated huff, but in truth, I appreciated the effort he was making. It was just lunch, and it didn't matter to me, but that wasn't the point. He knows how important it is for me to feel as though I'm in control. I'm no longer a supporting character. In this life of mine, I'm the lead.

This morning we've been hiking the Vernal Falls trail. We're following a gravel path that's blanketed by pine needles from the towering pine trees that hover over us. Our steps are hushed by the ground cover, and the only sound we hear is the wind as it weaves its way through the maze of branches overhead. The sweet melody of a bird catches my attention. I look ahead to call out to Jude, but he's too far away to hear me. He's gotten pretty used to nature distracting me, so I'm sure he'll discover I'm not behind him soon enough.

I follow the delicate chirping to a small clearing a few feet to my right. I crouch down and take aim, peering through the lens of my camera. Flitting about on tiny feet is a vibrant yellow bird. His beak sifts through the fallen foliage in search of food. Burrowing into the dirt, he yanks out a tiny bug. It squirms in his beak, but the little bird's moves are spastic. He cranes his neck, bobbing his head into the air and swallowing the bug whole. The act is savage, but it's also the very essence of survival. We navigate our way through life locating what we need, and once we find it, we consume it.

I hear a deep, throaty chuckle from behind me. I angle my head to see Jude walking down the path, heading my way.

Click! I snap a photo of him, but this one isn't for Blue Blaze. This one's just for me.

He strides toward me with his arms crossed and a look of

frustration on his face. But I know he's only pretending. His eyes tell me all I need to know. I can see pure adoration swimming in their cobalt depths, and I drink it in.

Stopping a foot in front of me, he lightly kicks at my heel. "There you are. You know, I was in the middle of a lengthy discussion about the evolution of pine trees when I realized the trees were the only ones listening."

I rise to standing and saunter over to him, wrapping my arms around his neck. "Well, I'm sorry I missed that. It sounds riveting," I deadpan.

The side of his mouth curves into a smile. His arms encircle my waist, and he pulls me toward him. "It was. But no worries, it's a passion of mine so I'll just start from the beginning. I don't want you to miss a thing."

I stand up on tiptoes and kiss the underside of his chin. "I wouldn't want you to overexert yourself, so how about we settle on a brief summary instead?"

He slides his hands up the length of my body and gently glides them around my neck. His thumbs work in lazy circles by my jaw. "Nellie, never settle for a summary when the best parts are in the small details." He punctuates his statement with a kiss that tells me this is one of those details he was talking about. And he's right, I've spent way too much time on the CliffsNotes version of my life. It's time to sit back and read every word.

The shrill song of the little yellow bird commands our attention, and we watch as he spreads his wings and takes flight. I tip my head goodbye as he soars through the air in search of his next adventure.

"Hey, Jude?" I'll never get tired of that.

He groans, but his eyes sparkle with amusement. "Yes, Nellie with an -ie."

His nickname for me serves as a reminder of how far we've come, and I can't help the cheesy grin on my face with the memory. "I just wanted to thank you."

"Thank me for what?"

"Oh, you know, loving me despite how broken I am, reminding me how incredible life can be, and never giving up on me no matter how stubborn I was. No big deal." I shrug in jest, and he chuckles.

"Nellie, loving you is the easiest thing I've ever done. It's as natural as these pine trees growing all around us. Which reminds me—"

I press my lips to his and stifle his lesson. His hands fist my hair as he deepens the kiss, letting me know he doesn't care that I interrupted him.

I know our lives won't be perfect. Perfect doesn't exist. There is no happily ever after, because happy cannot survive without a little sad to balance it out. But I'm not interested in "living happily ever after." I'm only focused on living. And standing here with Jude among these tall pines on this incredible adventure, living is exactly what I'm doing. Finally.

Author's Note

This is not an autobiography, not in the literal sense. But it is based on personal experience. I am very much like Nellie, and, if I'm being honest, I'm a little like Meg, too. When my mom was first diagnosed with Alzheimer's disease, I was determined to be an advocate for her in every way. I made her a priority in my life, and even now, over two years later, she's still a priority. But sometimes, I really just want to run away from this situation. I want to escape to some other part of the world and just pretend that everything is normal again.

It was important for me to write this story as I was experiencing it in my own life. I didn't want to wait for this season to pass. The emotions had to be raw, and I was afraid if I put this off, time might eventually soften how this feels. I didn't want to blur the edges. What you've read on these pages is personal and very real. Thank you for not looking away.

Alzheimer's is an ugly disease. It takes a person you love and twists them up like a pretzel until they are unrecognizable. People tend to shy away from this topic. It's hard to understand and it's uncomfortable, but it's a part of my everyday life just as it is for millions of others. I wanted to give a voice to the struggle in the hopes that maybe it might bring someone else a little comfort just knowing that they aren't alone in how they're feeling. I also wanted to bring awareness to this disease. The people who are suffering, both with Alzheimer's and from it, deserve to be heard.

Nellie made the ultimate sacrifice for her mother. She gave up living her own life and devoted all of herself to caring for her mom as well as every other person and animal who needed her. She shouldn't have been alone in her agony. She had a sister whom she needed desperately. I am lucky to have two brothers who haven't left me to deal with this on my own. I have a support system of friends and family who lift me up whenever I fall. And now Nellie has that, too, which is how I know she's going to be okay no matter where life takes her. As long as you have people behind you to support you, you can feel the wind on your face and know that they can feel it, too.

There are nearly 50 million people in the world who have Alzheimer's or a related form of dementia. And only one in four people with the disease have been diagnosed. That's a staggering statistic. It is my greatest wish that there will someday be a cure for this devastating disease, and I hope to see it in my lifetime.

If you have a loved one who's been diagnosed with Alzheimer's, I am with you. I know the pain you're experiencing and I want you to know that you do not have to go through this alone. Please contact the Alzheimer's Association at 800-272-3900 or visit them online at www.alz.org to find a support group in your area.

Acknowledgments

Adam—This all happened because you decided it was my turn. You're the Jude to my Nellie.

Stella & Jasper—When life gets dark, you are my light.

Mom & Dad—If only. I love you both, forever.

Angela & Marissa—My beautiful betas, my incredible friends. You are both the very best.

Traci—You took this book and whipped it into shape, sparing my heart in the process. You are magical.

Marla—Your eagle eyes are amazing.

Murphy—You're a true genius. This cover is gorgeous and I still can't believe it's mine.

My family, friends, fellow authors, readers—Your support means the world to me. I wouldn't be able to do this without you. Thank you for everything.

About the Author

Layne Deemer aims to push boundaries with her writing. Her stories deconstruct the ordinary until it becomes something else entirely.

She has a degree in Communications with a minor in English and has worked in the fields of public relations, marketing, and advertising, but writing has always been her true passion. When she isn't writing, she's reading. Her wish list of books will take her a lifetime to get through.

She resides in Pennsylvania with her husband, Adam, their two kids, Stella and Jasper, and their bulldog, Archie. In addition to Life Forgotten, she is also the author of Frayed, a psychological thriller.